TO MARGARET,

again

A*

THE EVIDENCE OF LOVE

By the same author

THE TRAP, 1955
A DANCE IN THE SUN, 1956
THE PRICE OF DIAMONDS, 1957
A LONG WAY FROM HOME, 1958
NO FURTHER WEST, 1959

THE EVIDENCE OF LOVE

a novel by

DAN JACOBSON

READERS UNION

WEIDENFELD AND NICOLSON

London 1961

This RU edition was produced in 1961 *for sale to its members only by Readers Union Ltd at Aldine House,* 10-13 *Bedford Street, London W.C.*2 *and at Letchworth Garden City, Herts. Full details of membership may be obtained from our London address. The book has been reset in* 10 *point Bell type leaded, and printed and bound by C. Tinling & Co. Ltd, Prescot, Lancs. It was first published by Weidenfeld & Nicolson Ltd.*

1

'IF WE DIDN'T believe each other, if we didn't trust each other, our life together would become quite impossible. We would all die, and very quickly, of war and hunger and cold and loneliness. You agree? I knew you would.

'Yet you look troubled. I'm not surprised. It is a troubling thing, our dependence on others for everything we have—even for our own most intimate ideas of ourselves. Little Johnny draws with a pencil on the wall, and Mummy says, "Naughty Johnny!" So little Johnny *feels* naughty, and, depending on the kind of naughtiness he goes in for, he hangs his head in shame or promptly draws on yet another wall. That's how it might begin; but where does it end?

'If, for instance, Jones tells me what a generous fellow I am, and if Smith tells me how mean and nasty I am, and if, like little Johnny, I make a habit of believing the things that people say about me, then what in truth am I? Probably (and this is a joke of a kind, I suppose) I'm generous to Jones and I'm nasty to Smith. That's the kind of animal I am. And the kind that you are too.

'Don't be offended please. You don't have to tell me indignantly that you're neither me nor little Johnny. I can see that you're an adult, a responsible person, a husband, a father, a man of position. Yes, I know that you are not in the least flighty, susceptible, spineless. I realize that by now you know pretty well your own nature—as you should, having lived with it for so long.

'Every weekday morning you get up at seven, you breakfast off cornflakes and milk, you watch your son go off to school, and then, with a newspaper in one hand and an umbrella in the other, you kiss your wife good-bye and walk to the station to catch the train to town. You greet the girls in your office, and you sit down behind your desk; at the end of the day you leave the office and take the train home, back to the house in the suburbs. That's the kind of man you are, I know; and a very fine kind of man it is too, if you'll allow me to say so: the kind without which we would most certainly be unable to live together. I most sincerely respect you; and I wish you well. Believe me, I do.

'And that is why I have a question to ask of you. I ask it precisely because you are so regular in your habits and responsible in your outlook. Say, one morning you get up and have your breakfast of cornflakes and milk and watch your son go off to school and take up your hat and umbrella and kiss your wife good-bye and go to the station to catch the train to town—say you do all these habitual, innocent and estimable things, as you have been doing for weeks and months and years. Say you arrive at the railway station in good time to catch the train you always catch, and you greet the ticket collector at the barrier as you have always greeted him—and say, for once, he doesn't reply to your greeting.

'He is a cheerful man usually, this ticket collector; he has a round red face and light blue eyes, and he wears a cap with a shiny black peak; and on every morning previously he has responded to your greeting with a smile of white teeth, a crinkling of the red skin around his eyes, and a fat forefinger lifted in a knowing and admonitory signal. But this morning he merely looks at your season ticket, gives you a stare from his blue eyes, and turns away, showing you the side of his plump and shaven cheek.

'You are already half-way down the steps towards the platform before you realize how sharply and deliberately you have been snubbed. You check your stride, think better of it, and continue down the steps. You decide that there must be something worrying the ticket collector, something pressing on his mind, to have made him so forgetful. And at the same time as you wonder what it can be that worries him, you feel a certain pleasure in noting how little there is that worries you. What could there be to worry you? You think of your faithful and dutiful wife; and the picture of her in your mind brings you a faint amused memory of desire that is also a premonition of delight: for your wife is not only faithful, but eager. You think of your son, and of how anxious he had been lest you should demean his manhood by kissing him in front of the friends with whom he walks to school every morning. You think of your work, and of what you hope to accomplish during the day. No, there is nothing uncomfortable on your mind, nothing at all, whatever may be the case with that ticket collector.

'You have reached the bottom of the steps. The usual people are waiting on the grey length of the platform, which looks as it always does: there are the benches, the barrows, the automatic machines, the gabled signal box at the far end. Most of the people on the platform you know by sight, for they, like you, regularly travel to town on the same train. You have spoken to most of them, at one time or another, of the weather, or of the lateness of the train. Now, as you move down the platform, you nod at the first familiar face you pass. The man does not see you nod. The next stares through your greeting. The third acknowledges it by turning his head aside, as the ticket collector had done, after the same cold stare.

'You halt. You look back at the people you have passed, and you see that they too have halted, and have turned to stare at you. Ridiculously, you wonder if there is anything amiss with your clothing: you feel your tie, look down at your trousers. But nothing seems to be out of order. Yet another familiar travelling companion walks towards you, and you lift your hand in greeting; his mouth turns down and his eyes fleetingly meet yours. Already he has gone past. You look at his retreating back, you become aware of your own hand half-lifted, and slowly you begin to lower it.

'Fear has come in a moment. The moment before you were not afraid: now you are. There is a faint burning at the back of your neck: in your chest there is a heaviness that you have to lift when you breathe. Fear has come like fear in a dream, so quickly; and, as in a dream, it imposes its own duration on time. For though your hand is still falling to the side of your body, it seems much later that you lift your head and see, with relief, Robinson a little way down the platform.

'The others on the platform are train-acquaintances merely, nothing more; but Robinson is a friend of yours, a visitor to your house, as you are to his. You call to him, and begin to make towards him, but your step falters when you see how pale Robinson is, how his mouth twitches as he retracts a painful smile: when you are no more than a pace or two away from him, Robinson suddenly opens his newspaper and lifts it in front of him; he shuffles his feet, and begins to walk away, still with the newspaper held foolishly open before him. Then, though you do not call again, Robinson halts and lowers the paper. You see his black hair, his wide frowning forehead, his tortoiseshell spectacle frames; but the eyes behind the glasses you hardly recognize at all, there is such a desperate appeal in them. And with a hideous dream-clarity you realize at once that Robinson is asking you not to hail him as a friend in front of the others on the platform.

'You turn, and you see that the people, the familiar and the unfamiliar among them, have all gathered a few yards off, and are watching you and Robinson. They stare at you with a hostility that is modified only by something worse, in its coldness: a sly and expectant curiosity. Behind your back, Robinson's footsteps begin moving away; they halt, move away faster; they are almost running now; they grow fainter. You clutch your shred of newspaper tightly in your hand, as if it were a weapon. In your mind, as you confront the crowd, there is only one tiny and uncertain hope—that you will wake in your bed to find the darkness around you and merely the sheet clutched desperately in your hand.

'But there is no darkness here: you are awake; and there is no escape. The noise of the train as it at last comes into the station seems to release the first mutter from the crowd watching you. Dazedly, incoherently, you imagine that if only you can get on to the train you will be safe, you will be taken away. You grasp at the handle of the first carriage door near to you, and immediately a cane is brought down viciously on your fingers; the swiftness with which the pain runs through your entire body is incredible. You struggle to get back to the carriage, but you are pulled away ignominously by the back of your collar; you are kicked and pushed aside; ten hands actually carry you through the air before flinging you down on the platform. You are a citizen, a husband, a father, a man of position; but who would believe it when they see the blood and the filth on your face, and your torn clothes; who would believe it when they hear the jeers of the crowd and see the fingers pointing at you; who would believe it when they hear the noises that you are making? Do you believe it yourself when you see your hands stretched out in an appeal for mercy, hear your own cries, "What have I done? Tell me what I have done . . ." Do you believe that you are a respectable and innocent man when you have exhausted your rage and have exhausted even your own terror, and in guilt and shame creep away on your hands and knees, hoping only that the crowd will let you go without further jeers, kicks, spittle on your bent and exposed back?

'Do you believe that under such circumstance you would still know who you are? And the next day?'

'But this is nightmare stuff, you say: of no interest to a man who lives in the daylight, a man of regular habits and a position of importance. Such circumstances don't occur you say.

'Of course, you are wrong. Have you already forgotten that what I have just described happened to millions of fathers, husbands, dutiful citizens, men of importance—and in Europe too, where you live? Yes, it did, you know. And these people were not merely spat at, jeered at, kicked, beaten. They were killed. Husbands who kissed their wives good-bye and walked to railway stations to catch the train to work—just such husbands stood in lines to be massacred, and stood meekly, because what had happened to them in streets and on railway stations and in camps and quarries had made them forget what they once had been: had made them, in fact, all that their masters declared them to be. And who were their masters? People: the people we must trust when they speak to us, or else we shall die.

'And what happened once, during a war, can happen again. Do you suppose that it isn't happening now? And I don't speak only of my own country, South Africa, or of the Southern states of the United States, or of a country like India where there are men so degraded that their shadows render uneatable the food of other men, or of those progressive countries where people plead sincerely for a bullet in the head to punish them for crimes they have never committed. For good or evil, with less violence or more, with smiles and handshakes and frowns and grimaces, as well as blows and cries and kisses, what I have spoken of here happens to all of us, all the days of our lives, wherever we may happen to live.

'Remember it next time the ticket collector greets you in the morning, next time Robinson tells you what a fine fellow you are. Robinson is probably right today: what will he be when another day comes?'

2

AT THAT POINT the earliest long entry in Kenneth Makeer's diary or journal breaks off abruptly, and is not continued: the subsequent entry balances his anticipated living expenses against the amount of money he had in the bank. Long after I had become friendly with Makeer, and with the girl whom I met unexpectedly in his room, this journal was shown to me; even then I hardly knew what to make of it. Now I know better: they have seen to that.

I had met Kenneth Makeer in a pub in a poky little alleyway coming off the Strand. We happened one day to sit at the same table during lunch, and when I asked him to pass me the salt, he recognized me immediately; and with a smile that drew into small folds the tight skin of his cheeks, he asked me which part of the Union I came from. We found out then that not only were we both South Africans, but that we were both at the Middle Temple—he as a student in the Inns of Court School of Law, myself as a pupil in chambers. We found out too that our lodgings were fairly close together, off the Finchley Road, in what Makeer, smiling again, called 'the poor man's Hampstead'—those excessively gabled and cupola-ed blocks of red brick that lie in the valley below the Finchley Road Tube Station. After that first meeting we met again several times—casually, on the Embankment, or at lunch, or in the Temple library, or while watching the workmen repair the bomb-damage to the Temple church—and a kind of friendship sprang up between us. When I think of Makeer as he seemed to me then, the picture I have of him is always set among the buildings and grounds of the Temple: the old buildings, the new buildings, the restored buildings, the grey flagged courts, the lawns that the cars nosed at where they were parked, the green of the trees along the Embankment, and the darkness and light of the river beyond. I see him in his dark suit, bareheaded, slight, alert in his stance, with his shoulders half-turned and his head lifted. He looked from a distance like a boy.

Actually he was in his early twenties; he was slightly-built, sallow-complexioned; and under a nose beaked a little at the end he wore a fierce black moustache that hid his upper lip completely. His eyes were large: too large for the size of his face, and too closely set together. But they were handsome, nevertheless—very dark and bright. With his eyes, moustache, prominent cheek-bones and drawn skin, his face looked almost angry, and it consorted oddly with the frailness and lightness of his body. He was really very small—even smaller, one realized on seeing him, than one had remembered him as being: his neck and wrists were thin, and both at his neck and wrists there were tight-drawn tendons, so that he seemed bound and straitened by cords from which he would never be able to free himself. But he moved easily and gracefully, nevertheless.

He never talked of himself, of what he had done in South Africa, of the kind of family from which he had come, of his plans for the future. We talked merely of exams, of the merits and demerits of the chambers in which he might serve his pupilage, of the weather, of events reported in the newspapers. Yet I liked him, and I liked him even more when I found out later that those weeks in which we had been getting acquainted were some of the most miserable and lonely through which he had ever lived, that as he walked among the placid and echoing courts of the Temple or on the great terrace of the Embankment, he was weaving his way through acres of doubt and self-suspicion, across a kind of lowveld of self-hatred and distrust, and still coming no nearer a ledge of feeling from which he could survey the path he had taken, and the direction he would have to take. For him time was passing, but nothing was passing with it, neither the castigation without fury, nor the malice without expression, nor the folly without freedom. He considered taking his own life—I was to find out later—considered it while staring out of the window of his room, or waiting for buses, or sitting in the darkened smoky cinemas in which he spent much of his time. What made him most consider it, he was to tell me seriously, was the taste in his mouth when he awoke; every morning there was this inexpressibly black and bitter taste in his mouth, as if all night he had sucked something foul. It was only his own listlessness, he was convinced, that sustained him through those days, got him up in the mornings, got him dressed, sent him into the streets, and to his lectures.

Until even that failed, and he did not come to the School or the Temple at all. Of course, I knew nothing of why he stayed away, I did not even miss him at first. Eventually, however, not having seen him for some time, I did notice his absence; and one afternoon

I went over to the Treasurer's office to ask for his address, thinking that I might look him up at home. I was late in getting to the office, and the door was already closed; I rattled at it, and after an interval it was opened by a clerk who held a cup of tea in his hand, and did not seem at all to resent my intrusion. The clerk was heavily-built and military in appearance; his greying hair was close-cropped, his face was purplish, his teeth were bad. 'Mr Makeer?—him, yes,' he said several times, drawing the last word into a sigh, as he led me down a corridor and then ushered me into a little carpeted, paper-stacked office. With care he put his cup and saucer on the desk, and then took a chair. 'Are you a friend of his?' he asked me.

'Yes, I am.'

On hearing this the clerk expanded—physically I mean, as well as conversationally. He breathed out heavily, he settled himself down more comfortably in his chair, he stretched his hands forward on the desk, and his legs forward under it. He told me that he had happened to take especial notice of Mr Makeer. That he always took especial notice of the best students—followed their careers, as you might say. And Mr Makeer was a very good student, *and* he had a good manner, especially for a colonial, if I didn't mind him saying so. Because it was his opinion that some overseas students lacked polish, as you might say, when they came in. But Mr Makeer was different. 'He's a clever young gentleman. He should do very well, very well indeed, whether he stays here or whether he goes back to Africa.' Then he lowered his head, and dropped his voice 'Provided his health holds out, that's all.'

'His health?' I was surprised.

'That's what I said.' For a moment the clerk grew heavily derisive. 'Here you are, his friend, you say, and you don't know about his health.' The derision had been long in coming and it was long in going; once it had gone it was as though it had never been. 'It's a cause of worry to me, thinking as highly of him as I do. He's delicate. You can see it in his frame. A very delicate frame that young gentleman has. And here's the autumn coming, the first cold wind, and he isn't in for his dinners, I just don't see him in the Hall. So my colleague here, Mr Hayward—you've heard of Mr Hayward?'

'Yes I have. From Mr Makeer.'

'Well, he's my colleague. And Mr Hayward—to whom I mention this, and to whom a nod, as you may say, is as good as a wink—gives me a look, and I know immediately what he is thinking of. He was thinking of that gentleman's delicate frame, I'll lay you two to one. However,' the clerk added, after a long pause, 'that mightn't matter so much, in Africa, what with the warmer climates you have out there.'

I was sorry to hear that Makeer wasn't well; and asked the clerk again for Makeer's address and telephone number. After some searching he gave them both to me—previously I had known only the name of the street in which Makeer lived. As I was folding up the paper the clerk told me, 'And when you see him, give him my regards. Tell him that Prance sends his regards.'

'I will.'

I was at the door, but Prance had not yet done with me. 'You do for Mr Makeer what you can,' he instructed me. 'I would. I have. I'm very fond of that Mr Makeer. Don't tell him that I'm worried about him, though—that wouldn't cheer him up. Just tell him that I send my regards and will do what I can for him.'

'I believe you,' I said. And I did. I had known Makeer for a shorter time than Mr Prance, yet I was surprised at how anxious I felt at hearing that he wasn't well; and I made up my mind that I would go to see him that evening. It's curious how many people—people like myself and Mr Prance, and others more important to Makeer—were to be drawn to him with a kind of anxiety; he had the knack of exciting solicitude. Yet none of those who felt solicitous towards him actually pitied him: he was too spare, too reserved, to be pitied. And people interpreted their anxiety in so many ways: Mr Prance felt it about his delicate frame; I towards his possible loneliness and isolation in London (though I had no reason to suppose that he did not have a great many friends closer to him than myself); others, who knew him better, had better reasons still for their solicitude.

Makeer's appearance shocked me. He was unshaven, he needed a haircut; he was dressed in a pair of stained flannel trousers and a sweater showing at its open neck that there was no shirt beneath it. His face was thinner than ever; it seemed altogether drawn down towards the mouth, like that of an animal. And his eyes burned darkly, under the hair fallen across his forehead.

He did not seem glad to see me. On swinging the door open his first words were, 'How did you find out where I live?'

'From the Treasurer's Office.'

He did not move, did not ask me in.

'What do you want?'

'The man there told me you were sick. Mr Prance, his name was.'

Again there was a silence from Makeer: he stood with one hand still on the door-handle, as if he might yet swing it shut in my face. 'Busybody,' he muttered.

I decided that I would take him to be referring to the clerk. 'I don't know,' I said, as pleasantly as I could. 'He seemed to be very concerned about you. He thinks highly of you—that's what he said. And he sends you his best wishes.'

Makeer's eyes moved, but that was all. 'Thanks,' he said sardonically.

'Can I come in?'

He hesitated again. Then he said, 'Why not?' and stood to one side, to let me in.

A flight of stairs led up from a tiled lobby; Makeer began to climb these stairs and I followed a pace or two behind. The paint along the sides of the stairs, and the pale strip in the middle, showed that there had once been a carpet down on them, but there was none now, and our footsteps were loud on the boards. We came to a landing; it was in darkness, though a line of light was drawn under one of the doors that faced on to it. Somewhere in the house there was a radio or television set switched on; a muffled voice talked and talked and no one made any reply; I could not make out a word that was being said. We climbed another flight of stairs, and when we came to the second bare landing, we halted. 'Here we are', Makeer said. He opened a door, letting me go in ahead of him.

The room was in a filthy mess; the bed was unmade, there were books and papers all over the floor; a pot with solidified food inside it stood on a table beneath the window; clothes were scattered about; a wardrobe door hung open; its own weight pulling it away from the top hinge. The room could never have been a pleasant one: the wallpaper was a dirty yellow, the carpet was shrunken and skimpy, the arm-chair was a beaten-in affair, its velvet cover worn away in patches like mange. 'What's the matter?' Makeer asked from behind me. 'Don't you like it? I didn't invite you.'

'No wonder,' I said.

He was smiling when I turned. He looked even more like an animal than before, showing his small white teeth. 'It's all right,' he said. 'It's how I like it.'

'Why?'

'Because it's what I feel like.'

'You must be feeling pretty bad.'

For a moment he did not reply. Then he said, 'I am.'

'Have you been to see a doctor?'

'A doctor? Oh——' He still smiled; the skin of his cheeks was drawn so tightly that the folds were shallow, merely creases now. The tendons at his neck showed up harshly. 'No. I haven't been to see a doctor. A doctor couldn't help me.'

'Are you sure?'

'Quite sure.'

'Is there anything I can do?'

'That's very kind of you. No, there's nothing you can do.'

'Shall I go away then?'

'If you like.'

I stepped towards the door, but he halted me. 'No,' he said. 'Stay here. Tell me about the Temple. Tell me about Prance. Tell me what's in the newspapers these days. I'll make you some tea. Tell me about the plays you've been to.' He came forward and pushed some of the clothes on the arm of the chair on to the floor. Then he kicked the clothes aside. 'Here, I'll tidy up.' He tidied up in a moment, by kicking everything that lay on the floor to the sides of the room, so that the carpet was clear; and by pulling a single blanket over the humps and lumps of the bedclothes. 'There you are. Sit down.' He himself sat on the bed. 'Tell me about your room,' he said. 'How much do you pay? Do they give you breakfast? How do you like England?'

His hands were working together, where he held them in his lap; his dark eyelashes twitched, too often. 'I'm in trouble,' he said suddenly, not looking at me. He could not sit still; it was painful to watch his hands, eyes, the foot that vibrated just an inch or two off the floor. He groaned; he got up and went to the window, and stood at it, looking out. He tapped with his forefinger at the glass, and the window shook with a faint noise in its frame. 'It's rotten,' he said. 'It's the putty—it can't last in this climate, and with all the smoke and dirt there is in the air.' He sat on the table, pushing the pot aside. 'I'm Coloured, you know,' he said. 'A Cape Coloured. Did you know?'

'No, I didn't.'

Then I added, because it was the truth—'I suppose I just thought that you were perhaps the sort of South African white who's got some Coloured blood in him. From somewhere way back. You know, like——' I said, naming a very distinguished

South African politician, famous for the violence with which he upholds 'White Civilization' and the 'purity of the race.' 'Or like ——' I said, naming yet another, almost as well known, and with the same views.

'There are thousands of whites like that, aren't there?' Makeer said. His voice was calmer. Then he smiled. 'No, I'm not like that. We never passed. Now we never will, what with the new identity cards and everything. I'm Coloured all right, always will be. And you should see my brother.' He turned to the window; he made the whole wide expanse of glass shiver again at his touch. 'Macmillan or Walker or someone—one of the historians, I don't know which—says that there is some Coloured blood in one in four of the 'whites' in South Africa. I wouldn't have thought it would be as much as that, would you? Still, white South Africans are pretty dark—you realize it when you see them here, in England. They don't look like Europeans any more, say what you like. Not that it matters; it doesn't help me, I mean. I'm Coloured. I couldn't pass now. And it isn't only the identity cards, it's the shame of it, of trying.' He put his hands to his head; his face was covered, hidden. 'I should know, Jesus Christ.'

Suddenly he got down from the table. 'But I promised you some tea. Let me make you some tea.' There was a gas-ring on the floor, next to the kettle. 'I'm just going to get some water,' he said, and went out of the door. He was back in a minute. 'The basin's just down the corridor,' he explained. He busied himself with arranging things for the tea; he lit the gas-ring and put the kettle on it; he took up two cups and saucers and a couple of spoons. 'I must get these things washed.' Again he went out. 'It'll soon be boiling,' he said, when he came back. He looked down, watching the flames that clung around the blackened edge of the kettle.

The gas-fire hissed; we were both silent. When the kettle screamed he swung it off the flame, and turned the fire down. 'How do you like yours?'

'As it comes.'

'That's what the English always say.'

'Well, I'm not English,' I said.

'You wouldn't be here if you were. You'd have waited for an invitation before you'd have dared to come into my room.'

The tea was ready and he handed my cup to me. Then he said, 'But perhaps the English aren't so stand-offish with one another. Perhaps it's only the colonials that they're so frightened of.'

'They can't be as frightened of us as we are of them, that's for sure.'

He smiled. 'No, I suppose not.' He lifted his cup. By the time he had finished drinking he was talking excitedly again, with a great earnestness about what he was saying and a complete indifference to me; he was obviously doing no more than conduct an old and harried debate with himself. I can't remember all he said, it came out so rapidly, but I do remember his repeated exclamation, 'Ridiculous! Ridiculous! And I don't mean just what's happening in South Africa. I mean—the whole thing—' and the vehemence of his gesture showed that he was referring to nothing less than life, his own life. 'There's no logic to it, no order, it has no reason, and the worst of it all is that there's no *truth* to it. No truth anywhere, no truth that lasts. From any rational point of view, the whole thing is hopeless—altogether . . . ' He leaned forward; he spoke fervently, yet with a hopeless attempt at reasonableness in his words, even in his voice: 'If people are pushed together then they should be like bees and ants altogether, don't you see? Or if they are ever to be alone, then they should be truly alone, so that they could know what they are without doubt or dependency of any kind. You understand? Either way then the truth would be permanent, it wouldn't change; it wouldn't be what it is now—it's never still, that's the worst of it; it's like closing your eyes when you're very tired, and your eyeballs jump under your lids, and you see lights, and stripes and shapes, and none of them keep still for a moment. You'd think out of pity alone——!'

His pallor was frightening, with the dark bristles of his beard showing it up. He looked bloodless, fleshless, skull-like where he squatted next to the gas-ring; yet he was horribly full of life, to the very stiffness of his growth of beard.

'You should rest,' I said, interrupting him.

'Rest?' He repeated the word. And with a surprising quietness he agreed with me. 'Yes, I should. I try sometimes . . . and I do sleep, you mustn't think I don't. In that chair'—he pointed at it, and I started up from where I was sitting. He looked at me. 'I don't want it now, you know,' he said. 'Sit down, it's all right.' He was still speaking quietly. 'It's the waking up that I'm afraid of. I could have imagined myself not wanting to fall asleep because of the dreams I might have. But instead, it's that moment when I open my eyes. I know where I was before, no further, no better. And the chances I've lost! Oh, you don't know what they've been. I could have had—I could have had . . . . Instead, all I have is that taste in my mouth.' He swallowed, as if it were in his mouth even as he spoke. 'It's foul, you have no idea. How could you? You don't know. It's rottenness, it's evil, the taste of evil, and I have it in my mouth. You think I'm boasting?' he asked me suddenly.

'I think you should pull yourself together,' I said.

He laughed abruptly, throwing his head back. 'That's good,' he said. 'That's damned funny. What do you do when you've got no self to pull together? It's like being in a hall of mirrors, that's all—trapped there, staring, frowning, screwing up your eyes, and every figure in the mirrors doing the same, and the same, and the same.' He muttered a few more words; he shook his head nauseously. Suddenly he said clearly, 'And imagine every figure a dirty little monster—nothing violent, nothing big. Just cowardice, ingratitude, spite, lies, lies, lies—imagine them all, every way you look, and no other voice in the world but their voices. My voice.'

He was kneeling; his face was lifted, his eyes were closed; he looked pitiful, like a blind man. And because his eyes were closed he did not see—as I did—the door opening. I got to my feet. In the doorway there was a girl: I could see nothing of her except that she seemed much too smartly dressed to enter the filthily disordered room we were in. Her jacket, her skirt, her little beret, were all navy-blue; her jersey was a light pink, her hair was fair. She stood in the doorway and looked at me in surprise. Then she saw Makeer, kneeling on the floor, his eyes still closed: to her he must have looked like a man in prayer. 'Kenneth!' she said. Her voice was so low that one heard the sound of her breath above the sound of the word.

He opened his eyes, and uttered a sound; it came deep from within his slight chest. 'Get away!' he shouted at her. 'I don't want you! I'm better on my own! Please, please, go away! I beg of you.' He had come up from the floor; he stood for a moment, and I saw how he shuddered; even his mouth seemed to shake itself open, he could not keep it closed between the words he uttered. He lifted one arm and staggered towards the girl: his hand seemed accusatory, pointing at her, or as if he were making the gesture of expulsion instead of the words he could no longer utter. The girl had not spoken. He came to a halt before her, his hand just a few inches from her.

She put out her hand, and met his with hers, in an absurdly, sadly, genteel gesture, as if she had just been introduced to him.

She pulled him gently towards her, and his head bent lower. She kissed him on the lips.

Needless to say, I left the room, very quickly, glad to get out of it. But, as I have said, this was not the last time I was to see Makeer and the girl; and even if I had not known them, I would later have heard of them, anyway. We have all heard so much about them; we have all been given the chance to honour or revile their names.

3

IN THE VEINS of Cornelius Makeer there flowed the blood of half the nations of Europe, and of a great many of the tribes of Southern Africa. The skin of Cornelius's face had the brown colour and the high shine of polished walnut; that of his hands was lighter and rougher. By trade he was a carpenter, a plasterer, an interior decorator, a painter, a bricklayer—he could turn his hand successfully to almost anything in the building and decorating line. His manner was not, however, that of a man who works with his hands: it was rather, that of a man who works with his head, or of one who does no work at all—the manner of a gentleman. This gentlemanliness Cornelius had inherited from his father, Kenneth's grandfather, who had certainly been gentlemanly enough both in the whiteness of his skin and in his refusal to do any work at all. Having set up in concubinage with a Cape Coloured woman—at a time when this was still legally permissible, though considered socially and morally unspeakable by other whites—Cornelius's father had seen to it that his woman paid for the upkeep of himself and the family she bore him, by dressmaking. And Cornelius's mother submitted to the duty; she did not once urge her man to go out to work. She admired him too much to urge him to anything—he was so white, so educated, so English. In fact, he was a tall, cranky, irritable, drunken Irishman, who despised the company he kept, the house he lived in, his concubine, his children, all the circumstances of his life. But he kept himself very clean, very dapper even, in his blue suits and polished shoes, and did not consort with Coloureds other than his helpmeet. He went to the 'white' areas of the town for his drink and his entertainments, and in bars there he talked of his 'investments' to people who did not know of his *mésalliance;* he sat in parks and sunned himself; he was a great figure at ratepayers' meetings during municipal elections, when he invariably asked questions relating to the 'education of the younger generation', which for some reason he had made his special topic. The education of his own younger generation was a matter of complete indifference to him, however; and Cornelius Makeer was taken out of school very early and attached to an independent Coloured builder as a kind of apprentice.

From his gentlemanly and unlamented father—whom Cornelius as a boy had either seen not at all, the gentleman being out so often; or else seen much too much of, the gentleman being short of funds and skulking irritably at home—Cornelius Makeer had thus inherited neither his name nor any money. It was to his father, nevertheless, that he owed his unusually good command of English, his stooped and reflective walk, his way of nodding his head when he was spoken to, even when he disagreed with what was being said to him, and a manner that was as condescending as it could be to his inferiors, as ingratiating as it could be to his superiors.

Cornelius Makeer was putty in the hands of any white man. He did not actually call a white man 'Baas' as the Africans did; his status as a Cape Coloured demanded that he call a white man 'Sah'—and he called any white man 'Sah' with a vehemence and a frequency that generally made most white men feel kindly disposed towards him. It was a word that punctuated Cornelius's speech like a kind of tic; it was slipped in anywhere, even in the middle of such phrases as 'You see' which became in his mouth 'You-sah-see', or 'Never mind' which became 'Never-sah-mind', rendering some passages of his speech almost unintelligible. To his fellow-Cape Coloureds Cornelius Makeer was much more moderately ingratiating when they were richer than he was; and moderately patronizing when they were poorer. To the black African Cornelius's patronage was so excessive as almost to deprive him of the power of speech. To Africans he would gasp, stretch out his hand and wave it in command, and nod kindly when they did what he wanted of them, frown when they did not.

Cornelius was the father not only of Kenneth, but also of Peter, both children being by his thin, low-voiced, and low-spirited wife, who was fierce only in her respectability. The family lived in a house that was made entirely of corrugated iron—walls, roof, inner walls, everything. It was a very small house, and it had a tiny garden in front of a tiny *stoep*, and it was right on the edge of the district which was known simply as the Coloured Camp. This name dated from the days when the whole of Lyndhurst—white, Coloured, and African—had been a diamond-rush town, had been in fact one large and dusty and ramshackle encampment on the veld. But while the bungalowed suburbs of the white inhabitants of Lyndhurst now went under such names as 'Kensington', 'Chamberlain,' and 'Milnerton', the Coloured Camp had remained the Coloured Camp. It was a large grey area of irregular and unpaved roads, of corrugated-iron shacks and pitifully plastered little houses; it was bounded on three sides by stretches of unkempt and rock-littered veld, which effectively quarantined it from the white suburbs beyond. On the fourth side the Coloured Camp almost abutted on the town centre, and its position was thus a curiously yet fittingly central one—unlike that of the African locations, which were all miles out of the town.

And in the Coloured Camp there lived the entire Coloured population of Lyndhurst, the richest among them and the poorest, cheek-by-jowl. The rich were never really rich—they had small shops, perhaps, or were successful artisans and petty contractors, or schoolteachers, or sempstresses; the 'rich' were rich only in comparison with the poor, who were very poor indeed, as poor as the Africans, poor to the point of hunger and near-nakedness. The real distinction in the Coloured Camp, however, was between those who were respectable and those who were not, though inevitably it was the somewhat better-off who were more respectable. Respectability was the true dividing-line socially; and it was a line treacherously easy to cross, and always to the wrong side.

There were so many invitations to a loss of respectability that enumeration of them would become nothing less than a description of the life of everyone who lived in the Coloured Camp. And one could leave out nothing, not one item—neither the scenes of drunken cheerfulness and drunken violence that took place every Friday evening on every street corner, nor the very lack of tar on the streets, so that every wind covered with a disheartening film of dust the sticks of furniture in every home. There were no electric lights in the streets; no water-borne sanitation in the houses; no parks, no pavements, no trees; not a handsome building nor a pretty garden in the whole of the Coloured Camp. There was no hope; and that was the worst of all.

Yet those in the Coloured Camp who were respectable, were respectable with a fervour that should have put the respectable whites of Lyndhurst to shame. Because they felt themselves continually on trial, the respectable Coloureds never took their respectability for granted. They had to prove it every day: in the decorations of their houses and the clothes their children wore to school, in the conversations they had when visitors came, in the attitudes they adopted towards the whites and towards the Africans; in their gestures, their religion.

Certainly, it was so with Cornelius Makeer and his wife. Every Sunday morning they went to church; Cornelius decorously attired in a dark blue suit, a high white collar, and a pearl-grey tie with a silver pin through it; and his wife in a black bombazine dress and a black straw hat. Altogether, his respectability and that of his friends, was decorous in a strangely old-fashioned way: it was very much an affair of church-going and dark clothes on Sunday; of bits of best china, potted ferns, and photographs in leather frames in the living-room; of talk about the weather and cricket scores; of hushed, scandalized gossip about relatives—preferably distant ones—who had failed to remain respectable. When he was a young man Cornelius Makeer, in spotless whites, had played tennis every Saturday afternoon at the Cape Coloured Tennis Club (one sandy court and a clubhouse made of tin); when he was older he still went along to watch the tennis, and cried out loudly, when the applause was merited, 'Oh, good stroke there.' He called his friends by their second names, even when he had known them for years; and invariably prefaced their names with 'Mister'. He never went out without a hat on his head. He did not smoke, drink, or gamble, and he permitted himself no public intimacy with his wife. When violence took place in the streets near by, or women screamed with lewd pleasure and excitement in the dark veld opposite his house, Cornelius Makeer remained seated and raised his voice in conversation.

And his wife scrubbed, darned, sighed; scrubbed, darned, sighed; she slapped the children, the two boys, often, unlovingly, and sadly, for their own good. As she grew older she grew thinner; her body shrank, her hair receded, the features of her face grew smaller, except for her eyes. They were large and set too closely together, and in the white or her right eye there was a fleck, a mark, like a blood-spot in an egg, and over this eye the lid came down in a twitch, as though the speck irritated her. Towards the end of her life this nervous habit became more pronounced and continuous: she winked as if she was in mocking colloquy with a bitter, disreputable spirit that stood close by her, while she scrubbed and darned and listened to her husband's conversation. But the colloquy was a silent one; and to the day she took to her bed she never relaxed or forgave the children for anything they had done wrong. Once she took to her bed, however—in the tiny bedroom, with its uneven floor covered with hard linoleum and one tiny, curtained window cut into the corrugated iron—she cried and trembled, almost without pause; and no one could comfort her, or find out from her the reason for the sounds of grief which came from her. At the end the eyelid of her right eye hung down slack, twitching no longer, and the tears seeped silently below the closed lid, while the other eye remained dry and open; so that young Kenneth Makeer was filled with horror at the sight of her, and ran from the house, and hid like a little animal in a *donga* in the veld. It was there that his brother, Peter, found him, and brought him the news, later that night, that their mother was dead; and the two frightened and uncomprehending boys sat together in the darkness, shivering, sobbing, hearing in the distance the noises of the town.

The funeral was, as Cornelius described it, 'satisfactory', for he had always paid his dues to the burial society to which he belonged. And then he went on in the same way as before. It seemed that time had no power over him, but to make him more what he was already. He did not change his habits; he went to watch the tennis on Saturday afternoons and he always went to church on Sunday mornings. More than ever he looked like a professor, a pedagogue, even when he was overalled, be-plastered, paint-spotted. Low down on his nose he wore small spectacles with shiny gold frames; on his hand there was a broad wedding-ring; his greying hair was always neatly combed, to the last ringlet over his temple. His brow was furrowed and there were heavy lines around his mouth; but his skin still shone, as though every time he blew his nose or passed his large handkerchief over his brow he was imparting a discreet polish to it. More than ever he said 'Sah' when he spoke to white people; more than ever he stooped when he walked.

And the boys grew up. No longer were they quite so trim as they had been when their mother had been alive; when she had kept them both, year in and year out, unchangingly, in khaki shirts and khaki shorts. Now they wore their father's old clothes, or clothes they themselves had bought in second-hand shops with the money they had earned wherever they could. Their education was neglected; they stayed away from school and worked as caddies at the golf-club; or picked up tickeys and sixpennies in the Market Square. When Peter at last passed Standard Six he did not go on to do his Junior Certificate, as Cornelius had hoped he would, and as he could have afforded to make possible; instead Peter announced that now he was altogether finished with school.

He would not listen when his father warned him that without education he would not be able to rise in the world. 'Rise where?' Peter asked. 'Rise where in the world?'

'You could be a schoolmaster,' Cornelius said.

'A schoolmaster! With a Junior Certificate, in a Coloured school? I wouldn't earn as much as you do.'

'Perhaps you wouldn't; but you'd hold a position of respect.'

'Who'd respect me? Who?'

'The members of the Coloured community.'

'What they respect is a white skin. And I won't get one if I stay at school for the next twenty years.'

'Please, to talk like that is to look for trouble.'

'Well, I suppose I'm the kind of fellow who looks for trouble.'

'Then it will come to you,' his father warned him.

'And what about Kenneth? Why don't you make a schoolmaster out of him?'

'Because you know quite well that Kenneth is coming to help me.' Makeer's voice was irritated now. 'It's an understanding.'

'Just like it's an understanding that I'm not.'

'Yes,' the father said, angered. 'That's quite right.'

Peter brought his hands to his head and waggled them in a humorous gesture of surrender and dismissal. 'That's how it's always been. All right, all right.'

'I offered to you too,' Cornelius said, clumsily defensive.

'All right, all right,' All three of them waited for a moment, anxiously. But Peter spoke again, without anger. 'Good luck to Kenneth; good luck to me; we go our ways.' And Cornelius was content to leave the matter there, feeling that he had done his duty.

Peter went to a firm in town and became a delivery-boy. 'You'll never become anything this way,' his father still said to him occasionally; but because he felt guilty towards Peter, Cornelius was secretly relieved to have some of the responsibility for the boy off his shoulders; now that Peter was earning his own money regularly he was so much more of a man. And already Peter showed what kind of a man he would be, in just a year or two—a handsome, light-skinned man, with the straight-nosed, hard-chinned aspect of his Irish grandfather; tall, well-proportioned, easy and casual in his movements, a little slouching in his walk, given to wearing his hat tipped over one eye and his shirt-sleeves rolled up, and many cheap rings on his fingers. Peter never got into trouble with the police, or with his employers; but he fought often, spent nights out of the house, spoke loudly, whistled at girls, never came near the church or the tennis-club. 'He is a great anxiety to me,' Cornelius told Kenneth, frequently.

'He's all right. He knows what he's doing,' Kenneth always replied. Others saw Peter only as the whistling and jaunty boy, the bare-armed young tough; but Kenneth knew him better. Cornelius favoured Kenneth, and the three of them knew it; yet when the father showed his preference, when Kenneth himself would be moved to protest against an unfairness shown to Peter—then Peter would be the one to say something flippant, change the subject, perform some bit of tomfoolery. And often enough the thing that Peter would say or do would bring down on his head a further reproof; and this made Peter's actions seem to Kenneth almost saintly in their quality of self-sacrifice. Kenneth knew that Peter acted as he did out of a deep and unrewarded courtesy, for by being flippant, reckless, or irritating, he gave the father a reason for preferring his other son, he put himself deliberately in disfavour, so that the father could feel justified instead of guilty and insecure, as he would have had Peter reproached him and shown his need for love.

But only Kenneth knew of this; and to Peter he could not speak of it. He could only try to show that he was not disturbed by his brother's 'wildness'; that he trusted his brother, wished him well, loved him well. He could best do that, he knew, and had known from his earliest childhood, by doing what his father wanted him to do, and yet remaining true to Peter, never speaking against him in the father's presence, and by silently supporting Peter when the boy raged, or cursed his father, or broke things in his hands. And in this way both Cornelius and Peter Makeer came to depend on the youngest and slightest member of the family.

Yet, as far as his family was concerned, Kenneth felt that for himself things had always been easier; and even being depended upon was not a hardship. If he supported his father and brother in their relationship, he was in turn supported by them, and by his duties towards them. He loved them both; and it was for this reason that his ambitions never came to him but in the form of a temptation, an invitation to betrayal.

It was absurd. There he was, sunk in the Coloured Camp in Lyndhurst; but when Kenneth thought of winning power and wealth and fame, of gaining the respect and love of people he did not know, then simultaneously he felt the guilt of betrayal and abandonment towards his poor and respectable and loving father, towards his violent and bewildered brother. For others ambition could be part of a continuity of desire and emotion; for others the fulfilment of ambition could be a way of actually serving the desires of those closest and dearest; others could bring home their rewards in pride and love. But not Kenneth Makeer.

For where in Lyndhurst, and the great country beyond, could the rewards and prizes and trophies be found? Where was there success and power and riches? Where was the fame that was read about in the newspapers and applauded in the streets? Where was there a love that was neither abashed nor violent? Not in the Coloured Camp, where Kenneth Makeer and his family lived. Not in the Coloured quarter of every other town in the country, where Coloureds had to live. In the Coloured Camp there was deprivation, poverty, and squalor; and even those who fought themselves to some degree clear of squalor and poverty, even those who attained learning (as doctors or schoolmasters), who gathered together some money in business, who went away as soldiers and were awarded medals for gallantry, even those who were physically beautiful or gifted as singers or dancers, remained despised and rejected and hated, for ever outside what seemed to Kenneth the circles of true reward. And they were rejected and hated for precise reasons, of which Kenneth Makeer at the age of eighteen—after growing up in Lyndhurst, having passed his Junior Certificate, and having worked for his father for two years—was fully aware. They were rejected and hated for being what they were; and what they were was in their blood, on their skins, their hands, their faces; they could not scrub it out of themselves, and they could never be forgiven for it. The rejection was made formal in the laws, statutes, and ordinances of the country; it was enforced by all the power of the state.

Was there no point then in being ambitious? Often there did not seem to be any, other than the opportunities it gave for day-dreaming and subsequent self-reproach. In both of these activities Kenneth indulged; and because he was working *with* his father, and so had the entry to a hundred Lyndhurst homes, he was able to build rooms for his fantasies, and furnish them, and fill them with the people he met and the books he covertly eyed and the ornaments his fingers slid over when no one was looking. Then, at the end of each day's work, he rode home on his bicycle, along the flat Lyndhurst streets, back to the noise and the half-light of the Coloured Camp, back to the corrugated-iron house and the oil-lamps on the table and the cloth-covered apple-crate next to his bed, back to his brother who ate hastily and then went into the streets again. Often the younger brother followed the older, despite the reproachful glances he received over his father's gold-rimmed spectacles, or the lectures about the dangers of going astray that he would be given at work the next morning. Cornelius could not bear to reproach his younger son directly, so the lectures were invariably abstract and general in their terms, and were interrupted by extravagant praise of the work that Kenneth would be busy with at the time. Yet when Kenneth was really restless, neither glances, nor the subsequent reproaches, could keep him at home, reading a book or listening to the little battery-run radio.

In the streets of Lyndhurst, and especially in its dustiest and most disordered streets, Kenneth Makeer and his brother ran freely. Kenneth made love to Coloured girls, crouching on his knees in *dongas* and quarries in the veld, the smell of ordure in his nostrils; he fought with Coloured boys in gangs; he stood outside the Coloured bars and jeered at the drunkards flung into the street; he saw police-raids, when men were clubbed and carried upside-down and flung into pick-up vans; once a group of white youths surrounded him in the wild and deserted veld on the outskirts of the town and told him that they were going to cut his balls off. There were six, eight, ten of them; and Kenneth screamed in terror, until Peter, who had been with him when they had fled from the white gang, and of whom Kenneth had lost sight before he had fallen—Peter came back, swinging an iron railing and screaming like a madman, and all of the group of whites turned and fled. Then Peter dropped the iron railing, and in the darkness groped on the ground, until he touched his brother. 'Come on, *ou* boy,' Peter said. 'They wouldn't have done anything. They were just talking big.'

Late, Kenneth said, 'Thanks for coming back, Peter. I thought you'd left me.'

'Don't mention it, man. You'll do the same for me one day.'

It was dark, they were walking over the humped and tussocked veld, towards the street lamps that marked the nearest street. Peter's shadowy figure seemed to lurch and plunge forward in the darkness as he spoke, and Kenneth's heart contracted gratitude, and fear for him. 'I'll try to, Peter. I won't forge. Kenneth said, making what haste he could to catch up with his brother. The street lamps drew nearer; they marked a whole suburb of well-lit and orderly streets; beyond that again, where the lights failed, there was more veld and then the Coloured Camp, their home.

The days passed in work, and the nights at home or outside it. Time went so insidiously; summer or winter the thorn trees were unchanging, and the bluegum trees shed and regained their leaves indiscriminately, and every day the sun rose in the east and set in the west, to be seen through its entire passage; as if here were a place where nature neither aged nor renewed herself, but merely slept. Yet ambition was not forgotten: nor could Kenneth put out of mind the one thing which made the ambitions he dared not acknowledge seem not entirely grotesque and pointless. This one thing was that Kenneth was light-skinned, for a Coloured, as light as many white men. In another country, or even farther north in this country, where there were so many fewer Coloureds . . . .

So the voice of treason and betrayal and ingratitude spoke, though to others it might have sounded like the voice of hope, of youth, of desire, which we are all entitled to hear at some time, and to live by, as well as we can, on the memory of it, the hope of its return. And what was strange too in Kenneth's case was that Kenneth knew it was *because* of this lighter skin of his that his people loved him. They were proud of him, he looked so much more like a white man than they did; they did not seem to realize that if he were ever to act on his gift he would have to cut himself off entirely from them, never see them, never speak to them, bring up his children in ignorance of them.

The whole speculation was mere self-torment, nevertheless. He could not go north, let alone leave the country; he had no money, and even if he had had the money, he knew that he did not have the nerve to try. Nor the ingratitude, the indifference, the callous lovelessness that he would need as much as nerve or money. He stayed at home, he went to work, he went into the streets at night.

When Cornelius Makeer got the contract for rebuilding the side fence of Mr Last's house, he was, as he said at the time to Mr Last, 'Sah, most gratified, sah.' To Kenneth he repeated several essions of gratification. 'We may expect even more racts,' he said, 'if we do the work well. He is so rich, o many contacts through the building society. We xpect almost anything to come of this.' To Mr Last lid not dare to speak of his hopes for the future; whe spoke to Mr Last, Cornelius positively simpered—greying, bent, and parsonical though he was; and he turned up the sole of his shoe and looked at it, as if afraid to look anywhere else.

So Cornelius and Kenneth came to work at Mr Last's house, along with a wizened little African by the name of Sixpence, who was employed to do the rough work, though he was even smaller than Kenneth. The job was a very simple one: they were to take up a ragged hedge of oleander bushes along the lane to the side of the house and replace it with a more dignified brick fence. Sixpence worked ahead of them, pulling up the bushes and digging the trench for the foundation of the fence; Kenneth and Sixpence then mixed the concrete for Cornelius, carried it in barrows, and poured it as Cornelius directed; Kenneth helped his father to level off the foundation, and lay the first bricks. Cornelius was grave and silent when he worked; there was no shade from the sun in the sandy lane; the days were hot and Kenneth worked in the smell of his own sweat. When they broke for lunch, or for afternoon tea, they sat under a cypress tree within the grounds of the house, to the side of a gauzed-in sleeping porch. And every lunch-time, when he came home from his office, Mr Last came to see what progress they had made; and in the evenings too he walked up and down, with Cornelius a respectful pace or two behind him. But though Cornelius walked behind, he was so much taller than Mr Last that their long shadows stretched head-to-head across the sand.

Mr Last was a self-made man, who had come to South Africa as a boy, and who still spoke English with something of a West Country softness in his accent. He had made his money originally as the owner of a shoestore; but that had long since been sold, and he now engaged himself in the far more gentlemanly occupation of directing a well-to-do local building society. Years before he had been injured in a motor accident, in which his wife had been killed; he walked with a limp, and with much movement of his shoulders, as though his shoulders could make up by their activity for the sluggishness of his foot. He was short, thickset, going bald; his stare was direct and unrevealing;

and because his eyes were hard and grey, his jaw was heavy, his mouth straight, the softness of his voice was curiously disconcerting.

Cornelius was altogether afraid of Mr Last; and Cornelius always watched Kenneth very anxiously when Mr Last was about, lest Kenneth should do something that would displease his employer. When they had first come to the house Mr Last had asked casually of Cornelius, 'Your boy?'

'Sah,' Cornelius replied, turning his head for a look at Kenneth before he replied, 'yes, sah.'

'He doesn't look like you,' Mr Last said.

Cornelius took this as a joke—a very good joke, the funniest joke he had heard for many days. 'No sah, that's quite true, he doesn't look like me, it's strange, sah, oh yes, sah,' said Cornelius, nodding his head as he spoke, and laughing in little chuckles between his words. Mr Last waited until the amusement subsided before going on to make a remark that had nothing to do with Kenneth or Kenneth's appearance; and Cornelius's brow had immediately furrowed deeply and professionally. Since then Mr Last had nodded at Kenneth a few times, had once said, 'Here, catch this,' flinging at him a tape-measure, which Kenneth, to Cornelius's consternation, had failed to catch. But Mr Last had not even looked to see where the tape-measure had fallen. Every morning, every evening, Kenneth formally greeted Mr Last; but as often as not his greetings were not returned.

Yet, despite this, Mr Last had in fact noticed Kenneth by feature, manner, stance, voice. There was something pathetic about the boy, Last had felt, though he could not have said why he felt this, other than that the boy was so slight, and young, and fair-skinned, and bound to his clown of a father. It was 'nonsense' of course even to give a moment to it; yet when Mr Last thought of the work that was being done outside his house, when he mentioned it to his daughter, and there came into his mind a picture of the trench outside, the foundation laid and the first bricks on it, Cornelius stooping over and the little African standing by with a spade in his hand—always, in this picture, there was another figure, distinct, isolated, irritating. It was the boy—yes, but what was it about him that made him so very much a part of the picture, and yet unassimilated within it? Mr Last stared harder than before at Kenneth when he next went to inspect the work; and Kenneth dropped his eyes; but it was too late. So that was it, then,

Mr Last decided, with his quick and indifferent intuition—the boy was unhappy. Mr Last gave him a moment's compassion: what it must be like, he wondered, to be not merely a Coloured boy, working in the sun, in overalls too big and mannish for him, with no prospect of becoming anything but what his father was, and at the same time to hope, to understand, to want? All this Mr Last had seen in the glance that his eyes had exchanged with Kenneth's; and he did not care to look for more. He turned away; but halted after he had taken a pace or two. 'What's your name?' he asked.

'Kenneth, sir.'

'And you're learning your father's trade?'

'Yes, sir.'

'Well, you could do worse.' Unexpectedly, Mr Last was moved to explain to Kenneth how little he had to grumble about. 'Your father's a good workman, I can see it. You be as good a workman as he is, and you won't go hungry, you'll always have work to do.'

'Sah, thank you, sah,' Cornelius, who had been standing near by, could not restrain himself; but the stare he received from Mr Last discouraged him from coming any closer. 'Sah is very kind,' Cornelius said, nevertheless, standing where he was.

'Don't you think so?' Mr Last asked suddenly of Kenneth. The three men were standing in the lane, Last and Kenneth confronting one another, Cornelius a few paces off. And though the effect of the question he had just asked was violent, there was something curiously defensive about it too. The white man waited for an answer; and Cornelius moved impatiently at the hips, then at the shoulders, as if beckoning Kenneth on.

The boy's answer came eventually, 'I don't know, sir.' He stood very straight and still, in his baggy brown overalls.

'Sah——!'

Last ignored Cornelius's interruption. He stirred heavily, turned again to go; and it was over his shoulder that he said, 'Then you better find out. It's all nonsense, everything else, let me tell you. This is the only life you'll ever have.' He gestured with one hand; his gesture took in his own large white house, open and fenceless to the sandy lane; and the two Coloureds in their working clothes; even Sixpence, who sang softly as he worked, unconsciously. 'You don't know, hey? You'll learn then, you'll have to.'

'Sah—sah—I don't understand—sah—how the boy——'

'Oh, I can *understand* all right. Understanding's easy.' Last glanced again in the direction he had to go, towards the house, before stepping with a clumsy dragging stride of his injured leg over the bricks that Cornelius had just laid. Some earth was dragged on to the wet mortar by the white man's boot; but Cornelius did not dare to remove it immediately. He stood on one side of the line of the foundation, the white man on the other. 'Anyone can see, can know . . . . But I can't change it. Nor can he,' Last said, and pointed at Kenneth; he knew that the boy could hear what he was saying, but he did not look in Kenneth's direction. 'And you—Makeer, I don't suppose you've ever thought of trying to change it.'

'Changing, sah? Changing what, sah?'

Last smiled, his lower lip protruding a little beyond the upper, bringing into prominence the heaviness of his chin. 'No, you wouldn't. Let's hope he won't either, when he's reached your age. For his sake.'

'Won't—sah—?'

'Won't waste his time with nonsense. Do what he has to do. Live the kind of life he has to live. There's no other for him. There's no other for any of us.' Then Mr Last saw Kenneth approaching; and his head settled more firmly on his shoulders. He looked like a man preparing to guard the house behind him.

But Kenneth had come only to apologize. There was a cleft inserted in the too-narrow space between his eyes, as if it had been driven there. 'I'm sorry, sir,' Kenneth said awkwardly.

'What for? I asked you a straight question. You gave me a reply. I didn't want any more.'

'Thank you, sir.'

Mr Last's smile did not change. 'Don't thank me, now. I haven't given you anything. Only—my attention.' And he turned and stumped away, along the length of the porch, around the front of the house, out of sight, where Cornelius and Kenneth had never been.

Cornelius immediately began scolding Kenneth; though the scolding merely took the form of extolling Mr Last. He was such a rich gentleman. Such an interested gentleman. The way he stopped and talked when he was so busy, a man with concerns, affairs, investments. It was gentlemanly, it was kindly, it was not at all common. Would Kenneth ever have expected that a man like Mr Last would be interested in him? Mr Last? In Kenneth?

'Interested!' Kenneth broke out suddenly. 'It cost him a lot to be interested. It's a hard life, yes, it's a hard life for him, I can see how hard it is, in his big house, with his big car, with all his money—it's the only life he'll ever have—oh, oh—that's the way it is, oh yes, oh sure, he understands, the old bastard. So go back to your bricks, you bloody *Hotnot*, it's the only life you'll ever have.' Kenneth began limping towards the bricks, in a cruel parody of the white man's limp.

Cornelius was the one who saw the figure vague and dark behind the gauze-netting of the porch. In a moment his hat was off his head, and his voice sang out, 'Good afternoon, madam. Madam, please, good afternoon.'

Kenneth had halted, one foot behind the other; behind him, scored into the sand of the lane, was the irregular mark of the dragging steps he had taken.

There was no reply from the figure behind the gauze. Then it had gone, though the two frightened Coloureds stood and stared in silence at the place where they had seen it, as if the very blurs and marks on the gauze might yet be good enough to give them the friendly and condescending greeting they had hoped for.

'What have you done?' Cornelius cried out in anguish. 'She'll tell her father, and then what will happen? Where is my job? And where is my opportunity?' Kenneth's face was turned to him, in fear and defiance, and the unhappiness he saw there made Cornelius cry out again, 'What have you done?' It was because of the love he felt for the boy, even as he shouted at him, that Cornelius could not restrain himself, but came to Kenneth and took him by the shoulders. He shook Kenneth backwards and forwards lightly, and then let go. He was shocked when Kenneth stumbled back and fell, sprawling in the dust.

It was just then that Miss Last came around the corner of the house. She halted abruptly when she saw them, but it was too late, for they had seen her.

With a clumsy, lurching movement, Kenneth got to his feet. He did not look up, but began dusting his overalls with his hands, moving back slowly. 'All right,' he said to his father, 'all right. I won't forget what you did. You see what you did.' He pointed at the ground, as if the evidence of his fall were still there. 'I'm going now. You saw me on the ground.' He turned his back on them and began walking away.

'Go!' Cornelius shouted after him. 'I don't want you! You bring disgrace on me.'

Kenneth suddenly broke into a run, his overalls flapping without dignity around his legs. Since Mr Last had made his first remark to him everything had had, for Kenneth, its own sharp point of humiliation; and his fall in front of the girl was the last. He did not expect it to happen, but his eyes suddenly stung with tears; ahead of him, at the end of the lane, the blue tar quivered in his sight, and as he ran he wiped the tears from his eyes. The gesture was seen by both Cornelius and the white girl, then Kenneth disappeared around the corner, and they no longer looked where he had gone.

Cornelius had taken off his soiled and broad-brimmed hat. 'Good morning, madam,' he said, struggling to control his breathing.

Little Sixpence muttered, 'Missus,' and remained half-crouching, as a mark of respect.

'Good morning.'

Cornelius was so much older and taller than Miss Last, and under such emotion, that the girl seemed embarrassed, and looked away. But there was only little Sixpence to look at, his features ancient and wrinkled, with the grey peppercorns of his beard stuck here and there on his chin, and his eyes clouded, like a blind man's. His feet were bare and his toes were hard and cracked; they looked almost like the feet of an animal. Slowly the girl turned to Cornelius again; and immediately he broke into speech.

'Madam, I am terribly sorry about what happened, what you saw that boy of mine doing. And saying, too, madam. I'm glad he's gone, madam; I don't want him here, I won't let him come here again. I'm going to finish the job by myself, madam; and so that Mr Last won't have to suffer because that boy isn't here, I'm going to work double-time to make up for it. Madam will see, I will finish the job at the time I said, I will work so late every afternoon, I will begin so early every morning with this Sixpence here. Your father is so kind to me, and I must show the madam how I hate what he did. I am respectable—with respect to a European gentleman like your father—madam, I try—'

Cornelius's voice had grown slower and slower, heavier and heavier, and so finally he stopped, as if at the muddy bottom of his own abasement. And the white girl seemed as abashed as he was.

But Cornelius wasn't done yet: he still had to go lower. He almost whispered, 'So the madam will not tell her father . . . ?'

'You mean——?'

'I mean you won't see him again, madam. He won't disturb you with his disgusting tricks, please, madam. And if madam will forget that she ever saw him that will be the best. I will hit him,' Cornelius cried, flinging his hat on the ground, 'if he ever puts his face in front of the madam again, after such insults—the fool, the loafer.'

'So I won't see him again?' Miss Last spoke loudly, her eyes opening wide.

'Never again, madam! So help me God! God strike me dead! A cheeky boy!' Cornelius picked up his hat and once again threw it down on the ground. 'God is my witness!' he cried. 'I hate a cheeky boy in front of a European gentleman. And the madam, too.'

His passion seemed to fill the girl with shame, to recoil upon her. 'Please——' she began to say; but then her voice rose. 'He had no business to be rude to my father. And in such a horrible cruel way. I saw him. I heard him. I've never seen anything like it. And from someone like that? Who is he? What is he?'

Cornelius answered her question directly. 'He is nothing. He is the dust in front of the madam.'

'And what am I?' she challenged him.

'Madam is the madam.'

'Ah, is that how it is,' she said, leaning forward and breathing deeply.

'Yes, madam, that is how it is.'

Then the girl drew back. 'That's horrible,' she said. She looked in the direction where Kenneth had gone. 'I want to do what's right,' she said. 'That's why I came out.' Irresolutely she began to move away. 'I didn't know——'

'Madam,' Cornelius called after her. 'Please, your father—will you tell him?'

'You've done what you think is right.'

Cornelius lifted a shaking hand in appeal. He could say only, 'What the madam wants is right.'

The girl shook her head. She turned her back and walked away. For a long time Cornelius stared after her; then, when she had gone, he fell furiously on his work. He worked until it was late, late in the afternoon; the rays of the setting sun showed up the dust that was in the air, and still he worked, to make up for the absence of Kenneth.

4

WHAT MAKES OF someone a 'liberal' in a country like South Africa is really a great mystery. Isabel Last, at the age of seventeen was a liberal; but, like most South African liberals, Isabel Last at the age of seven had then been a liberal too. Almost all white South African liberals begin very early: that is their trouble, or their glory, if you so prefer. Tiny little children, they can be, when they begin to 'feel sorry' for all the African and Coloured children who have dirty clothes and are so obviously hungry, neglected, spoken to unkindly; and though, like any well-brought-up white child, our little liberal is horrified by the snot that hangs from the noses of the black children, at the grime that is encrusted on the backs of their hands, at the very blackness of their skins—still, in a way he does not understand and does not even desire, he feels a large, unwelcome, and inexplicable responsibility for their cold, their hunger, their misery. It is a burden to him; a double burden: a treble burden, for he is burdened not only by his pity, and by his impotence to relieve the misery that arouses his pity; but also by his loneliness. Because he knows very well, our little liberal, and know it early, that most of the people around him do *not* feel as he does, that there is something singular and lonely in what he feels.

He is seven or eight years old, no more; he cannot express what he feels, he barely knows what he feels, and still less does he know whether it is right or wrong of him to feel as he does. More often than not, because he is lonely he feels that he is in the wrong; but he cannot change the flow of his compassion by an act of will. And he finds that it is not only the Coloured and African children for whom he finds himself feeling sorry: it is even, he finds, the Coloured and African adults who are making this demand upon him—huge though they are, frightening, black and impassably strange though they are. And it is not only them, either: there are claimants for his pity everywhere. He learns in his history lessons about the wars between the French and the English, and though the rest of the class applauds when Napoleon is finally sent to St Helena, or when the French are routed at Agincourt, he finds himself alone in the class in feeling sorry for Napoleon, for the ignominously vanquished Dauphin and all his armoured thousands. He feels sorry for the heavyweight boxer who loses the title-fight; for the boy at school who is chased out of the playground; for the Zulus at the battle of Blood River. All who have ever been worsted, defeated, subdued, condemned, despised, make their claim upon him. Of course, he shirks the claim guiltily; he joins the applause of the powerful, he joins the gang of schoolboys jeering at the one worsted in a fight, or those who make a piccanin crawl like a dog before giving him a piece of bread. Then guilt towards the oppressed, whom he has rejected, and guilt towards the oppressors, whom he knows he supported so reluctantly, both feed his loneliness; and loneliness feeds the compassion again—and so on, round and round in a circle from which there seems no escape.

There is an escape, ultimately, though it is learned only as time passes. In itself the passage of time blunts the edge to compassion, just as it blunts all the other emotions of childhood. No longer a child, the liberal no longer wonders what it must be like to feel the cold pavement against his own bare feet, he doesn't even think of desperately taking off his own shoes to give to another. And then time teaches him to take pride in his liberalism; it can encourage in him the growth of a feeling of sheer righteousness, which seeks only and always to satisfy itself, so that liberalism and loneliness become a pleasure, not at all the pain that they were before. And our little liberal is a grown man or woman, doing the work he has chosen to do, settled fast in his habits, secure in what he feels, unwilling to feel anything new, knowing what is right and wrong for him, and only very rarely—if at all—asking himself why right and wrong are what they are for him, and how they came to be what they are. And in this of course, as in so very much else, our liberal is in exactly the same boat as everyone else, unwelcome though the notion might be to him if he is one of the proud and self-righteous kind.

So when you next hear a little boy or girl in their play with their fellows taking on themselves the burden of the losing side, tell yourself not to despair on their behalf. They will suffer despair, it is true; their side will lose in the end, and so will they, in that and other roles, again and again. But out of it, as time passes, time will offer them the victories dearest and closest to them, the victories they most want.

Certainly, if Isabel Last hadn't been a liberal, she would have gone straight to her father with the story that the Coloured workmen doing the fence were being cheeky to him behind his back. As it was, being a liberal, Isabel had gone out with a confused intention of reproving the workmen simply by showing herself to them—as if, on sight, they might divine that she was on their side, and therefore be filled with guilt at having abused her father. She hadn't meant to make trouble between the father and son; she hadn't meant the old man to take extra work on himself; she hadn't meant to flaunt over them both the superiority of her position. But that was all she had succeeded in doing; and the momentary excitement she had got from doing it was no comfort to her when she was alone again. On the contrary, it was the source of the deepest shame she felt over the whole incident.

This story is as much Isabel's as it is Kenneth's; and it is her whom we must now follow—not only as she goes back into her house, or when she visits her elderly friend, Miss Bentwisch, and tells her what had happened with the two Coloured workmen, but through all the months, the years succeeding, when she lived ignorant of Kenneth and his affairs, and he remained ignorant of hers. For each of them had duties, families, and friends; neither Kenneth nor Isabel were ever alone, even when they feared they were, or wanted to be.

Fully and frankly, but with no anticipation of any kind, Isabel told Miss Bentwisch of what had happened between herself and the two Coloureds. She left out nothing of her own confusion and ambiguity of response; it was so very much the kind of story in which Miss Bentwisch was most interested. And when she had finished, Miss Bentwisch agreed that what had happened was, as Isabel described it, 'a horrible mixed-up South African kind of thing to have happened'; she sympathized with Isabel's confusion and guilt; she agreed that the boy, to judge from the way he had behaved, seemed to have some spirit in him; she agreed, too, that it was shameful that a man's soul should be twisted into the shape that Cornelius's seemed to be. 'But what about my own?' Isabel asked. 'The way I spoke to the old man was twisted enough. And as for them, Daddy's right!—that's the worst about it. All that boy can hope for, if he's lucky, is that he'll be like his father one day.'

'I wouldn't say that.'

'But what else is there for him?'

'I don't know. I haven't met the boy. But if he's got something to him, he might still find his way.'

'His way to where? To being a better bricklayer than his father? To saying, "Madam, madam, madam" all the time, like his father?'

'A good bricklayer is a useful member of society.'

'I know that. But there's no society here for him to be a member of. He could be the best bricklayer in the world, but there'd still be no place for him, except in the dust, as his father said. He still wouldn't be able to walk through the front door of most of the houses in Lyndhurst. He still couldn't sit on the front seat of a bus. He still couldn't go into a bioscope, or a concert in the Town Hall, or send his children to a good school—or anything. And what if those are the things he wants to do? And of course they are: they are the things that everyone wants to do.'

Miss Bentwisch reflected on what Isabel had just said. Then she said, 'In a way he's lucky. Fighting for himself really means fighting for others, there's no choice for him. And the fight for others is the only worthwhile fight.'

'But how can he fight? Who can he fight? His father? My father? He's already fought them, and all that's happened is that he's had to run away back to the Coloured Camp. He was crying, I think; and he's a man already, not a child. So what it must have been to him! He has no weapons, he has no opportunities, he has nothing. It's so unfair, when we have everything.'

'That's our opportunity, of course. That's our chance to join in a worthwhile struggle, to do something better with our lives than just live them.'

'And he can't even do that. Not what we'd call living.'

'No.'

There was a pause; both were silent, thinking of what they had said. Then Miss Bentwisch asked, 'And what does he look like, this boy?'

Isabel laughed, and blushed slightly. 'It's awful to admit this, but I don't really know. I've hardly had a chance to look at him. He's small.'

'I see. He's small.'

Isabel could not help saying, 'You sound as though you know all about him now.'

'Well, you've done nothing but talk about him for the last fifteen minutes.'

'I'm sorry.'

'There's nothing to be sorry about. I enjoyed listening to you.'

'I know,' Isabel said regretfully. 'You just egg me on, and then when I go away I feel that I've been jabbering away all the time instead of listening to you.'

'You jabber away very interestingly. And what you've told me today——'

Isabel interrupted eagerly, 'Would you think of doing something about it? I'd be so glad if something good came of what I did. Then I'd feel I'd made up for speaking like that. . . . Even if it's just a job for them. Have you got a job for them? A garden wall that you want fixed up? I can recommend them, they're very good workmen,' Isabel said, laughing at what she was saying. 'And you'd be doing me a favour.'

'Perhaps I'd be doing myself one.'

'Then you will——?'

'Then we'll see.'

'You'll see, you mean,' Isabel said. 'I won't. Perhaps you'll give them some work to do, and a bonus at Christmas, and all sorts of things, and I'll never hear about it again.'

'Perhaps I will, perhaps I won't. Perhaps I'll decide that the pair of them aren't worth a moment's thought, and that poor little Isabel has misjudged everything again. So you ought to be grateful to me for keeping my own counsel.'

'I'm grateful to you for everything.'

Isabel and her companion sat side by side on a broad swinging chair, covered with cushions, in a corner of a spacious wooden porch. Isabel had come to Miss Bentwisch's house for tea, straight from school, and was still wearing her school gym tunic, with its pinafore top; she looked demure, slight, very fair-complexioned; the sleeves of her white blouse were puffed out and transparent at her shoulders; her forearms were bare. Miss Bentwisch was a woman very much older than Isabel; her face seemed all lengthy cheek-bone and brow, with no beauty or refinement in it, until one looked into her eyes, and saw how deeply, darkly blue they were. Because of her eyes some people said Miss Bentwisch must have been a beauty once, which she had never been; she had always been gaunt, large-featured, plain. But because of her wealth, her parentage, and her loneliness, she was the kind of person about whom people were inclined to imagine such things as lost beauty and tragic love-affairs in the past.

Miss Bentwisch was a survivor of what were sometimes called 'Lyndhurst's great days'; the days when the whole of Lyndhurst had been even more dusty and disordered than the Coloured Camp now was; when the town had been a world-famous diamond-mining centre, rather than the minor commercial and agricultural centre it was more and more becoming. Miss Bentwisch's father, who had come to Lyndhurst as a penniless German Jew, had ended his career by being knighted by King Edward VII, and posthumously a bust of him stared out of a niche in the wall of the public library. Of the descendants of the half-dozen or dozen great mining magnates from 'the old days', Miss Bentwisch was the only one who still lived in Lyndhurst, though she took no part in the management of the Lyndhurst General Mining and Exploration Company, which was itself now merely one company of a group with its headquarters in Johannesburg. Indeed, important though the mines still were to its economy, the control of the public affairs of the town had largely passed into the hands of men like Isabel's father: self-made men of the middle-classes, engaged in commerce and industry, who were quite indistinguishable from their fellows in any other town in the Union. And even these men felt their positions to be insecure, for more and more their places were being taken by Boers from the country, eager to learn the ways to commercial success and social esteem. And beyond the Boers, again, were the Africans, whose turn, too, would surely come.

Yet Miss Bentwisch remained, and in a town where each hungry and self-made generation so quickly followed the last, she could easily have made of herself something of a souvenir: people would have been glad if she had, and would have forgiven her any eccentricities, which she might have cared to display. But she lived alone, and very quietly; she did no entertaining, and rarely went out of her house; the only thing which gossip had been able to seize upon was that she was in the habit of giving large sums of money to charities, especially those involving the welfare of the Africans and the Coloureds. The money was usually given anonymously, however; and the closest most of the townsfolk were ever able to come to Miss Bentwisch was when they stopped on their walks to stare curiously at her house. The house was a huge one, and had been built to Sir Lucius Bentwisch's own confused and Germanic tastes: it was two storeys (unusual in Lyndhurst); it had turrets; it had pinnacles; it had gables; it had wooden porches upstairs and downstairs, running fully around the house; and much fretted wood had been used to emphasize the exterior lines of every piece of decorative architecture. For such a large house the grounds in front were small; to the side there was much more space, most of it taken up by a series of hedges in a maze-like pattern, where Sir Lucius had been in the habit of walking at nightfall.

And there, after a lifetime of bachelordom—his moustache yellow with tobacco and his face and hands puffed-out and transparent, as though filled with water—Sir Lucius had wooed in his own fashion the young Scotswoman from Edinburgh who had come to be his nurse. And had won her, too, and in turn had been presented by her with a child, a few months before his death. There were many who said immediately that the child was not Sir Lucius's; but Sir Lucius seemed to think it was, because by the terms of his will he left his entire estate in trust to the little girl-child. On the publication of the will the young Scotswoman promptly decamped with all the clothes, jewellery and other portables she could pack into her bags; she left the daughter, who was undoubtedly hers, to be brought up by Sir Lucius's rather resentful relatives. The effective relative turned out to be the one closest to Sir Lucius: a younger brother, who had been handling the business of the family on the continental side, in Amsterdam; after his brother's death he had transferred his operations to London, and it was in a succession of boarding-schools and convents in England that the girl had been brought up.

No sooner had she come of age, however, than she had returned to South Africa, to which she was almost entirely a stranger; and not only to South Africa, but to Lyndhurst; and not only to Lyndhurst, but to the house in which she had been born. She dispossessed the last of the migrant families who had for so many years been renting the house, restored those parts of it which it was necessary to restore, and closed the doors on most of the rest of it. Since then she had lived in Lyndhurst; she had gone back to England a few times, mostly on occasions of a melancholy nature, for few of her uncle's children had lived to enjoy the money that had been left to them—they had been killed at war, or in motor accidents; a girl had committed suicide in her St. John's Wood home. The youngest daughter had married a military gentleman, by the name of Martin Bullivant, and their son (who also had the name of Martin Bullivant) was Miss Bentwisch's sole, close-surviving relative; and was known to be her heir.

This—then—was the lady with whom Isabel sat on the wooden porch of the large house, on a sunny Friday afternoon, having come for tea. The first time she had been to the house, Isabel had been very nervous, very much conscious of the visit as a 'grown-up' affair; and not at all sure that she would have been so anxious to win the Lucille Bentwisch Prize for an Essay on Race Relations if she had known that it would subsequently involve tea with the lady who had given the prize. On that first visit Isabel had been accompanied by prim little Miss Eastcote, the headmistress of the school, who for the occasion had put on her best flowered silk dress and most sharply pointed shoes, and had dabbed so much of her best scent behind her ears that she had smelt, as Miss Bentwisch later put it, 'like a trollop'. On the second visit, when Miss Bentwisch made this remark, Isabel giggled in an ecstasy of divided loyalties: by now, however, Isabel's loyalties were no longer divided.

Isabel admired Miss Bentwisch almost without reservation: if she had dared to she would have copied Miss Bentwisch's voluminous clothing and severe, almost mannish, hair-style, as assiduously as she copied Miss Bentwisch's views. Yet she pitied Miss Bentwisch, too: pitied her because she was old, unmarried, childless, lived alone in such a large house—though Isabel also managed contradictorily to be shocked, hurt and jealous when she found out that Miss Bentwisch was not quite as lonely as she seemed. Isabel found out, in fact, that she was only one among several young people who regularly visited Miss Bentwisch; and she could not understand why Miss Bentwisch had kept the existence of the others a secret from her. When she dared to tackle Miss Bentwisch about this, the older lady had simply laughed at her. 'Nonsense, there are no secrets. I haven't introduced you to the others, but I've never claimed that you're the only visitor I have. That would be absurd, I'm not that much of a hermit. And if I choose to have my friends come in one at a time, you can't really complain about that, can you, my dear? I prefer to have you singly; I find that you all go so much further when I spread you out in this way.'

Isabel felt that she had been very mean, begrudging her friend the company of others, in whatever circumstances her friend most enjoyed having company. Yet, in her hurt, she could not resist asking, 'Is there anyone else from High School who comes to see you?'

Miss Bentwisch smiled. 'I wouldn't tell you if there were.' Her smile softened a little, on her gaunt face, as she added, 'But I dare say that you would have heard any other girl talking about her friendship with me, if there had been one.'

'I'm not sure,' Isabel said. 'I don't talk to anyone about you.'

'Oh, why not?'

'Because I don't want them to know,' Isabel said simply and defiantly.

She was rewarded with an immediate understanding. 'That's a great compliment,' Miss Bentwisch said, 'considering what most people are like.'

'Exactly. And I'm not sure that your other friends feel the same way.'

'Well, I'd be flattered if they did. But let's talk about something else, Isabel. Just accept that I'm a very private old lady who enjoys her privacy. There's a great deal that I do that you know nothing about.'

'I've heard all the rumours about you,' Isabel said. 'About the charities, and all that sort of thing. You've never told me anything about them.'

'I shan't start now.'

When it was time for Isabel to go she still lingered on, each visit, unwilling to leave. She loved the house with its high, moulded, white ceilings and faded papers on the walls, the thickly-carpeted and much-shadowed passages, the massive polished banisters along the staircase; even the maze in the grounds seemed to her romantic. There was food for imagination in Miss Bentwisch's house; just as there was food for the imagination in Miss Bentwisch's appearance and manner, her very accent. And Isabel's imagination, stultified by the drab corrugated-iron roofing of the town, the drab conversations of the townsfolk, by the drab waste spaces around the town, was grateful for what sustenance it could get. Later in the afternoon, after they had spoken of Kenneth, Miss Bentwisch talked of her girlhood in England, and some of the names that Isabel had read of in her books—and there were hundreds of such names, names of places, people, trees, theatres—became momentarily real to the girl, illumined, available, things in possible world. They had talked of England before; but never had Isabel exclaimed, interrupting suddenly—'Why did you ever come back? I would never have come back.'

'Well, perhaps you will have a chance to go one day. And then we'll see.'

'But it's different for me. I mean, I was born here, and was brought up here—I'd be a stranger there. But you grew up there, it was all yours; and yet you came back. I can't understand it.'

'Perhaps you'll understand it better when you've been. I feel that here what I do can still make a difference; there, nothing I could have done would have made any difference, it's all so old, so settled, so established. Here, things are just beginning; there, they're ending.'

'But——'

'But what have I done here that could make a difference to anything? Is that what you mean?'

'No—I mean, yes,' Isabel admitted frankly. 'You live so quietly, you could have lived as quietly in England; and enjoyed all the other things. All the things there are in books.' And to show that she was being as simple as she might have sounded, Isabel laughed and said, 'Even if it was just having snow in winter.'

It was warm on the porch, the light lay heavy and yellow on a little dusty patch of lawn, and the fronds of a palm tree hung down at their ends. 'There's nothing to enjoy in snow,' Miss Bentwisch instructed Isabel. 'Not in the towns. In a moment it's all filthy slush; it gets into your shoes and stockings.'

'I don't know what I'll do if I ever see snow,' Isabel said wistfully. 'I think I'll think I'm in a book.'

'What an ambition!' Miss Bentwisch mocked her. 'I'd rather feel that I was in the real world.'

'Well, I'm glad you did come back, anyway, so I shouldn't be talking like this. I don't know what I would have done without you.'

'That's very kind of you, Isabel.'

'It isn't kind, it's the truth. You've made me think—and no one else ever did that.'

'You've always tried to think for yourself, surely.'

'Without you I would never have gone on, I would have stopped half-way, like everyone else does.'

'If they ever begin at all.'

'Most of them don't, that's true,' Isabel admitted, without regret. A little more reluctantly, she added, 'Even someone like Daddy, who doesn't care what other people think, he stops short, he doesn't do any real thinking for himself. All he thinks is *about* himself, and that's something quite different.' Isabel spoke hesitantly; she did not want to talk about her father behind his back, but to whom could she talk about him, if not to Miss Bentwisch?

In any case, Miss Bentwisch took up her remark in the most general way. "That's very good, what you've just said. Self—self—self—I don't mean your father particularly, I mean all the men like him; I mean almost everyone. There are so few people who seem to realize that there's no meaning to oneself unless one is busy with something much bigger than just what one is. A cause or a duty—something which doesn't begin and end inside one precious self-contained little personality. Don't you think so?'

'I don't know. I think so, yes. The thing is to find the cause or the duty.'

'There's no shortage of duties in this country, is there?'

'No.'

'And that in itself is a very good reason for living here. One can find a duty everywhere. What you've told me today—that story about that Coloured youth and his father—there could be a duty, too, if one wanted to make it one, and if the people deserved helping. People don't want to understand what the rewards are when you work for others.'

'So it comes back to the self in the end,' Isabel said.

Miss Bentwisch looked displeased. 'I suppose you can look at it in that way, if you like.' Her voice was thin, measured; her words were always beautifully articulated, with that fullness of vowel-sound and modesty of consonant which is perhaps the most lasting gift of an expensive education in England. And when she spoke one saw the movement of her throat, as if she would rather swallow her words than utter them. 'But that does seem too sophisticated for me,' she said. 'It's no good saying that things are the same when they are different. Someone who helps others *is* acting differently from a man who helps only himself. And their rewards are different in each case, so different that it would be ridiculous to call them by the same name.'

'You must be right. I suppose——'

'I know I'm right. It's to avoid an easy reward that I've always kept so quiet about the things I do, Isabel—it hasn't merely been a whim, an old lady's eccentricity, I assure you. I don't want to win the reputation of being a philanthropist. That would be the easiest reward possible.'

Isabel was frowning earnestly. Her voice, after the other's, sounded no younger; merely a little coarser. 'But there's still the reward. A harder reward is one that you value more, that's all.' Hastily Isabel added, 'I don't mean you, I mean . . . one, anyone.' Isabel looked up with a smile; but the smile went when she saw how the old lady looked down upon her. 'I'm only trying to understand,' Isabel said.

'Wait, Isabel, wait until you've lived as long as I have. Wait until you've learned the boredom and disgust of living inside yourself, with no escape from it, never any—just being what you are, day after day. And knowing yourself!—not like the others, who live within themselves, and who know so little that they think themselves interesting, admirable even. But knowing, knowing what you are: you couldn't bear it. You must live through others, you must live selflessly, always putting away what you are, otherwise'—and to Isabel's gaze the old lady had an almost prophetic aspect, she was so tall and old and so much in earnest about what she was saying—'you will find yourself in a prison, the narrowest, most stifling prison in the world.'

For a moment Miss Bentwisch's hand plucked at the lap of her dress; and Isabel gave a cry of pity and reached out, and brought the restless hand to her cheek. Isabel kissed the hand she grasped, she rubbed it against her cheek. 'I didn't know it was like that,' Isabel cried. She would not look up; already she felt shy, was afraid she was being impertinent. So she clung harder to the hand within her grasp. Then Miss Bentwisch drew back her hand, and Isabel did not resist. She sat with her head bowed.

'It's time you left, Isabel,' Miss Bentwisch said.

'I don't want to go.'

'You must.' Miss Bentwisch sounded as she had before—aloof, calm, ironical, patient.

'And you—what will you do?'

'You don't have to worry about me, Isabel.'

'Oh, I say the wrong things. I do the wrong things.'

'No—you don't. You are a sweet girl. I have great hopes for you.'

'What are they? Tell me, please.'

But Miss Bentwisch merely smiled, and sent Isabel home.

5

AND CIRCUMSTANCES DID so fall out that Miss Bentwisch's hopes of remaining in a position of friendship and patronage over the girl became, within a few years, something very like a matter of planning for the old lady. Among these circumstances was the fact that Isabel did not leave Lyndhurst to go to the university in Johannesburg or Cape Town, as most South African girls of her position would have done; but remained behind, to keep house for her father. And the second circumstance which became a part, very quickly, of Miss Bentwisch's hopes or plans was the conclusion—leaving him at a very loose end—of her young nephew's National Service in England. It was suggested by his father's family that he might come out to join the Lyndhurst General Mining and Exploration Company; and Miss Bentwisch agreed to use her influence to get him a good position in the firm. Once in such a position, it was felt, there was no saying to what heights the young man might rise, for the group of companies with which the Legemco was associated were all very large, very prosperous, and very powerful. And they all had a weakness for young men of good background and good accent from England.

Miss Bentwisch's plans were very simple: they were to bring together Isabel and her nephew; and Miss Bentwisch did consciously hope that their acquaintance might lead to marriage. From such a match Miss Bentwisch saw many benefits, for all parties concerned. Isabel, who, admittedly, was not by any means poor, would immediately become a girl of great expectations; and young Martin Bullivant would get an attractive, intelligent, sensible and loving-hearted wife. Miss Bentwisch, with her determined and lonely piety towards her father and what remained of his family, intended leaving her fortune to her nephew; but this did not make her feel any the less the need for a true heir. It was a role that Isabel in her capacity as Martin's wife would be admirably fitted to play.

So it was for her to introduce Martin to Isabel, which was accomplished easily enough, Martin at first knowing nobody in Lyndhurst but the people he met at his work; and Isabel still being a constant visitor to Miss Bentwisch's house. The relationship between the two women had not fallen into desuetude as Isabel had grown older: at the age of twenty-one Miss Bentwisch's friendship meant almost as much to Isabel as it had when she had been seventeen. In the years between Isabel had grown plump, and then grown thin again; she was now even slighter than she had been in her last years at school, but the thinness of her face was one of the things that made her look older, made her look most her age. Her clothes were smart, though unobtrusive; by choice she wore tailored linen suits and blouses, very trim and adult, almost too much so; she still used little make-up on her face. And her hair was cut simply—even shorter than before, in a close fair crop that emphasized the width and openness of her brow.

This was the young woman to whom Martin was introduced. They were both shy; for they had both heard much about each other from the person who was introducing them; and because they were both aware that in a town of the size of Lyndhurst there weren't all that many people of even potential interest to whom they might be introduced. But Martin's manners were good, and he was an agreeable and rather lazy young man, in whose company it was easy to relax. This Isabel soon did, and when she drove away in the little car her father had given her for a recent birthday, she left with the feeling that Martin was 'really very nice', as she put it to herself.

And so he was, in his way. From his mother Martin might have been expected to inherit something of the energy and nervousness of his German Jewish ancestors; from his father the blunt stolidity of purpose which over many generations had given officers for parade and slaughter to a county regiment of distinction. But Martin Bullivant was neither nervously energetic nor stolid and blunt. He was unambitious, he was charming, he was talkative, he was lazy, he was cynical to a degree. An education in one of England's most famous, ancient, and expensive schools had left him with a marked taste for gossip, which he was ready to indulge in even with people he did not really know well—thus he gossiped at work about his aunt; he gossiped with his aunt about Isabel; and he gossiped with Isabel about everyone. His cynicism was not at all harsh or desperate; on the contrary, it was smooth and cheerful and affable. Martin had simply never found anything really worth striving for, and he was amused by people who had. But he did not look down on such people any more than he looked down on himself; he was always ready, as Isabel was to say, to run himself down. And to help him, he had a large stock of denigratory turns of phrase, which he applied to himself and to everyone else, quite fair-mindedly; their effect was invariably to make absurd whatever he was talking about. A mildly angry man became in Martin's description 'absolutely apoplectic', and a very angry young man could be described (with a delicate smile of complicity) as being 'in a bit of a state'. Martin never took a chair; he always 'seized' it. He never laughed; he always 'chortled'—and when he used the word he invited you to 'chortle' with him at the very idea of anyone doing so. He could very easily become 'exhausted', 'flabbergasted', 'hysterical', and 'livid'; it was much more difficult for him to become enthusiastic. The most he would ever own to in that direction was that he was 'keen on'—and it was a phrase he used indiscriminately about food, motor-cars, holidays, money, Scotch whisky, and—more and more—Isabel.

Months passed, and Isabel, who had not before had a regular escort (she had been much dependent on the young men on vacation from the universities) found herself being smiled at in a special and unmistakable way when she went out with Martin. They were an easily recognizable couple; and there weren't so many places for them to go to. They went to them all, anyway: the bioscopes, and the two roadhouses outside the town, where there was dancing (but you had to bring your own liquor), occasional weddings, private parties, charity balls. People began to take it for granted that Isabel would be accompanied by Martin; Isabel very nearly began to take it for granted herself.

But not altogether. It was true that among the young men of Lyndhurst, Martin, with his English manners, his English voice, his English accent, stood out markedly, and stood out attractively. Isabel hadn't before heard a young man talk the way Martin talked to her; she hadn't seen a young man move the way Martin moved; she hadn't before been treated with the kind of quick and unostentatious deference that seemed to come naturally to Martin, so easily and quickly, as if there were no other way he could ever treat her. Isabel was flattered and soothed by his attentions; and they all spoke to her with a curious intimacy, as if some of her own hopes had at last been given tongue and gesture and body.

For Isabel had done more in the past few years than put on weight and lose it again. She had read, she had thought, and she had suffered a little—suffered boredom and frustration and a sense of uselessness. She had grown more sure of herself, but she was even less sure than before that she liked what she was or seemed to be becoming. It was of her own free choice that she had elected to stay in Lyndhurst; her father had urged her to go to the university, and she had refused. Yet now she could not help yearning sometimes, often, for what lay beyond the yellow and brown veld that surrounded the town—beyond even the big city of Johannesburg, beyond the half-wild and deserted continent to the north. And her yearnings left her dissatisfied and discontented, they gave her no freedom, they thrust her back among the sand and corrugated iron and brick.

But then, she would tell herself, Lyndhurst was what she would make of it. She had books, she had magazines, she had gramophone records, she had frequent holidays; above all, she had work to do. She had not taken a job, after leaving school; but she kept herself busy nevertheless. She was secretary to the Native Relief Organization, the Coloured Welfare Society, to the Non-European Higher Education Bursary Scheme; a lady Senator of formidable aspect and advanced views was in correspondence with her about the possibility of starting a branch of the Liberal Party in Lyndhurst.

But 'charity', 'good works,' 'social relief'—these did not content her. She told herself that she felt discontented because she could do so very little to relieve the distress which she saw on her visits to the Coloured Camp or the African locations, and which was so far beyond her comprehension as to be almost beyond her pity. In the sunlight, on the outskirts of sandy and peaceful Lyndhurst, Isabel had seen that terrible things were taking place: poverty and disease, hunger, violence and apathy, despair, dislocation and indifference, were embodied in the black faces and hands and histories of individual men and women who together made up the whole townships of people, and who lived and worked in such a wild confusion of instinct and law, of ignorance and hope, that sometimes Isabel felt enraged at them for their sheer pertinacity in going on, in continuing to laugh, curse, weep, couple, bear children, work, live as they could. And those were the healthy among them: the sick were twisted and racked; the babies lay in soap-boxes for cradles, and snuffed and turned and mewed and sucked at the sacks that covered them, and were nailed into the same soap-boxes when they died and were thrust under the sand. Into hut after hut Isabel went, down long lanes of sand, where the healthy watched her with resentment and the sick waited mutely in the darkness of shadows made by hessian sacking, corrugated iron, bricks of brown mud, packing-cases; where dogs once fought in the street over a piece of red bone and gristle, and Isabel started, in a daze of horror, thinking it was human matter that the dogs' teeth were closing into; where a smell so foul rose from the ground that it seemed to her the smell must surely fill all the space between the earth and the blue dome imposed above it. Then she would leave these places, and drive home to her father's house. His house, and all the houses near by, were clean and spacious; they had gardens, trees, parked cars outside; there was no smell in them but the clean smell of dust and water from the gardens, the scents of flowers and furniture polish indoors.

Yet Isabel knew, deeply, inwardly, that it was not only the infinitesimal scale of help she was able to bring that disheartened and even disgusted her. It was the activity of charity itself that seemed to her fundamentally false and suspect. It was false to the people to whom she extended her charity (why should they need to accept it?); it was false to herself (who was she to give it?). And this sense of falsity was puzzling, even frightening to her. For Isabel was anxious as she had ever been to do and to feel the right things; and she had no guide at all other than the claims that were pressed upon her from outside—whether from her father, from Miss Bentwisch, or from the poverty and misery of the Africans and Coloureds. If only, then, she didn't feel so dissatisfied, unfulfilled; if only she didn't think of herself with distaste as a 'charitable young lady'; if only there was some secure purpose in always responding, responding, responding, with all the sincerity of which she was capable, and all the kindness, and all the intelligence—whose exercise left her more than ever doubting her own worth. If only . . . if only—what?

If only she were married and had a home of her own? Would that make the difference to her? She really did not know. For a great many reasons it would obviously be pleasant for her to be Martin's wife. She liked him—even admired him—and was grateful to him for being the kind of gentleman he obviously was, for bringing so much of what was outside, to Lyndhurst. Her father approved of him, and the approval of her father carried great weight with Isabel. Miss Bentwisch made no secret of her gratification at the friendship between the two young people; and Isabel herself could not repress a feeling of excitement at the thought of becoming a member of Miss Bentwisch's family. And it was more than excitement she felt when she realized that Miss

Bentwisch thought of her directly as being an heir, a successor: the realization aroused in Isabel something that was close to awe, a sense of power and privilege, that yet was one of rightness, too, for she *was* already Miss Bentwisch's heir. She did already want what the old lady wanted, believed what the old lady believed; she would try to use her power as the old lady had used it: selflessly, anonymously, for the good of others.

All the same, it wasn't a prospect, it wasn't an inheritance, it wasn't a power, it was Martin whom she would be marrying. And Martin—well, Martin really, when you got down to it, was a bit—somehow—dog-like, Isabel felt. And not even dog-like in a sturdy St Bernard sort of way, but . . . Isabel's mind shrank from the image which presented itself to her: the image of a kaffir-dog, a thin-shanked, lean-bellied, tail-trailing kaffir-dog, all casual friendship and vicious disrespect. It was so unfair on Martin. He was quite pleasing to look at: his figure was tall, his face was lean, and his complexion had quite recovered from the first blistered-looking red that the African sun had inflicted on it, and was now decently tanned. He moved so much more gracefully than did any other young man Isabel knew; and his brown eyes were handsome in their pale way, even though they seemed to see so curiously little.

And he had, finally, proposed to her, between the steak and the coffee, at one of the town's roadhouses, at two in the morning, with the words, 'I'd ask you all right, if you weren't too brainy for me.'

She had been injured by this weapon of his before. Most of the other young men whom Isabel knew—tennis players, rugby-players, cricketers, cheerful fellows to a man—did not believe in hiding such lights as they had under any kind of bushel. But Martin insistently, naggingly, good-humouredly, shamelessly, continued to run himself down; and the longer Isabel knew him the more energetically did he do it. He played no games; but he made no virtue of it: he simply said that he wasn't any good at games. He said he drove his car badly; he said he was feeble, dull, not much of a wit; honestly, he said, there wasn't much to recommend him to anyone. All of which might have been true—but said by the man himself, in a shallow but resonant Cambridge bray, above clothes in perfect taste, in the best homes the town could provide . . . this was something against which Isabel felt herself almost powerless. She felt there was something 'deep' in it all; she suspected that behind it there was an idea of life or behaviour or manner with which she was not familiar, and for which, having none of her own, she had an exaggerated respect. And at the same time, even more difficult to resist, his self-scorn roused her pity, pressed another claim upon her.

'Why am I too brainy for you, Martin? Why do you say that?'

'Oh, there's all those things you're interested in.'

'What things?'

'Those books you read.'

'What books?'

'Jane Austen. That kind of book.'

'But you've read Jane Austen.'

'I know I have. I had to. But you read poor old Jane for fun. It's no good. You're too brainy for me. After a year you'd be so bored with me you'd want to scream when you saw me. If it weren't for that'—and here Martin repeated his proposal—'I would ask you to marry me. Here. Now.'

The rest of their party was on the tiny dance-floor. Only Isabel and Martin sat at the littered table, with the bottles and plates pushed to one side on the white cloth.

'But do you love me?' Isabel asked.

'Of course I do.'

So it ended with Isabel pleading with him to propose to her properly. He did it in the end, because she insisted that she wasn't too brainy for him. Then she said she would have to think it over.

'Oh, you can take your time, answering *me*,' Martin replied obligingly and cheerfully.

'I probably will,' Isabel replied, much less cheerfully.

That night—or early morning—Isabel responded eagerly to Martin's embraces, when he parked the car outside her house. But it was all willed response and reply, until half-desperately she pushed his head away from her bosom and ran inside the house without saying good night.

He called the next day again, undaunted—or no more daunted than usual. And the day after that, too. And so things continued between them.

Then Isabel's father surprised her. He fell deeply and unsuitably and shamefacedly in love.

Hettie Stander was a mature divorcee, with an Afrikaans background, a harsh voice, a pert manner, and a quick, light eye set in a tanned and inexpressive face. There was something strap-like about Hettie, she was so brown and thin and tough; and when she spoke it was as if a strap had been sharply cracked. She was new to Lyndhurst; she had been working as a typist in an office when Mr Last had found her, and the friendship between them proceeded in intimacy very rapidly indeed. Within days of their first meeting, Hettie Stander was sitting in the Lasts' living-room, with the heels of her stockinged feet coming negligently out of her black leather shoes, and her eyes moving in quick scrutiny from point to point about the room. When she drew her legs on to the couch her shoes remained on the floor, pointing to one another with an inch of carpet between them, as if they, too, were conferring as anxiously (and as silently) between themselves as everyone else in the room.

There was some audible conversation, too; for the most part Hettie talked, in abrupt speeches about the work she did, the people she worked with, the impossible house at which she boarded. She referred several times to 'Billy—that's my ex, God bless him,' and described briefly what Billy had done to her on certain different occasions. She drank heavily, like a man, from the drinks that Mr Last poured for her and carried to her across the living-room; but she showed no signs of the drink having had any effect on her. Later, she was shown around the house, and admired what she saw. 'You have done yourself proud,' she said vivaciously to Mr Last, in the kitchen, the breakfast-room, the dining-room, leaning her shoulders towards him but just not touching him with them, before continuing her inspection. 'Very nice,' she said in conclusion when they came back into the living-room. 'You should see the room I've got. God, it's like a kaffir's, and they make me *pay* for it, too. Well, that's what happens to a poor girl when she's got to look after herself.'

'Poor Hettie!'

Mr Last's tone was so mildly ironical that Hettie was able to ignore the irony altogether. 'You can say that again!' she agreed with him loudly. 'It's no life for a girl. But that's what they do to us,' she said, turning to Isabel, as one girl to another, and smoothing over her narrow hips the tight, tailored jacket of the suit she wore. 'When they want us we're queens, and when they don't—then it's just bye-bye baby.'

Isabel could not help smiling. 'I'll remember that,' she said.

'Then you won't go wrong!'

They were all standing up, in the middle of the room. Hettie looked at her watch, and gave a cry of agitation. 'They'll lock me out, as true as God, at that place. They don't like their girls to be naughty, staying out late. I must fly. I must run.'

'I'll fly with you, Hettie,' Mr Last said, searching in his pocket for his keys.

'I won't say "no thanks" to that.'

'No, please don't.' Mr Last's tone was anxious. 'Come,' he said. Hettie led the way out of the room, after shaking hands and saying good-bye to Isabel. At the door Mr Last turned and gave his daughter a glance. It wrung her heart, to see him so apologetic, like a boy, and so eager, too.

Despite the lateness with which Hettie was supposed to have left, it was many hours before Isabel heard her father returning. She had lain awake, in her darkened bedroom; she heard the car being reversed into the garage; she pretended to be asleep when she heard his footsteps pause outside her room.

The next day, and the succeeding days, Mr Last made no mention of where he was going, when he dressed in the evenings and took the car out; and Isabel did not ask him. She pretended to be asleep every night, when he came home so late; and in the mornings, over breakfast, before Mr Last left for work, they talked of everything but the one thing that preoccupied them both.

But father and daughter, through all the years of their having lived alone in the house, had never been able to sustain their quarrels; still less now could they sustain their silence. They needed each other too much; and needed each other more than ever, when both were thinking of the changes that might soon be coming upon them, and might diminish for ever their need for one another. Change was painful for them both, when their lives had run together so long. For Isabel those years had been the time of her youth, of her growing up, and her love for her father had been without guilt and without regret; for him, on the other hand, there had always been guilt and bitterness in his thoughts of Isabel. The years of Mr Last's widowhood had been the years of his financial success: yet more and more, as each year passed, he had felt that he was going nowhere, and was dragging his daughter with him. He was a man of strong sensibility and deliberately blunt manners: he would never have admitted to anyone his concern and anxiety about Isabel, affecting about her and with her a rather breezy and man-to-man indifference; but in the loneliness of his room and office and car, his heart shook at the thought of her, at the responsibility it was to have her. For himself, he had told himself, and had believed, he expected nothing: but for his daughter all he had was insufficient. His riches were not secure enough, his house was not strong enough, his heart was not loving enough.

And then, to have to own to her that he wanted to marry Hettie Stander! He struggled as long as he could against the necessity. What could he tell Isabel? How could he explain to her what he was doing? What did Isabel know of love, of physical passion? He hoped little, yet it was that that he had to tell her of, for it was physical passion that had drawn him to Hettie, against his will, despite his own determined lack of expectation. At breakfast one morning, when the sun came in through the window and splashed in white and yellow on the tablecloth, he did at last make his admission to Isabel, baldly and bluntly, trying to bluff the matter out, but knowing as he spoke that he would never be able to carry it through. Not with Isabel sitting opposite him at the other end of the table, in a bright blue dress patterned haphazardly with red leaves—the colours merely showing up her own pallor.

Isabel stared at him, after he had spoken, but made no reply.

'I do,' her father said. 'I do want to marry her.'

He waited for her to speak; when she kept her silence, he felt himself being judged and failing, as had always feared he might fail. And at the bottom of his sense of failure he recognized with a kind of disgust the softness of a certain inevitable relief, now that the failure was made public at last. Disgust was there, and anger; and these, obscurely, roused him to a sense of his own rights. 'I can't help it,' he said. 'I tried—I tried all sorts of things. I *want* her, don't you understand?' One hand clenched over the handle of a knife, and he gripped it tight, his fist resting on the tablecloth, and the blade standing up. The blade gleamed in his hand, shook with the force with which he was holding it. 'I can't tell you what it's like,' he said. 'I didn't know myself. But that's how I am. After all these years . . . . You must try to understand, Isabel, though I know you can't. It's so different for a woman. And for a girl!' he said loudly, and there was an ironic echo to his own voice. What could Isabel know of the hunger he felt for Hettie's lean, used body, on which the bones showed through so pitifully, under the flat, round breasts? He closed his eyes against the picture of Hettie that had come before him, as he had seen her only a few hours before; he clenched his teeth together; with one hand he felt for the knife he had dropped, fingers twitching. He could not reach the knife, and he would not open his eyes to look for it. 'Hettie wants the best for all of us. She's as anxious about you as I am. If you don't—she doesn't . . . perhaps she'll go away.' But he knew that if Hettie went away he would follow her: he would never let her go: she was his last chance: there would never be another.

'I'm so ashamed,' he said suddenly.

Isabel saw how he was suffering; and could look at him no longer. She spread her arms on the tablecloth, and rested her forehead on them, showing only the top of her fair head above the cloth, and her shoulders crouching behind. Her father could not go to her. He sat in his chair; and then his face, too, began working, and he covered it with his hands. So they sat, the only movement in the room that of the light flickering off the polished cutlery.

Isabel was the first to recover. She stood up and walked carefully around the table, one finger trailing along its edge, as if to guide her. She put her hand on her father's shoulder. 'Daddy——'

He would not look up; he did not take his hands from his face. Gently, Isabel touched his shoulders. 'Please, Daddy.'

'Yes.' The word came muffled from behind his hands.

'You must do what you want, Daddy. I'm glad you want to marry Hettie. I'll try to like her. I'll try my hardest.'

When her father took his hands from his face, Isabel could not bear to look at him, she could not see him with tears in his eyes; and when he spoke Isabel heard with a kind of shame, almost a horror, the nasal tone of his voice, like that of anyone speaking after he had been crying. He tried to tell Isabel more of what he felt about Hettie, though much of what he said was false; for he spoke of Hettie in terms of pity, as a woman who had been ill-used and misunderstood; whereas in fact the pity he did feel for her was almost entirely physical, and was bound up in a way he could not understand with his lust for her. And in spite of himself the true quality of his feeling did break through—in his trembling voice, in the expression of his face, in some of the words he used. He talked about Hettie repeatedly as 'a girl', and said how 'open' she was, how 'eager', how 'easy'; so that Isabel—who knew as little of true physical passion as her father had hoped—nevertheless felt stirring within her an unease, a jealousy, and a swift and voracious curiosity to know what it was that she felt herself ignorant of, disablingly so. The figure of Martin came before her, wavered, and was lost. Later, when she knew her father was waiting—hoping—for her to speak of Martin, she was silent.

The very next time they met, Isabel told Martin that she would not marry him. It was quite early one Sunday morning; they were sitting on deck-chairs in the back garden of the Lasts' house. The sunlight was bright, the sky was a sharp blue, the bricks of the fence that Cornelius Makeer had built years before looked very new—pale orange and yellow, like flame. Every dry colour had its own freshness and clarity; there was no sign of the weariness there would be at the end of the day, when too much light would have fallen without slackening or relief for too long. Martin was slumped in a deck-chair; Isabel saw his thin arms, and his lax figure, the side of his face. His hair was light brown and soft, combed loosely away from his forehead. He seemed to her too thin to break, too supple to knot, like a blade. Or he was like a hair about her throat, too fine for her to pluck away.

And he settled himself deeper in his chair to consider what she had just said to him. 'So,' he said. 'Well,' he said. 'It didn't really take you such a long time to make up your mind, after all. I thought it might be years and years still.'

'So did I, at one time.'

'And is it quite made up?'

'I think so. Yes.'

'Oh.' Then he said, 'Can I ask you why not? Is it that you don't like me?'

'No, Martin! I do.'

'But you don't love me?'

'No,' Isabel said, shaking her head slowly. 'No.'

'I love you,' Martin said, and the ease with which he said it made the colour mount in Isabel's cheeks.

She spoke with her head lowered. 'I don't think you do. If you did—you couldn't say it like that.'

'I can't say it any more passionately—here, now, on the lawn, after what you've just told me. But I do.'

Still Isabel's head drooped 'You don't. I know what it's like—'

'You mean you're in love with someone else?'

'No! Truly, it's not that at all. I couldn't be—all this time; it's you I've been seeing, no one else. You know that. But what there's been between us, Martin—it isn't marriage, I don't feel that it is. To be married to someone . . . it frightens me now, the thought of it, and Martin, please don't think I'm being funny—but I'm not frightened of you. Does that sound silly?'

'It makes me sound silly,' Martin replied eventually, without apparently taking offence.

Isabel was grateful to him for his reply. 'I'm sorry. I didn't mean it to.' And she was sorry for him, for her father, for herself. 'Martin, you won't mind—later, I mean. I'm sure of it. I think I'm the one who'll mind more, later. I don't know what I'm going to do.'

She hadn't intended talking of herself; but Martin took up her words immediately. 'Why?' he asked. 'What do you want to do? Can't you go on in the same way?'

'No.'

'Why not?' Then Martin surprised her. 'Because of your father?'

'Martin!'

'It's all right, there's no need to look at me like that. You're not the only one who knows that your father has—well, got himself involved. People are talking about it.'

'You mean you're talking about it!' Isabel exclaimed angrily. 'You're like an old woman.'

'That's quite the nicest thing you've ever said to me.'

Then they were both silent. Isabel felt how squalid it would be to part from him quarrelsomely. And he said, apologetically, 'Lyndhurst's such a small town really. These things get around so quickly.'

Isabel checked her reply: 'Helped along by people like you.' She said instead, without tone, 'Yes.'

'Anyway,' Martin said, 'it shouldn't make such a difference to you. I mean you're grown-up, you can do what you like.'

'I always have.'

Martin shook his head. 'No you haven't. You've done what other people have liked. I suppose that's one of the things that gave me the confidence to propose to you. For myself, I thought: well, perhaps she'll want to oblige me. And then I thought that your father likes me, and my aunt would like nothing better than to see us engaged—and I knew you knew all this—so I thought that perhaps even poor old me would stand a chance.' Martin was making a brave attempt to carry it off in his usual style; but it was hard going for him. And in his way he was struggling to tell the truth. Isabel saw his face obliquely, the bones of his jaw moving as he spoke, so much more slowly than usual. 'But I was wrong, I see. And yet—until just a little while ago, I would have thought . . . Well, it doesn't much matter, what I thought. I was wrong.'

'What are you going to do, Martin?'

'I can't do the traditional thing, can I? I mean, go off to Africa to console myself. I'm here already. It's rather absurd. And I don't want to go back to England. So I suppose I'll grin and bear it, right here in Lyndhurst. Perhaps I'll put in for a transfer, later, if it becomes too bad, too hard—seeing you, I mean, and not having you. And dear Aunt Lucille is going to be very fed up with me, I don't mind telling you. She'll blame me for it, not you. You can't do any wrong as far as she's concerned; while I can, I often do. So she'll think that it's because of my own'—he shrugged—'whatever it is, that you won't have me. Which is true enough, God knows.'

'She knows about us?'

'You know she knows.'

'I mean—how much?'

'Everything, I should guess. Except this.'

'What will she say? Oh, Martin, I'm so mixed-up, I don't know what to do. And it's not true that she'll blame you,' Isabel said. 'If she blames anyone it will be me.' Isabel spoke with conviction, though she did not know where her certainty came from. She felt empty, at a loss.

Martin was silent. It was his right to offer her no help, and she could not resent it in him. She got up from her chair.

'You want me to go?' he asked, looking up, remaining seated.

'Yes.'

'For good?'

'Please, Martin, you know it's not for good.' She waited for him to stand up, and together they walked round the side of the house, to the front garden. Martin's car was parked beyond the fence. The street was empty, not a car or a pedestrian moved on it.

'Give my love to your aunt.'

Martin smiled, as if he were about to comment on what she had just said; he looked down at her from his height. He veered away in silence. Isabel was proud that she and Martin were so calm; yet disappointed, too. It seemed that they had done so little, after all; as if they had been blank, numbed people. The blankness in herself—which seemed in accord with the somnolence and brightness of the morning—had been disturbed only by mere flickers of irritation, so small and commonplace. Yet deep within her, as she said good-bye to Martin, formally extending one hand to him, she felt a tremor, a premonition of the fear of which she had spoken to Martin.

She said calmly, 'Do phone me when you want to.'

'I will.'

They smiled at one another; her smile meeting his, in reflection. Then he was gone; and she turned and ran back into the house. When she reached her bed she flung herself down on it; she was trembling uncontrollably, as if the fear had expanded within her, filling her limbs, so that they shook and shook again, in spasms. She thrust her head under the pillow and cried. Later—though it was morning, and only a few hours had passed since she had first woken—she slept.

She was roused from her sleep by a light tap on the door. She called in answer, and her father came into the room. He stood almost within the doorway, coming no farther.

'Martin's gone?' he asked.

'Yes, he's gone,' she said, from where she lay on the bed.

'Oh.' He was about to close the door and leave her, for fear of intruding, but she halted him.

'Daddy, I'm not going to marry Martin.'

He looked down at her. He waited; then gently he asked, 'Are you unhappy, my dear?'

Isabel's head shook on the pillow. 'Not very. I'm tired.'

'Then I must leave you.' He lingered heavily for a moment longer. 'It is for the best, I suppose, if you weren't sure about him. I didn't really know that things had gone so far between you——'

'Daddy, please!' He had known; he had wanted her to marry Martin. He should own up to his disappointment.

But he did not. 'And I could see that you were not sure,' he said, as if she had not spoken.

'I'm sorry,' Isabel said, replying to what he had not admitted.

He smiled painfully. 'You don't have to apologize to me.'

Slowly he closed the door, leaving Isabel alone. She felt languid; she remembered how she had trembled when she had first lain on the bed; she wondered at it, for she felt momentarily light-hearted, as if released from a constraint. Then the fear returned, though not so fiercely as before. When she got up she arranged her clothes very methodically and hastily, as if dressing for an appointment. But at the door she stood for a moment, one hand lifted to the knob. She did not know where she should go.

It was only a few days later that Hettie Stander said to Isabel, when the two women were alone in the living-room, 'Why don't you go away?'

Isabel turned her head sharply, her mouth opening in exclamation.

'No, man, I don't mean it like that. There's no need for you to stare at me so.' Hettie lay back on the sofa, her thin, stockinged legs stretched before her. 'I mean go right away. Go somewhere else. Get out of here.'

Isabel did not speak; and Hettie repeated, 'I don't mean it like that. I know it must sound awful. It must sound as though I'm trying to get rid of you. But if you think that of me you'll think it whatever I do or say. But if you don't—well, then perhaps you'll see that I'm only trying to help you.'

'I don't need help.'

'We all need help,' Hettie said. 'I've never met anyone who didn't.'

This silenced Isabel. 'Go where?' she asked eventually.

'Hell, there's no shortage of places to go to. There's Cape Town or Johannesburg, for a start.'

'I don't know anyone there.'

'You've got some relatives in Cape Town, I've heard Harry talk about them. And anyway,' Hettie said, 'I knew no one when I came to Lyndhurst.'

'And look at you now,' Isabel could not help saying.

Hettie was not upset. She agreed with Isabel. 'Yes, look at me now. I haven't done too badly, have I?'

'No.'

'There you are then. You've got to take a chance sometimes, otherwise you'll never get anything, that's my experience. And if things don't work out for you, Isabel, you can always come back here. Perhaps if you go away and then come back you'll appreciate what you've got here all the more.'

'You mean Martin, don't you?'

'So what if I do?'

'I don't mind.' It was curious how frank the two women felt they could be with one another, though there was no affection between them. 'Tell me,' Isabel asked, 'what do you think Daddy wants me to do?'

Hettie thought for a moment before she spoke. 'He doesn't know. He's going to be miserable and guilty about you, whatever you do. Yes, he will be,' Hettie went on, over an interruption from Isabel. 'But that's the way things go. You just have to do your best with them, that's all.'

'That is what I want to do.' Isabel felt the need to say more. 'Martin proposed to me the other day,' she told Hettie. 'I said no.'

'Your father told me about it.' Hettie had crossed the room and was standing over the liquor cabinet. 'That's nothing. You're so proud of it, anyone would think you'd done something. All you've done is to say no to something you didn't want——'

'Everybody else wanted it.'

Hettie paused, 'That's true. And that is something, I suppose. But wait until you want to say yes, and can't! Or until you want to say no and have to say yes! Find your way out of that. Then you'll be able to feel you've done something. Then you'll have been in a real battle.'

Isabel watched Hettie pouring herself a drink. She wished she could like her stepmother-to-be; but she couldn't. Yet she respected her, even feared her. And suddenly it occurred to her to say,

'Well, I'm like that with you already.'

Hettie asked, 'You mean in a battle?'

'Sort of. Wanting to say yes and having to say no. Or the other way around.'

'Well—that's a beginning.'

'To what?'

Hettie shrugged her emaciated shoulders. 'I should know.' She held up her glass in a toast. 'You're young, we'll see. Good luck to you!' Hettie lowered her glass, without having sipped at it. She added deliberately, smiling frankly at her own cheerful malice, and expecting Isabel to do the same: '*Bon voyage!*' Then Hettie drank from her glass.

6

A YEAR LATER when Kenneth Makeer and Isabel walked side by side for the first time in a London street Isabel did not know in what way their being together was her doing. She was filled with the import of the words she had spoken to Kenneth a few minutes before; she had long forgotten other words she had said, on an afternoon years before, in Lyndhurst; she had forgotten the boy about whom she had said the words. She did not know him, the slight stranger who walked by her side; nor could she guess how much he knew of her, how much he owed to her.

It had been Isabel's words to Miss Bentwisch that had made the old lady, when she had next needed work done on the house, to seek out Cornelius Makeer and his son; and it had been Isabel's words, too, which had made Miss Bentwisch watch the son closely. Miss Bentwisch had not told Isabel that she was seeing Kenneth; and she had not told Kenneth and his father that it was on Miss Last's recommendation that she had called them in to shore up with new wood the back *stoep* of her house. It would not have been her way to tell either party of her interest in the other; she merely told Cornelius vaguely that she had heard he was a good workman, and to Kenneth she said nothing at all. She looked at him, and saw that he was small, as Isabel had described him. But Isabel had not seen what Miss Bentwisch noticed immediately—how white Kenneth was, for a Coloured. He could 'pass' in the Transvaal, very easily, she thought; but that was not at all what she would have wished for him.

At first she did not know if he was worth wishing anything for. He came to the house, he did his work, he seemed quite quick and nimble, spoke politely in a low voice, did what his father told him. His bare arms were frail; the elbows stood out in knobs when he crooked his arms, and his wrists were like a girl's. At lunch-break he lay in the shade with his father, and they ate sandwiches from the tin they brought with them, and drank tea from a gaudy vacuum flask of which Cornelius seemed very proud. Then both of them pulled their hats over their eyes and slept until two o'clock, when the work began again. It would have been very easy for Miss Bentwisch to let them be: to let them finish their work take their money, and go. But the easy thing to do had never appealed to Miss Bentwisch; and she felt that in some way she had undertaken an obligation to Isabel to follow the young man up. The fact that Isabel would never know whether or not the obligation had been met did not, for Miss Bentwisch, make it any the less weighty.

And then it was not only what she had heard about Kenneth that roused her curiosity; as the days passed Kenneth himself succeeded in doing this, for all the quietness of his manner. He seemed 'quite a little person', as Miss Bentwisch put it to herself, patronizingly and yet with respect; she found herself wondering what his thoughts were while he worked; what he looked like when he wasn't wearing those overalls of his. There was, unmistakably, something spare, defiant, and aloof about him; she thought he would look rather well in a dark suit, picturing him as a professional man or an administrator. But not even as she pictured him was he ever smug; and it was this quality of resistance or strain or ambition which she sensed in him that most attracted her.

One afternoon, when Cornelius had ridden off on his bicycle to purchase something that was needed on their job, Miss Bentwisch at last approached Kenneth directly. As an opening, and with no excuse for the inquiry, she asked him, 'What standard did you reach at school?'

'Standard Six, madam.'

His voice was low, and he spoke respectfully; he had stopped work at her approach. It was her right, his attitude had seemed to suggest, to take him away from his work: she was the employer and he the employee.

'Didn't you want to go on at school?'

'Madam?'

'Didn't you want to go on at school?'

'No, madam.'

'Why not?'

'My father wanted me to join him in the work, madam.'

He stood straight. Miss Bentwisch was a full head taller than he was. The two of them stood on the back *stoep*, in an isolation made more emphatic by the bright light and heavy shade of the yard behind her, the empty house behind Kenneth.

'And do you always do what your father wants you to do?'

He answered the question stiffly, without humour. 'I try, madam.'

'I see.'

'Yes, madam.' He waited to see if there would be more questions, before he could get on with his work.

'So that's what you say now.' Miss Bentwisch's head was thrust forward; her eyes stared into his. 'I've heard differently about you.'

'Madam?'

'I've heard that you aren't contented at all.'

'Madam?'

'Yes, I have,' Miss Bentwisch said slowly, persistently, as if the effort of her will went entirely into uttering the words, not at all into the effect the words would have on him.

'I have said nothing to the madam. I am doing my work. Madam has no complaints?'

'No, no complaints. Except that you aren't telling me the truth. What are you afraid of?'

Kenneth could assume only that his father must have been speaking about him to the old lady. He was angered with Cornelius at the thought, and yet he spoke with a kind of loyalty to his father, backing up what Cornelius must have said. 'I am sorry, madam. It means nothing if I complain sometimes.'

'What do you mean?'

Kenneth did not know what he had meant. 'Nothing,' he said stupidly. He was filled with resentment against the old woman in front of him; he was affronted by her very appearance. He thought she looked like an old brown fowl; he stared at her bare neck, above the brown dress she was wearing. His jaw set sullenly. 'I'm just a builder,' he said. 'I don't know anything except my work. Look, madam, this is what I'm doing.' He turned to show her what he had been working on, pointing with one hand. 'Is the madam satisfied with the progress? Yes? No? I'm just a stupid fellow,' he said insultingly. 'Not very good at my work, only trying, sometimes successful, sometimes not. Then my father is angry with me; and it's right that he should be angry. The madam would also be angry if she had such a stupid son, like me.' Kenneth's pronunciation grew more slovenly as he spoke; his voice grew louder. 'Now the madam understands? Do your best, even if your best is other people's worst. That's what my father says, and I try, madam, with energy, speed, strength.' The words ran together as they came off his tongue. 'If at first you don't succeed then try, try again, madam, is all I say——'

'Stop that!'

'Stop what, madam? Talking, madam? Yes, madam, at once, immediately. Look, now I've stopped.' He could not have been more insolent, in his stance, in his speech, in his humility. He brought up one hand to touch his cap. Then he stood silent, stupidly, passively obedient.

Miss Bentwisch was smiling. Her teeth were false, Kenneth was sure. He stared stonily at her from his black eyes. 'I can see what she meant,' she said.

'Who?' The question broke out from him.

'It doesn't matter. Not in the least.' Nothing he had said had in the least discouraged her. She leaned farther forward, seeking to meet the defiant stare from his eyes, and smiling again when she did so. He thought she was going to speak; but she remained silent.

'What do you want of me?' he asked simply. He had dropped his voice.

'The truth.'

Kenneth's eyes flickered. 'That's a big thing to ask for, madam.'

'I always ask big things of the people I'm interested in. The very biggest.'

'Does the madam always get it?'

'No, not always. There aren't so many people who have anything big in them. But you might be one.'

Kenneth shook his head. 'No, madam. There is nothing in me.'

'Haven't you just shown me what there might be in you——' She paused, then said slowly, with the same effort and persistence as before, 'if you had a chance in the world?'

'A chance in the world?' he repeated wonderingly.

'I can see that you know already what I'm talking about. Or you would not have said it as you did. Nor,' she said slowly, 'would you be looking at me as you are now.' Again there was a silence; Kenneth's expression did not alter, his eyes did not move from hers. 'A chance in the world—it's something you have thought about, haven't you?'

'And if I have?'

'Ah! You have! Then why do you deny it? Why do you pretend to be what you aren't?'

'Because no good can come of being anything else.'

'Is that what you say? Have you no courage? Where is your determination?'

Kenneth's lips twitched. It was as if he smiled; yet he answered her gravely, 'To do my job of work.'

'Is that all you want to do?' This work? Her hand pointed to the side of him.

'Yes.'

'You're lying again. Why do you say it?'

'What's the good of wanting? For me to want? Want what? To be rich?'

'To be white?'

'All right,' Kenneth said defiantly. 'White, too.'

'And you never can be?'

'No.'

'You could be white,' Miss Bentwisch said. 'You could try, in the north.'

Kenneth's future hung on the answer he then made. He said, 'No.'

'No?'

'No.'

'Why not?'

'I don't want to explain.' He turned away; and then felt Miss Bentwisch's hand on his shoulder. To his knowledge it was the first time he had ever been touched by a white woman, and he stood quite still, with his back to her.

'You must explain.'

Just then Cornelius Makeer pushed open the back-gate; immediately Miss Bentwisch's hand fell away. The corrugated iron of the gate scraped noisily on the ground, and both Kenneth and Miss Bentwisch turned to look at Cornelius coming in. Cornelius's face gleamed across the yard, his glasses reflecting the light. Kenneth nodded in his father's direction. 'There's the explanation,' he said.

She got it all out of him, though sometimes he would not speak; he would be sullen and silent; or at other times he would be jeering and self-pitying. Yet, when he did speak frankly, it was with such eagerness and rapidity that Miss Bentwisch could not but be moved by what he told her, by the expressions that followed one another so vividly across his face. She heard him speak of books, of people, of places with a longing that was almost a lust, a passion more distant and less hopeful than that felt by any lover. For the objects of Kenneth's love seemed to be all around him; and he saw them possessed and enjoyed by others, while his own senses starved, his own hands remained empty, there came nothing against his own body and mind that was not meagre, distorted, misshapen, spent. He burned with a barren desire: as innocent and as lecherous as a boy, he lusted yet never entered the centres of warmth and response. Sometimes jealousy shook him in spasms, in fits of hatred: hatred not only against the possessors, the lucky white lovers, but hatred against the objects of their love, too. At these times he wanted to make of himself something low, vulgar, brutish, unknowing; he was seized with a terrible desire to destroy all the things he couldn't have: he wanted to smash the glass of the houses he could never enter, to destroy their furnishings; he wanted to burn down the public library to which he was never admitted; he wanted to put glass on the roadways, to bring to a halt all the cars he could never ride in; to put boulders on the railway lines to derail the trains that passed through the city; to deface the public monuments in the city and defecate on the steps of the Town Hall. In these moods he never thought of power but as the power to destroy; he never thought of the world but as a collection of objects to be destroyed.

Then that mood would leave him; and often it was succeeded by another much less violent, yet not less ultimately despairing. Knowledge and power and possessions then seemed to Kenneth as lovable as they ever did; so lovable that though his love could never be reciprocated, though there would never be any response or reward for him in his love, he felt that he should still seek to make himself the best lover that the world—in all its places, in all its appearances—had ever known. And he would have read the books he intended to read if he could have got hold of them; but because he was a Coloured he was not permitted to join the public library. He would have gone to the recitals and the lectures given by celebrities from Johannesburg or Cape Town, or from Europe; but because he was a Coloured he was not admitted into the halls where they were given. He would have gone to the plays put on by local groups, or by visiting troupes; but because he was a Coloured admission to these was barred to him. He would have looked at the pictures in the little local gallery; but because he was a Coloured he was turned away from its doors. And nowhere did there seem to be anybody he could talk to about the things he wanted to do, and read, and to understand, and to feel; there was no one to answer his questions, or to ask him questions; no one to guide him and encourage him. Kenneth felt that Peter, his brother, would not have understood what he was after; Cornelius would merely have worried about it; and the friends that Kenneth and Peter had were all much more like Peter than they were like

Kenneth. In the end, inevitably, Kenneth would put aside his plans to learn and understand and appreciate; he would fall into a kind of wistful, idle stupor; he would be gentle and obedient with his father, distant from Peter; he would sit with empty hands and empty head at the window of the little living-room, staring out across the veld. In summer he watched the grey swift evening gathering the darkness to itself, in winter the lights of the town shining so distinctly and brightly beyond the strip of veld; until after days, weeks of idleness, this mood would be succeeded by the other: destructive, vindictive, despairing, and the more so for the high intentions which had gone before.

All this Miss Bentwisch now heard from Kenneth; and all that he told her of, Miss Bentwisch had hoped to hear. But it would not have meant to her what it did, if it had not been accompanied by another persistent and unexpected strain in his talk, the nature of which he had indicated to her the first time she had spoken to him. After all, why shouldn't an intelligent young Coloured have been ambitious, greedy, resentful despairing? There was no surprise in that; it would have been surprising if he had not been. She could have gone to the Coloured schools and collected half a dozen such, who would have wanted what Kenneth wanted, and would have talked about it in the way that Kenneth did. But it was not only of his ambitions and disappointments that Kenneth spoke; but also of loyalty. He spoke of his father, of his brother; and of his determination to stand with them. In justice and love he felt that the conditions of his life should be the same as the conditions of their lives. He was not prepared to dissociate himself from them, even if the opportunity were given to him; he would not take himself what they could not share.

It was this—together with the other—that made Miss Bentwisch feel that Kenneth's was a rare, a fine spirit. Each by itself would have been nothing, would have been commonplace; but to find both the ambition and the love, both the despair and the loyalty, in one narrow youthful breast—Miss Bentwisch felt that this was a find indeed, that Kenneth was far more worth while, truly, than Isabel could ever have guessed him to be. Having heard Kenneth talk so much of his brother, Miss Bentwisch was curious to see Peter, and had him brought before her, and saw him for the handsome, slouching, disrespectful fellow that he was. Peter did not make a good impression on her—he spoke badly, he was incurious as to why she had wanted to see him, he winked at Kenneth, he left as soon as he could, with his hands in his pockets and his shirt coming out of his trousers at the back. Miss Bentwisch thought that at Peter's side, Kenneth—who had obviously been embarrassed by his brother's presence—had shown an alertness and acuity that could be seen like light against darkness. Yet she would not have wished it otherwise: she would not have minded if Peter had been a drunkard, an idiot, a criminal. For Peter's lack of worth (and it was Miss Bentwisch's quick conviction that Peter was worth very little) merely made Kenneth's loyalty to him the more admirable. Not that she said anything of this to Kenneth. On the contrary, she told him that she could see why he had so strong a feeling towards his elder brother; she said that she could understand his loyalty to his admirable and devoted father.

Miss Bentwisch believed that she could answer both Kenneth's ambition and his loyalty, his desire and his guilt. The answer was complete and detailed; and it was, she was convinced, reciprocal with the movement of his own mind and heart. She did not consider that her answer was reciprocal with the movement of *her* mind and heart; that she was fitting him into her own moral styles, whether they suited or not. How could she suspect it, when she acted always for the good of others, and not her own?

And she asked no more of Kenneth than that he should follow, in his very different way, the path that had been hers. She did not put it to him in these terms; she did not know that that was what she was asking of him. She merely told him the truth as she saw it; with the conviction that her truth was the truth indeed. 'You must not be offended at what I am saying,' she said to him more than once; and went on to tell him, more than once, that he had never been anything but a selfish boy, and that it was from his selfishness that his unhappiness had come. 'I know, I know, you have been no more selfish than anyone else: in fact, you have flattered yourself that you have been more generous than most. And perhaps you have.' But what had his standards been? His standards had been those of the people around him, whose lives were given over entirely to selfishness and self-seeking. Selfishness was the governing idea of our society, our world; our relations between people, our politics, our morals, our economics, even our literature, were so dominated by self-seeking that people had ceased even to be aware of it. They thought it 'natural' and obvious that everyone should try to grab for himself what he could, as if he were at war with everyone else; as if there were nothing else that a man could do but to increase his own wealth and power, his own success and fame. 'And you have never questioned this,' she told Kenneth, 'you have thought only of yourself and what you can do for yourself.' So he had found himself in a trap; he had become merely one more trapped rat or fox, writhing, twisting, snarling, biting his own limbs in a hopeless attempt to set himself free.

What did Kenneth want for himself? He wanted riches, and power, and learning, and the admiration of others. And the only way he felt there would ever be any hope of him achieving these was through 'passing', through becoming a white man, to whom all doors, if he knocked long and hard enough, would open. And yet—and here there was hope for Kenneth, this showed that within him there was the germ of a true freedom, though it was unknown to him—he did not want to commit what seemed a betrayal of his father and brother, of those he loved, and thus a betrayal of himself. Had he never realized that here lay the answer to the problem: in the very emotions that as far as he was concerned merely made the conflict so acute, so apparently insoluble? Let him not think only of his father and brother; let him think of all those who were like his father and brother in the colour of their skins, or darker, and so alike too, or even more brutally penalized, in their deprivation, their poverty, their lack of education, the insults and humiliations that they had to endure. Let him think of them *all* as his fathers and brothers; let him think of himself as involved with them all in the same way and with the same passion as he was involved with Cornelius and Peter Makeer. Now did he see his way out of the trap?

No, not yet; but he soon would, if he would listen to her. And Kenneth did listen to her, with wonder and gratitude. He hardly knew himself when he sat in a room with tall hanging curtains of blue and gold drawn aside at the windows, a white moulded ceiling high above, a great stone-blue vase in the middle of a table, and all the colours in the room glinting again from mirrors and the glass doors of cabinets. The light came in through the windows, and retained its strength until the very end of each afternoon when it suddenly grew weak and faded; then shadows were heavier in the room; Miss Bentwisch's face became featureless, pale, abstract; yet she did not switch on the lights and he did not move from his place until she would dismiss him at last. How many such afternoons Kenneth spent with Miss Bentwisch he could not later have said. Every evening the sluggish warmth of the air was the same when he came out of the house, and the homeliness and the familiarity of the streets outside surprised him in the same way, each time, as if all had been said between them in the course of one long conversation.

Let him think—Miss Bentwisch said—let him think of all the oppressed and humiliated as the brothers he could never abandon: the weary men cycling or walking back from work at the end of every day in factories or coalyards; the men in the mine-compounds, lying on concrete bunkers, singing their songs together; the barefoot convicts working in gangs, passing in gangs through the streets; the women carrying their children strapped to their broad backs, or carrying the bundles of washing that they collected from half a dozen white homes, and took to the locations to boil and bring back for shillings at the end of each week; all those who were cold and hungry and barefoot; those who grew embittered, drunken, careless, slovenly, in their bitter surroundings; those who cried with impotence and hurt when they were struck in the face by police who asked for their permits and passes, and carried them to prison when they could not respond. Let Kenneth have power and learning, all that he wanted, all that he could earn or learn from the world—*not* for himself, but only and always for the service of the others: all his fathers and brothers, his family, his people. Now did he understand what she meant? Now did he see that there was no true conflict, no real disjuncture between his loyalty and his ambitions? Could he not realize that each, when his purposes were worthy, fed the other, supported the other, became the other?

Then he would be free, truly free, free not only of all that degraded and humiliated him from outside, but free of all that most dissatisfied and embittered him from within; then he would be free of himself. Then any learning he might gain would be sweet to him, not a source of shame; then his power and his position would be triumphant, not rotten, precarious, having no end but their own miserable preservation. He would have to learn, to struggle, to reach; it would be harder than anything he had yet done or thought of doing, harder than living in Lyndhurst and being a builder's boy, harder than going to the north and passing himself off as a white man. Was he man enough to try for it? Did he want what she was offering him? Did he realize what it was that she was offering him?

When Kenneth came out of the house the sheer height of the sky above the streets was dizzying, as if he stood above it and looked down. He walked slowly, carefully, at first; then he began to run. He ran home through the streets, like a schoolboy, trotting, swinging his arms; from his lips there came snatches of song, words that Miss Bentwisch had said to him that he repeated until they had lost their meaning, obscenities that he uttered for sheer joy. Once he halted, on a half-made road, picked up a stone, and threw it at a metal lamp-post yards away: the stone flew straight and struck against the steel with a resonant clang that was like the loudest utterance of his own heart; and, like the deepest, was the vibrant long-lasting hum that followed. Then he ran on, through the dusk.

It was suddenly that he found himself home, for all the anticipation with which he had been running. To the left was the veld that divided the Coloured Camp from the nearest white suburb; to the right the Camp itself stretched in a slow decline of dust and twilight. The gate of his own house was in Kenneth's hand; a tiny paved path led from the gate to the *stoep* and the walls of corrugated iron, with a little corrugated iron gable standing up perkily above them. It was a box-like place, almost toy-like; it looked as though it could be crushed between two hands; yet it had always been maintained with great care, and the garden—small though it was—was divided into minute beds, each marked off from the next by whitewashed stones. There were ferns in wire baskets hanging within the *stoep*, and a trailing plant grew inside the suspended half of an old motor-car tyre, painted white. At one time a fashion for these tyres as decorated objects had spread through the Coloured Camp; and Kenneth could remember his father painting the tyre with the same care that he took over every job that came into his hands. There was nothing Kenneth could see which Cornelius's hands had not touched and worked on, many times; the house was his own property, and, as Cornelius had often remarked to his friends, it was the house that gave him the right to call himself 'a man with a stake in the country'.

They were waiting for him, as he had anticipated, in the little living-room: Cornelius with a newspaper in his hand and gold-rimmed glasses low on his brown nose; Peter sitting at the window, next to the radio, his feet tapping to the music that came out of it.

'Ah,' Cornelius said, looking up. 'Here at last.'

'How's the girl-friend?' Peter asked. His feet still tapped against the linoleum. 'So do we eat?'

'Yes. Come, boys.' Cornelius rose to his feet, slowly. He was tired and stiff from his work, and stood a little bent before at last straightening himself.

'Wait!' Kenneth cried. 'There's something I want to talk to you about. I can't go in and eat supper as though nothing has happened. Because something has happened—something big—the biggest thing that there could be. It's Miss Bentwisch——'

'Ah, the girl-friend again,' Peter said.

'You shut up.'

And Cornelius said gravely to Peter, 'I want you please to show some respect.'

'He will, when I've told him.'

'Told me what? Speak, man, we're waiting.'

Kenneth sat down. He spoke at first without emotion. 'Miss Bentwisch wants to educate me. She says she'll pay for me to become anything I want. A doctor, a lawyer, anything, a teacher. She says she'll send me to university if I work hard enough, and pass my matric.' When Kenneth looked up he saw his brother's face was grave. Kenneth could not meet the glance; he looked away, and using the same words, speaking more quickly, almost gabbling at the end, he again told them what Miss Bentwisch had offered him. Then Peter smiled.

'She must be mad about you. What have you got, man? What have you got that I haven't got?'

This was the question that Kenneth had most feared from Peter, who rose from his chair, and took Kenneth by the arm, gripping him tightly. 'I'm glad for you, if you want it,' Peter said. His chin was thrust forward, but he was still smiling. 'Man,' he said, and his grip became even tighter, so that it hurt Kenneth, with a pain that he did not resent, but rather felt grateful for, 'I'm proud of you,' Peter said. 'Christ! When you're a big lawyer or a doctor—Dr Makeer!—then I'll say, "You see that bloke, he's my brother, he's clever, you must watch out for him, he's got it!" That's what I'll say.' For a moment Peter's hand held firmly on to Kenneth's arm; then he stepped aside.

When Cornelius did at last speak, he said, as if unimpressed, 'I could have made you a teacher.' His voice was unsteady. 'A teacher is nothing. To be a teacher you only need the Junior Certificate.'

'That's the kind of teacher you wanted me to be,' Peter said loudly. 'That's no kind of a teacher at all. And who says he wants to be a teacher, anyway? No, man, I fancy him to be a doctor, that'll be best. He'll make lots of money, carry a little black bag—a doctor's the thing for you to be, Kenneth, you listen to your big brother.'

'I am listening,' Kenneth said.

'You're listening now. But wait a couple of years, when you've matriculated and at the university and everything, then you won't listen to me any more. You'll say, "Who is this Coloured fellow who speaks in my ear so loudly? I don't know him, take him out of my sight. I suspect," ' Peter said, still imitating Kenneth as he would be, pulling down the corners of his mouth and thrusting his nose into the air, ' "that he is nothing but a *skollie*." Then I'll say, "What! Don't you know your own brother, who——" '

'Quiet!' Cornelius shouted, and immediately Peter was silent. But Cornelius's bafflement had found its vent. 'Why do you always play the fool like that? Can't you be serious when there are serious things to talk about? You're a fool, a loafer, you make me sick. Here's Kenneth with something that we have to talk about properly, and what do I hear from you? Rubbish! Shit!' Cornelius shouted. He could not control himself now. 'You're full of shit, nothing but shit, I don't know why you don't get out of here and stay out!'

Peter had slumped into a chair; to all three of them the situation was painfully familiar. Only Cornelius, pushing his glasses back on his nose with a trembling hand, was still so angry as to be unaware, hardly conscious. But the outburst had served its purpose. When he was able to speak again he could do so almost calmly. 'You must tell us all about this business, properly, quietly, without interruptions'—Peter did not look up, despite Cornelius's stare at him, and Cornelius went on—'then I'll be able to tell you what I think.'

'There isn't so much to tell. You know I've been going to see her——'

'Don't we just!' Peter interrupted; then hastily, mockingly, brought one hand to his lips. 'Sorry, sorry, not another word.'

'Yes, I could see the madam took a great interest in you.' Cornelius was now on his very best behaviour; Miss Bentwisch might have been in the room, the way he spoke of her; and both his sons knew that he spoke as he did because of his embarrassment at the filthy word he had used a few minutes before. 'I did not stand in your way at all,' he went on. 'How could I, with a lady like Miss Bentwisch interested in you, and so rich, too? Sometimes I was afraid of what people would think, if they saw you visiting her so often, like a white man, but I comforted myself with the thought that nobody knows who goes in and out of Miss Bentwisch's house, she lives on her own altogether. So I didn't interfere, isn't that so?'

Kenneth had listened patiently to his father putting himself in the right. 'Yes, that's so. Well, anyway, she likes me . . . And she thinks I'm promising——' Kenneth brought the word out with embarrassment, and Peter took advantage of it.

'I promised you,' he sang, 'and you promised me; but what we promised will never be . . . ' The tune was his own, as the words were. Then, before Cornelius could say a word, Peter sprang from his chair, ducked exaggeratedly at the door, as if from a blow, and had gone out of the room.

'Thank God!' Cornelius shouted after him.

Peter put his head in through the door. 'Look! I'm back again!'

Kenneth said, 'Come in, Peter. And stop playing the fool. No,' he said to Cornelius, cutting off his expostulations, 'I want him to be here.' Cornelius kept silent, and Peter came back into the room. 'I think you should listen,' Kenneth said to Peter. 'I need your help, too.' Without a word Peter went back to the chair he had left a moment before.

'Help?' Cornelius said. 'What help can we give you? You have already made up your mind what you want to do. Do you think I can't see it? How can you go back to being—to what you were?'

'You could stop me,' Kenneth said. His voice, too, was low.

'And what will my payment be? Do I want you to hold it against me for the rest of my life that I stopped you? I'd rather you looked down on me, you thought what an ignorant old Coloured your father is, that you couldn't walk with me in the street—it would be better than keeping you when you want to go. We'll stay behind. It's all we're good for, so we must be content with what we are. Like Peter said, I'll also say, "That's my son!" But I'll say it softly so that no one will hear me, and you will need not be ashamed of the old man with paint on his trousers.' He fell silent, unable to go on.

Kenneth exchanged a glance with Peter, and slowly, Peter winked at him. Then Peter said, "All the same, it's right, there's nothing else for us. But I'm glad for you. Hell, man, if I had a chance like that——!' Peter was lost in the thought; in silence he shook his head. 'But I'm too stupid. Also, I suppose I look too much like a *skollie*, altogether. So bye-bye Kenneth, and good luck to you.'

Kenneth got up from his chair. 'I don't know what's the matter with you people,' he said, and at the note in his voice they both looked up. 'Why do you speak like that to me, both of you, in the same way? Have I said anything about having nothing to do with you? Have I? Tell me! Why do you push me away? Don't you want me? Dammit all, don't you love me?' His hands were in front of his chest, fingers crooked towards himself, his elbows tucked close to his sides. 'What kind of a person would I be if I did what you say? Is that all you think of me? Have I ever spoken like someone who would? And you tell me that I don't need your help! Of course I need it, I need it more than ever; and instead of help, what do I get? *Voetsak!*—that's what I get. Get out of this house—that's what I hear. You're not my son—that's what you tell me. Why? What have I done? I love you, don't you know what that means? Look, I thought that Miss Bentwisch would want me to break away, to cut myself off, so that there would be nothing between us; and I wasn't interested. I tell you, I wasn't! Do you believe me?' Kenneth dropped his voice, stretched one hand towards them. 'But she explained to me that that wasn't what she wanted. You're both making the same mistake that I made before Miss Bentwisch explained to me. Now I know better, and I want you to know, too, so that you'll understand. You'll see that what she wants me to do can put us together closer than we've been before, and not only us, but other people, too, all the people in the Coloured Camp; and others, even farther away. She showed me——'

'What did she show you?' Peter asked simply.

Kenneth looked around the familiar, cramped little room. How could he explain to them what Miss Bentwisch had told him of? Peter and Cornelius waited attentively for him to speak. He said, 'Look,' and gestured with his hand, but no words came. He tried again; he said, 'You must pay attention——'

But they were paying attention, and he was not speaking. 'It's difficult,' Kenneth said. 'You mustn't laugh at me. Just to say it like this is hard for me.'

'But Miss Bentwisch said it?'

'Oh yes, she did. And I believed her. And you must believe her. You *must*.' But assertions were meaningless until he spoke. He wished that they could all be taken into the high-ceilinged room in which Miss Bentwisch had spoken to him, with the blue vase on the table, the dark cabinets against the walls, the light fading swiftly against the tall windows. Then they would understand; if they heard Miss Bentwisch, the white, rich, lonely, passionate woman speaking to them. But she was in her room, and he was in the room in which he had grown up; and the disparity between the two rooms, the disparity between his ambitions and the bare facts of the life he had led, the life that Cornelius and Peter would continue to live—the disparity was suddenly too great, it was mocking, yawning, derisive, it made him look a fool. *This*, this in front of him, was the life Miss Bentwisch had been talking about; and what could he do to change it? And then what about the Coloured Camp? If he could do nothing within the room, what would he be able to do outside it? It was absurd to think of trying: let alone to think further yet and further, to the Africans in their locations scattered about the town, and to the other towns in the country, with their Coloured quarters and their locations. Words, words, words—that was all he had had from Miss Bentwisch; and he had taken those words to be truth, to be reality. But now he woke, and the reality was about him, totally incommensurate with what the words had told him he could make of it. He was a fool; Miss Bentwisch was a madwoman; there was no redemption in the world. A man was what he always had been; and if he changed, he changed himself and not the rest of the world, too.

'So?'

'Kenneth?'

They both spoke, almost at one time, and in one tone.

How good they were to him! This Kenneth knew at least, suddenly, as he stood empty and silenced before them. And he had reproached them for the way they had spoken to him earlier! It was their love that had spoken. For all their anxiety for him, and their distress, they had not said a single word of anger, of resentment, of jealousy. Peter especially—who was to remain behind without hope. And his father, too—no, there could be no distinction between them, between the love they bore for him. Kenneth cried out; and what before had been empty within him was now filled with sweetness. 'As true as God,' he cried, lifting his hand above his head, a man taking an oath, 'as true as God I'll show you that I'm right. I'll show you that it can be done. If I do anything, except for you; if I take anything, except for you; if I learn anything, except for you, then let me die where I am. There must be a way for us to live together and I will find it.'

7

KENNETH WENT AWAY to an Anglican boarding-school for Coloureds. The senior staff of the school were members of an Anglican community—gowned clerics from England, with aloof sunburnt faces and restless hands, who were given to rare outbreaks of sudden and endearing hilarity, before silence and diffidence closed down again on them. Then there was the Coloured staff, none of whom were in Orders, all of whom were married, middle-aged, and respectable to a paralysing degree. And lastly, there were the temporary teachers or 'helpers', as they were called: young South African-born whites, who came from a nearby university for months on end, to teach and live in the community. Many of the 'helpers' were thinking of taking Orders; but among them, invariably, were a few of a different kind, who came for political reasons, anxious to do something for what they mockingly called, 'the Cause'. And 'the Cause' was well-served, they felt, by mixing on terms of equality with the students, and talking sedition among them. They mocked everything, these young whites, who thought of themselves as 'liberals', 'intellectuals', 'socialists', and despised every form of authority set over them, whether it was that of the Church on whose property they were living, that of the government which watched them, or of the university they were supposed to be attending.

From them all Kenneth learned: from the bitterness of the liberals, though he did not share it; from the faith of the religious, though he did not understand it; he learned much from the very Englishness of the Englishmen. He learned, too, from his fellow-students, who were, as he was, not boys but young men, to all of whom education had come tardily, and was the more prized for it. Kenneth could not have helped learning, even if he had not wanted to. But he did want to learn, eagerly, passionately, and took every chance that came to him or to which he could reach: in the classrooms with their battered, donated desks; in the little tin library, where he spent so many afternoons, his head reeling from the heat and the sight of printed pages; in the talks in the dormitories at night, the rooms of the helpers, the monastic cells of the clerics, the living-rooms (so much like Cornelius's) of the Coloured staff.

Learning, the acquiring of knowledge, was not at all what Kenneth had imagined it to be, before he had had the opportunity of finding out. Before he had thought of knowledge simply as a block to be consumed, like an ice-cream or a slab of chocolate; or as a house that a man could take possession of; or, at its most arduous, as a mountain to be scaled. But it was none of these—if it was like anything at all, it was like a sea, in which one had to struggle to keep afloat, of whose depth one could never be sure, whose size one could never measure. But if the sense of size, wildness and shapelessness was dismaying, Kenneth has not anticipated the delight of those other times when the current of the sea took him with it in its own direction, and carried him on its surge, as if with no effort, on and on, until the wave at last slackened and lost itself again, leaving him as breathless and exhilarated as a surfer brought back to the shore. History was Kenneth's favourite subject; and next to history, English literature; and this in itself was a surprise to him, for he would have liked to think of himself as some kind of forward-looking social scientist, and not as one who found his deepest satisfactions in going back into the past of the race and the nation, in going back into his own past. But he did well in all his subjects.

Miss Bentwisch was paying for his tuition, she paid for his board, his clothing, his pocket-money. She did all as tactfully as possible; and Kenneth appreciated it that there was no one but her, his family, and the school authorities who knew what she was doing. The tuition and board were paid directly to the school, and he had a bank account in which there appeared at regular intervals a sum of money sufficient to cover all his other expenses. Miss Bentwisch never inquired as to how he spent this money, of which he had free use; but Kenneth kept a detailed account for her nevertheless. He was careful in his spending, and was able to return a balance to her at the end of his first year. Then she told him to put the money he had saved in a savings account; she said that she had worked out how much he would need, without extravagance, and that that was what she gave to him, neither less nor more. Kenneth showed her, too, his school reports, at the end of every term, and she declared herself fully satisfied with them. He came to see her regularly, whenever he was in Lyndhurst.

His feelings towards the old lady had deepened and changed:

he was not only grateful to her, as he had always been, but he wanted now to help her, too, though he did not know in what way she might need help, and knew still less how he would be able to offer his help, should she ever show that she needed it. It seemed that he could do no more for her than to fulfil the ambitions she had for him—to do well at school and spend as little as possible of her money; to show her that the lessons she had taught him had been taken to his heart and would be expressed in his actions. All this he would do, gladly and conscientiously; yet he felt that it was not enough. He wanted to touch her, to grasp her arm in his hand, to trace with a forefinger the line of her brow, above her fine eyes. It was not love he felt for her, not even the love of a son for a mother, which might have been the closest parallel to the relationship he felt he was having with her. No, in a curious way, he began to feel that he was the older; he felt that in some way he should protect her, warn her, counsel her. But he did not know what it was that he wanted to protect her from, nor what course he should advise her to follow; he wished merely that she were more at peace with herself, and with the world.

Yet he knew if she had been at peace with the world she would never have taken any interest in him.

During his holidays Kenneth put on his overalls and went out to work with his father, as he had done in the old days; and of this Miss Bentwisch fully approved. Kenneth's absence seemed to have helped Cornelius and Peter to get on better with each other: Peter was quieter with his father and Cornelius was more patient with his elder son, and a kind of trust grew between them which there had never been before. And this made the house a pleasanter place for Kenneth to come back to.

But when the train took Kenneth away from Lyndhurst at the end of every holiday, he had to admit to himself that he was glad to go. There, at the end of the track, beyond the scrub of the Karroo and the mountains to the south, there in the grass and the rolling hills of the Eastern Province, was his present opportunity; and Kenneth came back each time with a sense of pleased familiarity to the tin-roofed, brick buildings of the school settlement, and the depressed-looking and shadeless gardens in which he had to work in his spare time, like all the other students.

A year passed, a second, a third; he matriculated. He went back to the school for the post-matriculation year which the school provided for those of its students who would be going on to one of the universities. Then that year ended, too. For the last time Kenneth passed through the mountains, then across the wastes of the Karroo; he entered the grassveld of the Northern Cape, where the thornbushes were like dark tufts suspended here and there above the low, pallid grass. On the horizon there rose up the mine-dumps of Lyndhurst, as big and as irregular as *koppies*; a huge location passed alongside the railway track, with half-naked piccanins begging for pennies from the moving train; then there came the corrugated iron roofs and wide streets of the town itself. Railway lines ran to the right and left, the iron roof of the station drew nearer. The train plunged into shadow, and Kenneth's father was waiting for him on the platform. 'You haven't put on any weight,' he said. Then, 'Marvellous to see you again.' He stepped back to look at Kenneth, but did not release his grip on Kenneth's arm. 'You aren't in trouble, are you? That business in the location that you wrote about——'

'I don't think I'm in trouble, Dad.'

'You don't *think* so. Don't you know?'

The two of them stared at one another. Then Kenneth shook his head.

Cornelius frowned. 'And what will Miss Bentwisch say, if she hears about it?'

'She will hear about it. And she won't mind.'

Kenneth was right, though by the time he went to see Miss Bentwisch he knew that he was indeed in trouble of a kind.

When the people they were watching were young enough, the Special Branch of the South African Police made a habit of calling on the parents of the suspects, rather than on the suspects themselves. These approaches were ostensibly made as a matter of courtesy, out of a desire to be helpful; the parents were always told that there was no wish or intention to take too seriously what was (no doubt) merely a boyish prank; but the threat to the children beneath the courtesy was also made very plain.

It was one of these visits that was paid to Cornelius within a day or two of Kenneth's return to Lyndhurst. In the course of the visit Cornelius was told that Kenneth was known to have talked abusively of the government in such-and-such rooms at the school on such-and-such dates; that in a debate against the university Kenneth had led a motion opposing the government's *apartheid* policies; that Kenneth had sold copies of a radical weekly within the school; that Kenneth had persistently consorted with 'helpers' at the school who were already under the scrutiny of the Special Branch. None of these activities was actually criminal, though they were unwise; they might have been overlooked—Cornelius was told—if Kenneth had not taken part in a leaflet raid on the location of Regina village, some thirty miles away from the school. There had been trouble in Regina location over the burning of passes by African women; and the leaflets that Kenneth and his companions had scattered over the location had in effect incited the women to repeat their defiance of the law.

In taking part in this raid Kenneth had laid himself open to prosecution under the Incitement to Violence Act, the Suppression of Communism Act, and various acts relating to the entry of unauthorized persons into locations. Under these acts Kenneth could be charged in the courts, and if found guilty could be flogged, put in jail for several years; he could subsequently be banished to a remote part of the country, at the discretion of the Minister of of the Interior. It was not proposed, however, to bring a charge against Kenneth at the present time; but Cornelius was warned that if his son should ever again do anything which would bring his activities to the attention of the Special Branch, his past offences would be taken into consideration in deciding what steps would be taken against him. It was hoped that Cornelius would use his parental authority to prevent this ever happening; if he did not, and Kenneth should again break the laws of the country, not only would Kenneth be punished as the statutes laid down, but it would be assumed that Cornelius had abetted the boy in his crimes, and Cornelius himself would come under the gravest suspicion. The authorities were acting more than fairly towards Kenneth; they were acting as kindly and as considerately as they could; but their patience was not inexhaustible.

Having delivered themselves of these warnings and exhortations to a shattered and trembling Cornelius, the two Special Branch detectives then left his house. They left Cornelius as ashamed of their visit as he would have been had they come because his son had been involved in burglary or brawling. The only distinction Cornelius made was to be even more thoroughly terrified of the offences Kenneth had committed than he would have been of any other, for these involved so many things he knew nothing about, and among which he felt himself altogether powerless. He cursed himself for ever having let Kenneth leave home; he cursed Miss Bentwisch; he swore that he was going to put the boy back in his overalls and take him out to work every morning until the nonsense was knocked out of him. He wanted Kenneth to go to the local office of the Special Branch and apologize for what he had done; he suggested that Kenneth write a long letter in the humblest terms direct to the Minister for the Interior, explaining to the Minister how he had been led astray by bad companions. Cornelius saw all his hopes of Kenneth educated, Kenneth wealthy, Kenneth respected, becoming a reality of Kenneth a criminal, Kenneth a convict. But he was going to put his foot down this time, Cornelius swore, and no mistakes.

And then poor Cornelius found that there was nowhere for him to put his foot; that beneath him there was only a moral swamp (as it seemed to him) in which he had to struggle to keep himself from sinking. Kenneth was frightened at hearing that the police had been to the house, but he was proud, too; Cornelius could see that Kenneth did not feel in the least guilty, humiliated and repentant. (And Cornelius had drawn his only comfort in the whole situation from the thought of how he would forgive Kenneth after the boy had repented.) In the end tears sprang into Cornelius's eyes, as he pleaded with Kenneth not to bring disgrace upon himself and his father and his brother, but to live quietly, as other people did. 'What business did you have in that location?' Cornelius asked. 'What were you looking for? Why did you do it, please Kenneth, tell me, when you can live a lawyer, a respectable man, a member of the community? Don't stand there like that! Don't smile at me! Kenneth, don't I mean anything to you?'

And Kenneth, who was himself overwrought and distracted, for all the grin on his face, shouted out in reply, 'Not when you speak like that!' Hastily Kenneth added, 'I mean nothing to myself, don't you see, unless I *do* something to help in the struggle—that's how I feel. Dad, I didn't say it like you think——' But the words came too late and were too incoherent; Cornelius turned away in despair, and Kenneth averted his eyes from the sight of Cornelius's shaking back.

Kenneth went into his room to change. He put on the shirt and tie, the grey flannel trousers and English tweed sports coat, that he had bought with Miss Bentwisch's money. He had to see her, immediately, he had to tell her of what had happened to him. When he came into the living-room, Cornelius was standing at the little window, as he had been when Kenneth had left the room. 'Dad,' Kenneth said awkwardly, 'I'm going to see Miss Bentwisch, I'm going to tell her what's happened.'

'And what will she say to you? Is this what she educated you for? Is this what she spent money on you to become—a criminal, a convict?'

'Dad, you don't understand at all. Miss Bentwisch won't feel that I'm a convict or a criminal. I don't feel that I'm one. We went on that raid for the right reason, we did it for a cause, we did it because it was worth while doing it. We didn't rob anyone or hit anyone over the head. Can't you see the difference? We did it because we *cared*—we cared about those women burning their passes. We wanted to show them that they weren't alone, that there were people who wanted to help them, and who admired them for what they were doing. Don't you see? Try to see my point of view, Dad.'

'Are you trying to see mine?'

Kenneth gestured with his hand. 'We have the same point of view, Dad. We must. It's the same battle, for you and for me, as well as for all those other women. There's no difference between us. We're together in this, all of us.'

'I don't care about those other women!' Cornelius shouted. 'All your fine words mean nothing to me. And those women in the location mean nothing to me. What do I care about women I've never seen? It's all a madness in your head. Why should you care about Kaffir women in a location when you don't care about me? You're my son, and you see how unhappy I am, but that doesn't mean anything to you—no, no. I'm only here in front of you. I'm only your father, so I don't count.'

'Dad——'

'Don't call me that. Don't speak to me, I don't want to hear you, until you tell me that you're sorry for what you've done, and that you won't do it again.'

'I can't promise you that.'

'So now I know what it meant, when you came home that very first night, and told us how much you loved us and cared for us. Now I see what your words are worth.'

Kenneth turned and left the room. He had to see Miss Bentwisch; she was the only person in Lyndhurst to whom he felt he could turn. He could not believe that she would be angered by what he had done; she would understand, even if his father did not.

From Miss Bentwisch Kenneth did indeed receive a response something like the one he had hoped for, though it came with an intensity he had not anticipated. Kenneth was so full of his own news that he could not wait, once their greetings had been made, to begin to tell her of what had happened to him; but, self-absorbed though he was, he very soon noticed that a change seemed to have come over Miss Bentwisch since he had last seen her. The change was not so much in one in her physical appearance; it was in the gestures of her hands, which were looser than he had seen them before; in the inclinations of her head, which were quicker and at the same time more erratic than they had been; in the eagerness of her tone. She seemed to listen to him with great attentiveness, yet he became aware as he spoke that the expressions on her face did not respond directly to what he was saying; she looked away when he most wanted her to be looking at him, yet at other moments he unexpectedly found her staring at him with a voracity that was almost ugly, wolfish. He thought she had aged much in the four months that had passed since he had last seen her, though the lines about her mouth were no deeper, and the light in her eye was as clear as it had ever been.

And the terms in which she approved of his actions came as a surprise to Kenneth. 'You've burned your bridges,' she said. 'You're known. You've been noted. Now you're committed, and I'm glad, do you hear me, I'm glad. I'm grateful to the police, and you should be, too.'

'Grateful? I don't understand. And I was committed anyway.'

'No you weren't. You thought you were, but you weren't. A commitment that's inside your head isn't worth nearly so much as a commitment that's inside someone else's head. Or down on a Special Branch file—even better.'

'I committed myself to you,' Kenneth said.

'You speak as if I'll always be here,' Miss Bentwisch said.

Kenneth was silent. For the first time in his acquaintance with her Kenneth felt a kind of fear, but whether it was a fear of her of himself, he could not have said.

'I don't want you to go back, ever,' Miss Bentwisch said. 'It worries me—sometimes, often—it worries me what is going to happen when I'm not here. Do you understand what I mean? I think of the people I know,' Miss Bentwisch went on, 'all the people I've tried to help; and I think of them—backsliding.' Her hand gripped tightly in the air, and fell. 'I've just had a disappointment, with someone I know. I had hoped—I had planned—it's a girl I know, you don't know her.'

Kenneth was surprised to see a smile, like a grimace on Miss Bentwisch's wide mouth; her lips showed up bluish against her sallow skin. 'You do know this girl. Does the name Isabel Last mean anything to you?'

'No,' Kenneth said.

'Yet you do know her. It was through her that I heard of you, without her we would never have met. You would have still been in the building trade, if it hadn't been for Isabel Last. I'm to see her this very afternoon. She's leaving, she doesn't want what I was offering to her.' Miss Bentwisch broke off, rising from her chair, and then sinking back into it, as though the effort to stand were too great. 'People must commit themselves, I want to see them commit themselves. Then I'll know that it hasn't all been wasted, that they won't turn their backs on everything as soon as they can, as soon as I've gone.' The muscles about her eyes did not quiver; she stared without embarrassment at the boy in front of her.

'You have no faith,' Kenneth said suddenly.

For a long moment they were both silent. 'And you have faith?' Miss Bentwisch said. 'What in?'

'Myself,' Kenneth said. 'In the things you have told me of. In the things that have to be done. In my determination to do them.' Kenneth spoke up loudly, the louder for the fear he felt. 'Don't you know what I am? *Whites Only, Whites Only*—do you still see those signs? I do, everywhere I go. And what about the hundreds of places where they don't put up the signs, they take it so much for granted I won't go into them: bioscopes, swimming-baths, hotels, restaurants? If I don't spend my life fighting, pulling down the signs, then it'll mean that I accept them, don't you see? That *I* believe—not just the whites—that I don't deserve to be admitted, because I'm dirty, degenerate, disgusting, stinking. I know there's a history to this country; I know it has an economy, a sociology; but I'm not fighting just for a better history; a different economy, another sociology. It's dignity I'm fighting for, personal dignity: my own, my father's, my brother's, my children's, when I have children. And the dignity of all the others who are treated as I am. I'm committed, you don't have to worry about me. I'm committed to here—' Kenneth said fiercely, bringing forward one clenched fist, and with the fingers of the other hand plucking at the skin of his wrist—'here!' He clasped his hands together; still they were stretched forward to the woman opposite him. 'They commit me, wherever I go. This isn't the first time the police have interfered in my life; they've been doing it since the day I was born a Coloured, and shoved out, and shoved away, by every law that it's the duty of every policeman to see obeyed. When I met you these things looked differently to me—I admit it—I didn't know anything. But I can't go back. I won't go back. I began learning in this room, and I've been learning ever since. And you ask me if I've got faith? You ask me what I've got faith in? You don't frighten me with that kind of question—not now, not any more.'

Miss Bentwisch rose from her chair. She began pacing back and forth, stooping, turning abruptly, crossing the room again. She came to Kenneth and took his face between her hands. 'Thank you,' she said. 'I do believe you, and it means so much to me, I can't tell you.' Her face was only a few inches from his own, she was leaning forward as if about to kiss him. She did kiss him on the lips, and the blood mounted darkly in his cheeks, but his eyes did not waver, they met hers fully. She stepped back a pace. 'It's not true that I have no faith. I do have faith in you, Kenneth, I believe what you tell me.'

It was as though the kiss she had given him had set her free to talk. For the first time she told Kenneth about some of the other people she had helped—of this young African who had become a doctor at her expense, of that young Coloured girl she had sent to ballet school, of the family for whom she had bought a house, of the bursaries, essay prizes, sick-relief funds she had established, of the sums of money she had covenanted to give away through the regular distributors of charity in the town, of the support she had surreptitiously given to certain African politicians and trade unionists. Kenneth heard her with the greatest interest and yet with uneasiness too; she spoke with no apparent awareness that she had never spoken like this to him before, and it was just this lack of awareness that made him uneasy. She offered to him no explanation of her sudden frankness; she did not apologize for it: she talked simply as if she were afraid of silence, afraid of loneliness, afraid of time.

And again she spoke to him of Isabel Last. 'You would have loved Isabel if you had known what she was like then, as a girl,' she told Kenneth. 'She was so *anxious*—that's the only word for it, anxious to be helpful, and right, morally right I mean, in the deepest sense; it was lovable altogether. With you, for example, she thought she'd done wrong to you, and she came to me to make it right—could anything have been simpler, sweeter? It's only lately . . . I don't know what has been happening to the girl. She's changed, she's restless, she thinks of only herself. I've seen it happen so many times before it shouldn't shock me any more; but with Isabel it still does . . . And I had such hopes for her.'

Kenneth moved in his chair; he wanted to be released and yet he wanted to hear all that she had to tell him. And there seemed to be nothing that she would hold back. 'You must know that there were people who said that I wasn't entitled to the money, that my father had been deceived. You have heard the gossip about it. It's never given me any choice but to hand on within the family what was given to me. Do you understand what I mean? Oh, it isn't what people think . . . it's what my father thought. He was loyal to me. I must be loyal to him, don't you see? But I'd thought of Isabel as being with Martin; she shared all my views, she felt as I feel about everything, and I had hoped that she would carry on the work.'

'Isn't Miss Last going to marry your nephew?'

'No, that's just the point.'

'Perhaps she doesn't love him.'

'She liked Martin well enough. And she knows how I felt about it. No, she's full of will, full of self, a kind of grittiness, you'd hardly know her.' Miss Bentwisch looked up. 'But of course you don't know her anyway, you only owe your life to her.'

'Tell me about it,' Kenneth said, his curiosity greater than his discomfort. And on hearing of the incident that had brought him and Isabel together, Kenneth remembered it—remembered the lane, the fence he and his father had been building, the blue tar of the road beyond, the stumping figure of Mr Last, the argument with his father, his own flight. He remembered it all as one remembers a picture in its frame—bright, small, irrelevant; and because of this irrelevance he was the more surprised at how moved and grateful he felt towards the girl who had been so concerned about what she had done, and had gone to someone else with the story in the hope that good might come of her actions. Even if nothing had come of it, Kenneth felt, there still would have been cause for him to be grateful. She had been a rich white girl, and he a poor Coloured boy; Kenneth knew how easy it would have been for her to take for granted the abyss between them. Instead this girl had worried about it, had been—in Miss Bentwisch's words—anxious about it, as though she were not on the safe and sunlit side. God, how rare that kind of anxiety was! And when Kenneth thought of the consequences to him that her action *had*, in fact had, the disproportion he felt was all within himself: he was not worthy, he had never been worthy, of what had been done for him.

'Well, I'm sorry,' Kenneth said eventually, 'that things haven't worked out as you had hoped they might.'

Miss Bentwisch shrugged. 'I am sorry for Isabel.'

'For her, too,' Kenneth agreed. Then he asked, 'What is she going to do?'

'She's going to England.'

'To England!' Kenneth's eyes widened. 'Lucky girl!'

'They way you people talk about England, one would think that it's the promised land.'

'Well, it's the one country in the world I could walk into and be a full citizen immediately, a free man, more than I am in my own country—with a vote even! I do envy Miss Last. And I'm grateful to her, too. It's absurd how things come about. Does she know anything about me?'

'Nothing.'

'I'm relieved,' Kenneth said, though he felt oddly disappointed, too. 'What a burden of—of—something it would be for her to carry, knowing how much she's changed someone else's life.'

'You needn't worry about that. Isabel is busy shedding her burdens as fast as she can. And don't you ever think of what a burden it is for me to carry, knowing how much I've changed your life.'

'I do, indeed. But you've got something out of it.'

'What?'

'Me,' Kenneth said. This time it was Kenneth who came forward and stooped over Miss Bentwisch, taking her hand in his. With a finger of her free hand she touched at his hair, at his chin. 'I must go,' he said. He looked towards the window. 'Will you be very ashamed of me if I tell you that I'm nervous in the streets now? I think—are they watching me, are they following me, are they going to come up to me?'

Miss Bentwisch replied gravely, 'Perhaps they will one day. Not now, for the moment you needn't worry, I'm sure of that. If they had intended taking action against you now they would have taken it. But they're right to watch you, Kenneth: you are a dangerous man to them. You won't surrender. You won't go back, dear Kenneth, whatever happens to me. It's my happiness to know this: I know it so deeply, I could know it no better. Your life is as safe to me as my own.'

Kenneth stooped, and kissed her, awkwardly but as a right,

after what had passed between them. 'So it should be,' he said. 'You've given my life to me.'

It was only after he had left Miss Bentwisch that Kenneth remembered guiltily that he had said nothing to her about how upset his father had been at the intervention of the police. Nevertheless, Miss Bentwisch did learn how Cornelius felt.

Cornelius had decided that he would go up to the front door of Miss Bentwisch's house, and ring on the bell, like a man with a right to do so. He put on his blue church-going suit, he polished his shoes, he thrust a white handkerchief into the breast pocket of his jacket. But when he stood in the street outside Miss Bentwisch's house, its size overawed him, and he changed his plans; he walked around the block and approached the house by its private lane at the back. To the African servant who came out in response to his knock at the kitchen door, Cornelius said that he wanted to see the madam; the African servant disappeared, returning eventually with a young white man whom Cornelius had not seen before.

'Yes, what do you want?'

'Please, sah, I wish to see the madam.' Cornelius held his hat in both hands, in front of him.

'She's busy.'

'Can I wait, sah?'

'Is it urgent?'

'Sah, it is most urgent. I can wait here until the madam can give me a few minutes. I won't mind waiting, sah.' All Cornelius's habits of mind and character were urging him to apologize deeply for his intrusion, and then to retire immediately; but he was afraid that if he ever walked out of the back gate he would never be able to summon up his resolution to come through it again. So he stood where he was, though he yielded as much as he could without actually stepping back; he began slowly to crouch over his hat. 'Madam is kind,' he said. 'Sah is kind. If sah will tell the madam that Cornelius Makeer is waiting to see the madam—he doesn't mind waiting, he is glad to wait, anything not to disturb the madam, sah.'

'What did you say the name was?'

'Cornelius Makeer.'

'I'll tell her.'

'Thank you sah,' Cornelius called out, behind the young man's retreating back; then he breathed deeply and waited without any alteration in his posture, until the white man came back.

'She says you should wait. Come inside, sit down.' Cornelius was left sitting at the kitchen-table, his hat on the floor beside him. He sat patiently, only occasionally stirring in his chair and sighing heavily. The servant banged and whistled in the scullery nearby; the sun came into the kitchen through a large window, and its light made vague the pattern of pale brown and white tiles on the floor. Cornelius did not know how long he was kept waiting, before he was summoned by the young man into the interior of the house. There, in a room that seemed to Cornelius all shadows and size, he saw Miss Bentwisch, and with her a young white girl. The man who had called Cornelius from the kitchen stood behind him.

'Madam, madam,' Cornelius greeted each of the ladies in turn.

'You know this lady,' Miss Bentwisch said. 'This is Miss Last.'

'Madam. Madam.' The name meant nothing to Cornelius, at that moment.

'And that is my nephew standing behind you. Mr Bullivant.'

'Sah.' Cornelius turned. The young man made an indecisive gesture greeting with his hand, extending it and then halting it, which so confounded Cornelius that he dropped his hat. They both stooped to get the hat and collided with one another. 'Sah——' Cornelius gasped, rising from the floor, clutching his hat desperately. 'Madam,' he said .'My apologies. My fault. My mistake. Sorry, sah, I am interrupting. I will wait at the back for the madam. There is no hurry, I am sorry, madam.'

'Wait! Don't go! Do you remember him?' The old lady turned to the younger.

'No, I'm afraid not. Should I have remembered?'

'No, it doesn't matter. Martin, if you will show Isabel out.' Her tone was peremptory, and the two young people exchanged an awkward, miserable glance.

'Then I must say good-bye.'

'Yes.'

The girl stooped quickly and kissed Miss Bentwisch on the cheek. The other woman did not move her head in response. Draggingly, the girl turned to go; and with a movement of sympathy, the young man crossed the room to her. But before she was half-way to the door the girl had broken away, and gone back to Miss Bentwisch. She sank on the floor in front of the old lady and cried out, 'I can't go in this way. Please, please, don't send me away like this. I have done nothing wrong. Martin doesn't feel that I've done anything wrong. Why are you so unkind to me?'

'Please, Isabel, come,' the young man said. He stood uncertainly in the middle of the room; he did not look at either of the two women.

'No, no, I can't go without a word.' The girl threw her head back, trying to meet from below Miss Bentwisch's gaze. 'I'm still Isabel, Miss Bentwisch. Please look at me. If you look at me you'll see that it's just Isabel who came here so often, and who loved coming here so much. Do you want me to go away thinking that it was wrong of me to do so? That you didn't love me to come? I don't want to believe it. You know what you have been to me, don't make nothing of it now.'

'Isabel——' the young man said.

The girl turned at the sound of her name, and shook her head in bewilderment; it seemed that she did not have the strength to get up from the floor. The young man went to her, and helped her rise. Yet still she could not leave. She leaned towards Miss Bentwisch, she stretched out her arms, and when Miss Bentwisch at last spoke the girl darted forward and fiercely embraced the other. 'Oh, Isabel,' Miss Bentwisch said wearily. 'Leave well alone. Neither of us are what we were. I don't hope you will be happy in England. You see, Isabel, I want you to come back, after all. I'm still hoping you'll come back. Isn't that enough? Could I say more?'

The girl pressed Miss Bentwisch's hand to her lips. 'No more,' she said. 'It doesn't matter, you have spoken to me. I was right not to go until you did.'

'Don't write to me,' Miss Bentwisch said abruptly.

'No? Then I won't. Perhaps I'll come back sooner instead.'

When she passed him near the door, Cornelius saw the tears in the girl's eyes. He had himself been much moved by the parting he had witnessed—so much so that he had almost forgotten his embarrassment. No sooner had the door closed behind the girl and the frowning young man who followed her, than Cornelius's embarrassment returned. But Miss Bentwisch gave him no time to linger in it.

'Did you see that girl?' she demanded. 'Did you see her?'

'Ah—mad—ah.'

'I wanted you to. That's why I brought you in before she had left. She thought it was an insult to her, that you should have been here—a stranger—while she was saying good-bye to me, as if I didn't care at all. I know that's what she thought. But she was wrong. I know why you have come; and when you stood there it was as if your son stood here, stood with me, reminding me of all that that girl could have done with her life. And of all that your son is still prepared to do.'

Cornelius had caught only one phrase among those she had said to him. 'The madam knows why I have come?'

'Well, it's about Kenneth isn't it? And it's about the police? Kenneth was here this morning and told me that they'd been to see you.'

'Yes madam, they did come. And did Kenneth tell the madam what I said to him——'

'Wait, I must see.' Miss Bentwisch got to her feet, crossed to the window, and looked out. 'Poor Martin,' she said. 'He did try, in his way. You can't ask too much of him, I saw that immediately. Martin thinks that she's going to come back, that's why he is . . . Yes, you were saying?'

'I was saying about Kenneth, madam.'

'Yes.'

It was an effort for Cornelius to repeat the sentence. 'Did Kenneth tell the madam what I said to him about the visit of the police?'

'No. He didn't say a word to me.'

'Ach!' Cornelius cried out. 'It means nothing to him, what I say. Madam, for God's sake, help me. You are the only person in the world that I can come to for help. Kenneth will do anything that you tell him, madam. Madam, tell Kenneth to stop this business that is getting him into trouble. Does he want to break my heart? I have lived all my life in peace, madam, obeying the law; I want my children to do the same. Listen to me and help me, madam. I am an old man; we are two old people, madam, if you will allow me to say so—you know what it is to be old, you must know what it is to be hurt, and to be disappointed, so that you don't know where to turn or what to do. That is how I am, madam, at the end of myself, and all because of this boy of mine. Never before, madam, have I spoken so much to you, how could I dare? But they said they would flog him if he went on. What will it mean to us if Kenneth is flogged?' Cornelius was in tears, he spoke without thought, he gestured with his hands, now beseechingly, now despairingly; when he spoke of flogging his shoulders shrank inwards. 'Let him be poor, madam, let him be ignorant, let him be what he used to be, as long as he is safe. For me there is only one boy like him in the world.'

'Yes, for me, too, there is only one Kenneth in the world.'

Cornelius lifted his glasses to wipe his tears with his hand. 'Madam will help me?' Then he dropped his glasses on his nose, and groped with his hand for the handkerchief in his breast-pocket.

'How?'

'If the madam wants to help she will know how.'

Miss Bentwisch said, 'He can never again be what he was.'

'No, madam. The madam has done her work too well, I can see. But how old is he? Why should this be happening to him when he is so young, still a boy really, not yet a man? Is it fair? Is it right? When there are so many boys—white boys, Coloureds, all kinds—who are living now without any of this on their heads? Doesn't the madam feel what I am saying? Doesn't the madam want justice and fairness to Kenneth? If he cannot be changed, if there is going to be trouble in his life, let it come—but, madam, let it not come now, when he is so young. Give him a few more years, madam. That is all I hope for. Afterwards, when he is a man, he will do what he wants to do; but as a man, not as a boy.'

'So you feel it, too? You know that Kenneth will never surrender?'

'I don't understand the madam. I know that he is a determined boy. That he will do what he wants to do, not what his father wants him to do. That he is going to suffer. But let it not begin now, madam.'

Miss Bentwisch said slowly, 'I've said that I trust him. I am not afraid to show how I trust him.' Miss Bentwisch fell silent; and Cornelius, too, did not speak. He stood yards away from her, with his head bowed.

When Cornelius left the house the strain of the entire visit had been so much for him that in his weariness he was hardly able to feel any relief at the plan that Miss Bentwisch had suggested Kenneth should follow. He had not understood much of what Miss Bentwisch had said to him, least of all her references to Isabel Last—'that girl, enjoying what she has done nothing to earn, escaping scot-free, just at her own wish—and poor Kenneth so wistful, expecting so little, having only hardship and deprivation to look forward to. Why shouldn't he be free, too?' she had demanded of Cornelius. 'For a while, for a few years, so that he will know what it is to be free, know what he is struggling for in his own experience, in his heart and his head, in his past? Then you will not be able to reproach me. And at the end of that time we will both see Kenneth come back with his will all that it is now, but stronger, even more dangerous.' So she had gone on; until suddenly she had dismissed Cornelius with the command that he should say nothing of what had passed between them: that she would divulge her plan to Kenneth when next he came to see her.

Cornelius did what she asked of him; he was glad that there was something he could do, small though it was, to oblige her. He hoped merely that Kenneth would fall in with Miss Bentwisch's plan. Cornelius felt that any price was worth paying to have Kenneth out of harm's way; and harm, Cornelius was convinced, was everywhere, at every corner, at every discriminatory signpost, at every instance of maltreatment of black by white, harm for Kenneth was embodied in every policeman on his beat.

When Kenneth came back from his next visit to Miss Bentwisch with his face pale, almost grey, and his eyes glowing, Cornelius for a moment feared that he had just had a quarrel with her. But Kenneth stammered out excitedly what Miss Bentwisch had offered to him; and Cornelius was able to feel truly glad and relieved for the moment; he was able to embrace Kenneth whole-heartedly and wish him luck. 'There's nothing better that I could think for you,' Cornelius said sincerely, and it was this very sincerity that made him add bitterly, 'What a mixed-up business!'

'England!' Peter said, when he heard the news, 'Man, how do you like that?'

'I don't know yet,' Kenneth replied, smiling. 'I'll tell you when I've been there.'

8

WHAT IT MEANS for a South African to come to England can perhaps best be compared with what it means for a provincial in England to come to London, or a provincial in the United States to come to New York. But the comparison is untrustworthy, no more than a dim metaphor. How can one explain what England is to the South Africans who come to the country as visitors, tourists, immigrants, students? To them England is truth, and it is dream; England is reality, and it is pure vision. England is like a mirror in which they see their deepest selves reflected, the selves they have sought for and never found, and have known only by the sense of incompleteness that haunted all their previous days; yet England is chillingly, vastly, uncomfortably strange, with a strangeness made only the more poignant by the sense of dream-familiarity that accompanies it. England is their own past; yet they have never seen it before: England is all they have hoped for; yet it is a disappointment that endures and endures, long after they have left her or settled in her. England contains nothing less than the meanings of the words they have used all their lives; yet they understand them no better for having seen her. England makes unreal all they have done, all they have been, outside her; but grants no reality to what they may become within her. They would not have her any less than she is; yet they can never forgive her for being all that she is.

If they stand in an English street and look about them, there is a secret, insistent whisper in their ears, inescapable—the echo, the resonance of that past which is altogether theirs and yet not theirs at all. They do not know if they see because the voice speaks to them; or whether the voice speaks to them because of what we at last see. '*This*,' says the voice, 'is what I meant: and *that* is what I meant; and *now* do you understand what I meant?'

The voice claims the trivial and the imposing, the ugly and the beautiful; claims even the lettering above shop-fronts and the bricks of the buildings, the stucco around the windows and the chimney-pots above; claims everything that they see and hear. For so long it has talked to them; in books; in the pictures that were on the walls of their rooms, their schools, their galleries; in films; on the radio; through the mouths of their teachers and the memories of parents; the letters of those who preceded them here. It has told them of the sky, so different from the high and glittering arch they have known before; it has told them of the subtle and manifold light, so different from any light they have seen before. It has told them of the seasons which come in the months it has spoken of—October no longer bringing the heat of summer, nor May the first chill of winter. It has told them of the destinations of passing buses, of parks, bird-calls, counties, colleges, accents of speech, trees whose leaves they see for the first time. 'These,' the voice now whispers, 'are some of the things I meant, some of the simplest; there are still so many others, there is no end to the things I have told you of and that now I can show you. Through all those years, over all those distances, you have heard my voice in the voices of others: come, let me show you more of what I meant when I spoke to you then. I have a world to show you—nobler streets and streets much meaner; palaces and tea-shops; rivers, harbours, factories, fields. Come, it is all yours now; but wherever you go my voice will go too, to show you that what you see isn't yours at all. For if it were, you would not hear me. I am the voice of the country you will never own; I am the voice of your most secret ambition; and I will never be silenced.'

So speaks the voice of England, to the South Africans who arrive in boatloads, every Friday morning, and are taken in their special trains to Waterloo, and are then dispersed into the grimy and incomprehensible wastes of London and beyond, where they wander, some for weeks, some for years. And the voice speaks the truth, for it is never stilled; it murmurs to them by day and night, wherever they go, whatever they do; and if they return to South Africa it takes up the tone it had used before, before they had gone to England, and seen their truth become dream, their dream become truth. It is this voice that we must think of as always being in the ears of Isabel and Kenneth, as we follow them to England, and see them meeting there. Sometimes the voice spoke more loudly; sometimes more softly; but it was never silenced. It spoke within the sound of the traffic and the aeroplanes passing overhead, beneath the cries of schoolboys and bus conductors, the scurrying noise of trains, the speeches that were addressed to them, the words that they themselves used to each other.

9

THE GRANGE SCHOOL of Languages (English for Foreigners a Speciality) was in a mean little street that ran south from Oxford Street—one of those streets that make hopefully towards Mayfair, but never get there, running instead into the blunt cul-de-sac of a building site, or the back of a great new office-block. This particular street was occupied for most of its length by little shops and cafés; the school itself was above a ladies' hairdressing establishment. To get to the school one went straight up a narrow, uncarpeted and ill-lit flight of stairs, until one reached a door on which was painted the warning *Kindly Descend One Step After Knocking, as Door Opens Outwards.*

Once one had descended and the door had been opened, the lights and white-painted walls within positively assaulted the eyes, after the dimness of the stairs. 'We have to keep up standards,' Mr Randall, the headmaster and owner of the school, frequently told members of his staff, and standards of brightness and whiteness at least were maintained to a pitch that was close to cruelty. The lighting was fluorescent: long bluish tubes burned beneath hoods of stainless steel in the passages and the offices, in the classrooms and the lavatories, and every wall in every room glared shadowlessly. The desks in the classrooms had been bought second-hand, but a yellow varnish had been applied liberally to them all; the desks in the offices and the staff-room were of stainless steel, and they, too, contributed to the general glitter. The effect was overpowering; certainly it overpowered the continental maids and '*au par* helps', on whose anxiety to learn English the school almost entirely depended. There was hardly one of these girls who, having come up the stairs to make inquiries, left without having signed to take a course at the school, and having paid down a deposit, too. Then they went blinking down the stairs again, clutching their receipts, which were signed by Isabel Last, in her capacity as headmaster's secretary. A week or two later they would be back, to commence their classes. There were three grades in each of the languages taught—Elementary, Intermediate, and Advanced—but there were several classes in each grade, particularly in the 'English for Foreigners' group; and every class was in a state of flux, for the girls came and went erratically, and so, too, did their teachers.

The problem of staff was a constant anxiety to Mr Randall. 'It isn't only English that I want to teach here,' Mr Randall told prospective members of staff. 'I want our pupils to take away something more—ah—an understanding not only of the English language, but of England, of the English way of life. That is why I insist on the highest standards, the very highest; but how can I maintain them if I cannot rely on my staff?' How indeed, when he offered only part-time appointments at the very lowest wages, so that those who came to him to teach English were inevitably failures, sub-teachers, renegade young men from the universities, older men who had been discharged from better positions for irregularities of a financial nature; females of advanced years who were given alternatively to crying in the lavatories and laughing too loudly in the staff-room. The Grange School of Languages was no more than a few years old: Mr Randall had opened it with a legacy that had come to him comparatively late in his life, after a lifetime spent in someone else's school of languages; and he had been completely unnerved by his immediate and considerable financial success. The more money came in, the unhappier Mr Randall became about spending any of it; he had soon reached the point where he could not bear to part with any money that did not buy him something that he could *see*. Thus it was that the two floors he occupied were so bright and well-kept; thus it was that he paid his staff so badly, and never found anyone on whom he could rely. He worked like a slave for his school, for he did not have to pay anyone anything when he himself taught classes; but he could not, as he confessed bitterly to Isabel, do everything himself.

In appearance Mr Randall was a long-nosed gentleman with a little sandy hair on the top of his oval head, and many blue veins protruding through the transparent skin of his hands. His eyes were pale blue, and tears continually brimmed against their lower lids, which were pouched forward, as if to receive the moisture put into them. But they could not contain all the tears he shed, and sometimes the tears rolled over on to Mr Randall's cheeks: then they were wiped away without haste by the back of his hand. Mr Randall was Isabel's first employer, and she was determined to make the best of him; but it wasn't altogether an easy task. For he did not only weep; he also coughed. The sounds of his coughing could be shrill, like some kind of neighing; or hoarse, like a series of groans; a single cough could rumble on interminably, like a conversation; or it could be as brief and abrupt as a bark. When she had first heard Mr Randall coughing Isabel had gone immediately into his office, asking in alarm, 'Can I get you a drink of water? Is there something you should take?'

'It doesn't mean a thing,' Mr Randall replied, when he was able to. 'I've been coughing for forty years, and I'll be coughing for another forty yet.' He might have been talking of pipe-smoking, or card-playing.

'Are you sure?'

'Quite sure. Sound as a bell,' Mr Randall said, tapping his waistcoated breast. 'And as noisy as one, too.'

Even when he said this, Mr Randall did not smile. Mr Randall never smiled. He hardly ever altered the tone of his voice, which was always that of a man who spoke reluctantly, against his will. Yet he seemed to find it difficult to stop himself once he had started: the words came out, one after the other, each apparently shaken out by the slight and continuous up and down nodding of his head as he spoke. And when he wasn't complaining to Isabel about the inadequacies of his staff, the cost of heating and lighting and the rent he had to pay, and the flightiness of the girls who came to the school to learn English, he was lamenting what he called 'the decline of standards'. With a nodding of his head and the shedding of a tear Mr Randall spoke of 'keeping up traditions' and 'the heritage of the past'; he spoke of 'honour', 'decency', self-respect', and 'England'. 'Youths!' he would exclaim when he read his newspaper. 'Look at the youths of today! And they call themselves Englishmen!' His newspapers seemed to contain few reports other than those which described the arrest of juvenile delinquents for crimes ranging from assault and battery to prostitution—especially prostitution. 'It's all this modern namby-pamby, lovey-dovey, smoochy-poochy,' was Mr Randall's summary of the problem. 'It's all flashy cars and cushy jobs and neon signs and smart clothes on their backs, even if they haven't paid for them; it's all grabbing drinks and going to the pictures and listening to American crooners; it's all sex and smart talk and showing off. Spoiled children, spoiled parents, and all of them with too much money in their pockets. That's what they're making of England; that's how much anyone cares nowadays. Well, *I* care, and I'm going to go on caring; and if you tell me that I'm old-fashioned I'll take it as a compliment.'

Isabel did not tell him that he was old-fashioned. She waited, pad in hand, for him to continue with the letter he had started to dictate, or she looked up from her typewriter, with her fingers poised, ready to strike, or she avoided the eyes of any of the other members of the staff who happened to be present with her in the staff-room, when they were all drinking tea and Mr Randall was holding forth. Isabel particularly avoided meeting the eyes of her fellow-South African on the staff, his expression was so openly mocking. But it was not only Mr Randall whom he was mocking; Isabel knew that it was herself, too.

Mr Makeer's was a temporary appointment. This in itself was not enough to distinguish him from the rest of the members of the staff, whose appointments also had a habit of turning out to be temporary. But Mr. Makeer's was formally temporary, which none of the others were, for he was a student at the Inns of Court of Law, and had been taken on only for the period of the Long Vacation at the Bar. Mr Randall had been grateful to take him, for the Long Vacation coincided precisely with the summer migration of young girls and men from the continent, when the school was at its busiest. Then, just at the time of Mr Makeer's arrival at the school, two members of the staff—two young men of brilliant enunciation who had arrived together and had always shown an excessive fondness for one another—had quarrelled bitterly and jointly handed in their resignations: one was going back to Bath, he said; and the other (in tears) said that he couldn't bear the memories which were now associated with the school. Mr Randall was in despair when they made their announcements to him; but though he had hired Mr Makeer immediately and gratefully, he had not done so without some misgivings. 'The fellow,' as Mr Randall said later to Isabel, 'isn't English.'

'Nor am I,' Isabel said.

Mr Randall heard her with distaste. 'There's no need for you to spring to the fellow's defence,' he told her. 'You aren't teaching anyone, anyway. My pupils come to my school to learn the English that is spoken in England, by Englishmen. And so they get other benefits—something of England itself!' Mr Randall's head nodded up and down, but for the moment no words came out: the movement was one that frequently followed his proudest utterances, and its effect was rather like that of an empty salt-cellar being shaken. 'While a colonial—well, you never know where you are with a colonial. I've had them before . . . Australian painters, if you please! Canadian loafers. There was a fellow from

Kenya once, spoke like a military man, and tried to borrow five pounds off me when he'd been here barely a week. Nowadays . . . next thing you know I'll have darkies knocking at my door, telling me they want to teach English. "Teach English?"—I'll say to them—"Learn English, you mean." ' The recital of this imaginary conversation seemed to cheer Mr Randall a little. He was even more cheered by what he went on to say. 'Still, there's the Empire, you know. And the people who come here might as well learn what it's all about. And what better way than by seeing a young man from the colonies—a son of the Empire as you might say—come back to the mother-country? Won't that just show them that the Lion still has some roar to him!'

So spoke Mr Randall, several weeks after he had given Mr Makeer the appointment for which Makeer had asked, on the first afternoon he had come to the school. Isabel could remember clearly the puzzlement she had felt on seeing Makeer that afternoon: his face had been so familiar to her, and yet she had not thought that she had seen him before.

'Can I help you?' she asked him, in her official manner.

'Yes. No.' He started when she spoke, though he had been staring at her intently ever since he had walked into the office. His eyes were dark, Isabel saw, and they looked at her with an expression she could not understand. Was it fear? Was it hostility? Then he dropped his gaze, and stared at the edge of the desk, bringing his hands forward to touch it, as if to steady himself. His hands were small, and the tendons showed up, stretching back from his fingers, and between his thumb and wrist: the desk might have been an instrument on which he was about to strike some kind of chord. 'You're Miss Last,' he said. 'Miss Isabel Last.'

When she heard him speak, Isabel knew why his face had seemed so familiar to her; she knew where she had seen faces like his before. 'Yes, I am,' she said. 'Can I help you?'

'I don't know.' For the first time since he had come in there was something like a smile about his lips; slowly, the expression passed from his face. Then Isabel was aware again of the darkness of his eyes, and the fear or hostility in them.

'I'm Kenneth Makeer.'

'I'm sorry——' Isabel smiled, from behind the desk.

'The name doesn't mean anything to you?'

Isabel shook her head. 'You're from South Africa, aren't you?'

He seemed to consider for a moment before he answered,

'Yes.' Then he was silent. Isabel waited for him to speak; but she was the first to break the silence between them.

'I thought you must be, from the way you speak. Do you want to make an inquiry about lessons?' Only then did it occur to her to ask, 'How did you know my name?'

'I heard about you.' Again there was a long pause. 'Someone told me about you. You're at that club, aren't you, the one for girls from the dominions?'

'Yes.'

Was he merely someone on the prowl for a date? Isabel began speaking very quickly, in her most business-like way. 'What can I do for you? What language are you interested in? We offer tuition in several languages—English, of course, but you won't want that—we have regular classes in French, German and Italian; the other languages we teach by arrangement, depending on the number of people who might be wanting——'

'No!' He interrupted her loudly. He had moved away from the desk, he was closer to the door.

'Then what?' Isabel asked simply. Their glances met; Isabel lowered her head. 'That's all we do here,' she said softly, shyly.

'I don't want that from you,' the man said, shaking his head. 'I've come because I had to——'

It was at that moment that Mr Randall burst in through the door. 'What do you think of it?' he exclaimed at Isabel, taking no notice of the man at the door. 'Reynolds and Primpton are just clearing out! Like that! They've gone already, the pair of them, down the stairs. And here I am, classes to teach, other classes to organize, I can't send the people away. You'll have to help, Miss Last. You must come in and teach the beginners. There's nothing to it. A chair is a chair, a table is a table, any fool can teach them. I open my book, I close my book.' Suddenly Mr Randall was pronouncing his words with great care and loudness; he seized a dictionary from Isabel's desk, and opened and closed it. 'This is my jacket and this is my tie.' He pointed rapidly at his jacket and tie. 'That's all there is to it. You must come.'

Then he noticed the man at the door. 'Good afternoon,' he said. 'If you want to enrol I'm afraid you'll have to wait, or come back later, we're frightfully rushed. And the things that happen! Like children they were. And the one of them blubbering—I was astonished.' Mr Randall's head was nodding violently. 'At four o'clock in the afternoon they tell me! In midsummer! With the classes there, waiting for them, now, two classes.'

'Perhaps I can help you,' the young man said from the door.
'What do you mean? Who are you?' Mr Randall stared at the stranger. Then he said, 'Enrol later. We'll be glad to have you. Our fees are reasonable—oh, for heaven's sake, I haven't the time now. Miss Last, please do what I tell you.'

'Perhaps I can help you,' the young man repeated more loudly. 'I've come to make application for a position as an English teacher.' He spoke very firmly, but he kept his head averted, his glance away from Isabel. 'I can take a temporary appointment during the Long Vacation. I'm a student of the Inns of Court School of Law. I can give you references if you want them.'

'Where are you from?' Mr Randall asked suspiciously.

'From South Africa.' The stranger nodded his head in Isabel's direction, then looked away again. 'Like Miss Last.'

'Do you two know each other?' Mr Randall looked from the one to the other.

The young man spoke out, before Isabel could open her mouth. 'Yes, we do,' he said coolly. There was neither fear nor hostility in his gaze, when he looked down at Isabel: only a kind of mockery at her bewilderment.

'And can you recommend this man?' Mr Randall demanded.

'Well——' Isabel said in confusion.

'That's not fair to Miss Last really,' the man interrupted, his voice even more confident than it had been before. 'I should go out of the room. Then Miss Last would speak more frankly.'

'There's no need for that, if she's got nothing to say against you. Have you got anything to say against him?'

'I hardly——'

'Shall I go out?'

'No! Stay where you are. Come into my office. I'll talk this over with you. Come, we have no time to waste.'

Five minutes later, when Kenneth Makeer came out of Mr Randall's office, he was already on his way to the first class he had to teach. He winked at Isabel as he passed through her office, but did not speak to her. Mr Randall came in soon after. 'He'll have to do until we can find someone better. But in the meantime I want you to check up on these references he's given me. Here's somebody at the Middle Temple, and here's a Dr-Somebody at the university. You write to these people. Still, I don't suppose it's really necessary seeing that you know him and can vouch for his good character.' Isabel was too irritated with them both to speak. 'I've sent him to the Beginners,' Mr Randall was saying.

'And I'll double up on the other two classes. And draft an advertisement for the *Evening Standard*, for someone else. The usual thing: reliable, experienced, highest standards . . . Box such-and-such. And we'll see what kind of scum turns up this time.'

Muttering bitterly, his head preceding by several inches the rest of his body, Mr Randall went out of the office. And Isabel stayed behind and drafted the advertisement as Mr Randall had suggested. She was not really angered by what Mr Makeer had done—more piqued, irritated, put out. She felt that she had been made a fool of in some way, and did not know why he should have done it to her, when she had never seen him before.

When she had typed out the advertisement and the accompanying letter, Isabel looked at the two references that Mr Makeer had given Mr Randall. The one—that in the Middle Temple—meant nothing to her, except that it seemed respectable enough. The name of the Dr-Somebody at the university was more interesting; for the name in question was that of a man she had read about in the South African newspapers: a South African academician of repute, whose departure from South Africa several years before had been a *cause célèbre* of some kind. Isabel could not remember the details of the case: she remembered only that because of his political views the man had been denied a passport, or had sued the government for impounding the passport he already possessed, or had left the country without a passport. So that was the kind of company Mr Makeer kept, Isabel thought, turning his own name over in her mind. But it meant nothing to her—no more than that it was a South African name she had heard before.

She asked him where he came from when she saw him again.

'From South Africa,' he replied, smiling slightly at her.

'But where in South Africa?'

'Oh—all over.'

His voice was quite flat, and polite. His class had just ended; he was on his way out of the building.

'Who told you that I worked here?'

He hesitated for a moment. 'A girl I know.'

'What's her name?'

Again he hesitated. 'She's at the same hostel as you are.' With an effort he said, 'I was—I was speaking to her the other day; I told her that I wanted to take some kind of teaching job during the Vacation. So she said I should come here and ask you if there was anything going.'

'So you did come here to ask for a job?'

'What else did you think I came for?'

He was challenging her; and she had no reply to the challenge. Yet she attacked as well as she could. 'And why did you tell Mr Randall that we knew each other?'

'Well, we do now,' he said reasonably.

'You could have got yourself into trouble. I might have said that I'd never seen you before, and then where would you have been?'

'Out of a job.' Makeer shrugged suddenly, stiffly. 'I thought it worth the chance—there seemed to be a job going, and I wanted it when . . .' his voice died away unexpectedly. 'You don't begrudge me the job, do you?'

'I think it was a pretty dishonest way of getting one.'

'You should have said so then.'

Again Isabel was caught out. 'You think you're very clever,' she said bitterly.

'No,' he said—'No. I think you're very kind—to have helped me.' Isabel was not looking at him, but at her desk. She heard him say, 'I must be going now. I'm sorry that I've made this kind of impression on you. I didn't mean to. I'm as surprised as you at what's happened.' Then, with no further explanation or word of farewell, he was gone.

He was back again, in the afternoon of the next day, to take his class. He was still very polite, with a mixture of aloofness and diffidence that Isabel could not penetrate. She did not try very hard: once bitten, twice shy, she told herself. Yet at the same time she knew that a relationship had been established between them, and she was ready to wait for its development. It was a kind of tact or guile that kept her silent.

There was no need for Mr Randall, however, to be silent about Mr Makeer. Mr Randall continued to voice his doubts about Mr Makeer, and these doubts referred not only to Mr Makeer's colonial background or efficiency as a teacher, but soon became more immediately personal in character. And they were personal not only about Mr Makeer but personal in tone towards Isabel. Previously, Isabel had always been spared any kind of criticism, direct or otherwise, by Mr Randall; so much so that the teachers of the staff had been driven to ask her at different times and in different tones, 'What have you done to deserve it?' 'How do you get around him?' 'Aren't you ashamed of being the headmaster's pet?' Isabel had always kept to herself her answer to these questions: she believed that Mr Randall respected her because he knew that she did not need his job or his money, as all the others did. That was all there was to Mr Randall's 'respect', Isabel had believed.

It was Mr Randall himself who disabused her of this belief. For Mr Randall made it very clear that the rest of his employees had been right in supposing that he had a regard of a rather special kind for her. He soon betrayed the fact that he was jealous of Kenneth Makeer—bitterly and exorbitantly so. He suspected that between Isabel and Mr Makeer there was an intimate relationship; that Mr Makeer was Isabel's 'boy-friend' or 'young man'; and that that was why Makeer had come to the school; he suspected, too, that Isabel was 'leading him on'. And in the gravest tones he warned Isabel against permitting herself any kind of intimacy with 'that law-loafer'; he said that Isabel should keep her distance from him; she should 'tell him where he got off'; she should 'send him packing'. As a matter of fact, Mr Randall said, he would do so himself, if he ever caught that fellow making any kind of nuisance of himself with Isabel; and he would—he had to say—do the same to Isabel if he ever found her neglecting her work in order to 'carry on' with him.

That was the first tone Mr Randall adopted—it was avuncular, if not paternal, in a severe kind of way. The second was bitter, disillusioned, despairing. Isabel was young, far from home, alone in London, in a frighteningly exposed position, much too exposed for her to avoid being attacked and damaged in a way Mr Randall did not need to specify. Age, Mr Randall told Isabel, always warns youth; and youth always scorns the warnings of age; but that didn't absolve age from the duty of giving its warnings. And solemnly and frequently Mr Randall performed his duty. He warned Isabel that Makeer was flighty, unreliable, dangerous, not to be trusted, untruthful; he told Isabel that Makeer looked like a gambler, a drinker, a taker of drugs in jazz cellars, like one of those people you read about in the newspapers. Makeer was physically unhealthy—you could see it in his thinness; he was morally diseased—you could see it in the way his eyes were set so closely together. Makeer, Mr Randall told Isabel, made a habit of molesting the girls in his classes; there had already been several complaints about him from young girls—and from one old woman, Mr Randall added. As a matter of fact, he told Isabel eventually, he was going to give Makeer a week's wages in lieu of notice ('And you know what that means to me') so that he'd be rid of the fellow immediately. And Isabel, if she knew where her own interests lay, would be deeply grateful to him. 'The financial sacrifice alone,' Mr Randall pointed out to her, 'is considerable. But it's worth it to me, feeling about you as I do. And feeling about him as I do. I was never one to shirk my duty.'

Isabel did not know what she had said or done to justify Mr Randall's belief that there was a liaison between herself and Mr Makeer. It was true that Makeer had, on his first day in the office, claimed that he knew Isabel (and she could not forget the ambiguity of his glance when he had made this claim); it was true, too, that since then Isabel had made a habit of covertly watching Mr Makeer at tea-time, when he would be talking to others, and that she had liked what she had seen of him. But Isabel was as surprised as Mr Randall when she heard herself replying to his ultimatum with the words, 'If you give Mr Makeer notice, I want you please to accept mine, too. If he goes, I won't stay.'

'What?' Mr Randall stared at her.

'Yes. I mean it. I will not be bullied in this way and I don't see why he should be either. It's absurd. Even if there was something between us it would be absurd. But as it is——!'

'Do you know what you're saying to me?'

'Yes.' And Isabel did, now that the words had been spoken. She felt almost grateful to Mr Randall for forcing her to admit fully to herself her interest in the stranger. But she showed neither surprise nor gratitude, only a flushed and rather schoolgirlish defiance, as she waited for Mr Randall's reply.

When Mr Randall spoke again his voice was soft and sad, almost peaceful. 'No,' he said, 'you don't know what you are saying. I wouldn't let you go. You're invaluable to me. You're the only person here that I rely on. I cannot let you go, for your sake, as much as mine. At least, while you're here——' Mr Randall did not finish his sentence; he was looking down at his colourless hands. And Isabel walked out of his office.

In this way, then, Mr Randall entered the third stage of what he was to refer to later as his 'martyrdom'. For Isabel the third stage was far more uncomfortable than the two previous stages had been. Now that his worst fears were confirmed, Mr Randall lost the respect which he had previously so ostentatiously felt for her; he regarded her as a lost, as an abandoned, as a shameless creature. And the thought—or the knowledge—of her abandonment and shamelessness inflamed him to a degree which her virtue had never done; inflamed him to the point where he began to make physical advances to her; and yet at the same time confirmed in his own mind his conviction of his own probity and purity, his own uprightness and moral restraint. 'My conscience is clear,' Mr Randall said to Isabel, many times.

Probably he was telling the truth. Certainly he said it with great sincerity, right from the beginning of those encounters that were eventually to lead to Isabel's departure from the school. 'You don't understand,' he told Isabel. 'You think I mean harm, but I don't, at all. I don't want to hurt you. I want this business to be finished with as much as you do, can't you see? It's got nothing to do with me,' he explained, and seeing Isabel's fear and incomprehension Mr Randall was suddenly shocked, prudish, disapproving: he was even able to shake a scandalized finger at her. 'Why do you look at me like that? It's all your fault, not mine. Without a word I'd——' Isabel crouched away from him, her hands protecting her bosom, and Mr Randall cried out, his hand suspended towards her, 'There you are! You're the one! You're lewd, you're dirty, you've got no respect for anything. I'm old enough to be your father. I'm not a hooligan you've met in the street. I know the difference between right and wrong. But you don't! You drag me down!'

At night, when the last classes had ended, and desks stood in empty rows facing the scribbled-upon and abandoned blackboards, and books lay in piles on top of cupboards, the silence of the school had a deep, almost haunted quality that Isabel had once enjoyed; she had made a habit of dawdling, in putting away her things, so that she could have the building to herself for a few peaceful minutes, before leaving it to return to her room in the echoing and noisy club. But after Mr Randall had made his approaches, at first coughing, remarking tentatively upon the weather; later growing bolder, and standing beside her; later still sliding himself against her, so that she had to retreat; and at last nakedly and angrily beseeching her—after Mr Randall had made these approaches, Isabel left the school when everyone else left. Despite this, Mr Randall sometimes accompanied her, when she walked towards Oxford Street, and while they walked he alternatively pleaded with her and abused her: at the corner, however, he would stop, smile, lift his hat like a gentleman, and make off in the direction of his own home. And then there were the times when he met her in a corridor at the school, and darted at her directly and unashamedly, like a man seeing a coin he had dropped; or when she was forced to go into his office to get from him a piece of equipment or take down a letter, or when he came into the office while she was working.

Yet Isabel still came to the school. She tried laughing at Mr Randall, crudely and impertinently and harshly; but though the effort for her was painful, it produced no other effect than to make Mr Randall smile with hope, and put his head at absurd angles and pull faces to amuse her more. Isabel tried abusing Mr Randall: she told him that he was a 'filthy old man', told him that she would sooner die than let his 'scaly old hand touch her', and warned him that the police put 'people as foul as you in prison'. The words dried in Isabel's mouth as she struggled to produce them; they made her lips ache; and their only effect was to drive Mr Randall into an ecstasy of self-righteousness. *He* was filthy? *He* was dirty-minded? *He* was a police-case? Leaning over the table that Isabel had taken care to put between them, he told Isabel that she and she alone was responsible for what was happening, that she wouldn't oblige him because she *liked* him to worry her, that girls like her should be whipped at the cart's tail, as they had been in the old days. And the things she did with that Makeer fellow! If her father knew of it he would surely come to London to take her away! Or perhaps her father would be so filled with disgust that he would decide to have nothing more to do with her, ever again, but would let her sink deeper and deeper into the mire. And to think that his, Mr Randall's, school should be used for such purposes! It filled him with shame, the thought of it. 'Go!' he shouted at her one night. 'Go from my school! You hear what I say? And yet you don't go; because you want to torture me. If it's so hateful to you, why do you come here every day? Why haven't you left? You want to make a martyr of me, you enjoy tormenting me.'

'No!' Isabel shouted.

'Yes,' he said, approaching her. 'You don't leave me alone.' In the harsh artificial light, between the glittering walls, Mr Randall came closer, his body bent and swaying from side-to-side, his face protruding palely out of his dark suit. Isabel stood where she was and watched him, afraid to turn her back, lest he should spring at her. Then she opened her mouth and shouted, 'Leave me alone!'

The noise frightened her, she had not known it would be so loud or so desperate. Her hands came to her mouth; Mr Randall halted, still crouching.

The door opened, and Kenneth Makeer came in.

'What's the trouble?' he asked.

Isabel was too ashamed to speak. Mr Randall turned abruptly and walked out of her office.

'What's going on? What's he doing? Is he worrying you?'

'Yes,' Isabel said, drawing in her breath, released at hearing the words from another. Her breath left her in a long shuddering sigh. 'He has been. For weeks and weeks. It's been driving me mad, I can't stand it. You don't know what it's like.' Still her breath left her body quiveringly; she felt as though she were going to faint, and closed her eyes. The darkness that came down behind her lids was like a void. Where was the man she had been speaking to? Had he left her alone again? 'No,' she cried, 'please no! Don't go!'

As if from a distance she heard his voice. 'I'm still here. What can I do?' She could not open her eyes; the darkness pressed upon her, it filled her ears with a rushing sound; she had to fight violently for light, for breath, for silence.

Then the light came back, dazzlingly; and she saw Makeer standing in front of her, over her. She was sitting down and he was holding something in his hand, a glass of water. How the water glittered, how dark his hand was around it. 'Drink this,' she heard him say; his voice still came as if from a distance, but once he had spoken everything was so silent that she thought she could hear the water lapping minutely against the sides of the glass, where it quivered in his hand. Then the glass was against her mouth, and the cold water touched her teeth, her tongue, went down her throat, forcing her to swallow. 'Ah!' she breathed when the glass was taken away; and reached out for it again.

'Feeling better?'

She nodded, resting with her head to one side, almost touching her shoulder.

'You seem to have had a time,' she heard the man say. She made no reply, the effort to do so was too great. 'How long has this been going on, for heaven's sake?' Still she did not reply, it was so much easier to rest.

Then she heard: 'Why did you put up with it? Why didn't you tell him to go to hell? You don't need his lousy job. Why didn't you walk out?'

It was painful for Isabel to rouse her will to speak again. Yet she had to, now, otherwise she never would.

'Because of you,' she said.

She was not looking at him, he was standing somewhere to the side, a shadow in the light.

'What?' It was like a bark, like a command.

'Yes. He said you must go, and I said I would go, too. So he let you stay. And I stayed, too.'

'For me?' His voice was softer, and she heard it shake. She was filled with a kind of gladness, but she was too weary to enjoy it.

'Yes, for you.'

There was no reply, and she turned her head, to find him. There he stood, dressed in a grey suit; he was frowning as if angry at what she had said.

'So you put up with that! For me?' he repeated, and the anger that was on his face was in his voice, too. He did not draw nearer to her.

'Yes, I've told you.'

He did not speak, he made some kind of noise in his throat, an exclamation of rage or pleasure—she could not tell which. Then he said quietly, 'I stayed here because of you, there was no other reason. Did you know that?'

'I hoped so, sometimes. But I couldn't believe it.'

'You must believe it,' he said fiercely.

'I do, if you tell me so.'

He said merely, after a pause, 'Let's go.'

'Go?'

'Get out of here. We've got no business here. Get your things.'

'But what about——?' She could not say the name of the other man.

'To hell with him.' Makeer laughed, without humour. 'He can find another teacher—and another secretary—tomorrow.'

'Aren't you going to tell him we're leaving?'

'No. Are you?'

Isabel hesitated, before answering, 'I couldn't bear to see him again.'

'Then I'll wait for you.' He stood near the door. Isabel began looking for the few things of her own which she kept in the desk—her handbag, a book or two, a plastic mug. There was an open packet of biscuits, its wrapper torn, in one of the drawers, and she stared at it, not knowing what to do with it. She was ashamed to leave it, ashamed to take it with her. 'What's the matter?' Makeer asked from the door.

'I don't know what to do with this packet of biscuits.'

'Oh—for Christ's sake!'

Isabel began crying. The tears ran down her cheeks, and she wiped them away, but more came. She looked up at the man near the door. 'Why don't you help me? Don't you want to help me?'

He came to her, bending forward. 'Come,' he said. He took her hand. There was no resistance in Isabel: she rose at the touch of his hand, awkwardly clasping her belongings in the crook of her other arm. He led her to the door, where she put on her coat and a little cotton scarf; she had given her bag and the few other things to him, and he held them with both hands. 'I'll hang on to these,' he said when she turned to go.

'No, me,' Isabel said quickly, taking them from him. She put her other hand in his. 'You see,' she said.

'Oh, is that what you want?' He smiled at her, and she saw how tired he now looked, like an old man, wearied before he began.

'Yes.'

They stood in silence for a moment, in a repose without peace; their hands trembled where they were joined, and their eyes did not meet. Then they left the office together.

10

WHAT DID I want of her?' (Kenneth wrote later in his journal.) 'Why did I stay? Shouldn't I have known enough to get out? And then, when she told me that she'd been staying on for my sake——

'Well, I told her the truth then, I had stayed on because she was there, for no other reason. But I didn't tell her that it was because of her that I'd come, in the first place. So my truth was a lie, too, even then, one more lie among the all others.

'That morning, when I woke and found that my mind was made up—that I was going to look for and find Miss Isabel Last—I was quite calm about it, as if it were the obvious and natural thing to do. It's extraordinary the way the mind can leap to its decisions when you think you're sleeping. I opened my eyes, and in the very act of opening them, it seemed, the decision was made, as if the words had been written in chalk on the wall. I was going to find Miss Last.

'I dressed; I shaved; I was calmer than I'd been for weeks; I ate my bowl of cornflakes and milk. And then that Norwegian came in—on this morning of all mornings. Imagine the pair of us, the Norwegian and me, standing there, in a room in London, and him talking to me about his fish. Fish! I stared at him. It was as though he had come in on purpose, to show me why I was looking for Isabel Last, to show me what I was running away from; the sheer haphazard inconsequence of the life I was leading, had led, would lead.

'And the Norwegian went on, as serious as a man could be. "I am here to apologize, you understand," he said. "To assure you that I do not make a habit of what you saw me doing. Believe me, sir, I do not. It was once that I did it, and once only. I was in a very difficult situation, and that is why I committed this unforgivable act. My china bowl, you understand, was broken." '

'Your china bowl?'

' "Yes. That is what I usually work with." There he stood, with that face of his that should have been fine and open and frank; and instead crawled with a hundred faint lines of doubt and indecision and evasion—there stood Hr Kandidaat Dr Phil Hansen: nothing less. Such was the resounding title given to him on the envelopes of all the letters that came to him from Norway: but what I knew of the candidate-philosopher was that he slept late, drank a great deal, watched television interminably, and entertained various frightened and shamefaced girls whom I'd seen scurrying down the passage and into the bathroom early in the mornings. And whom I'd sometimes heard crying in his room late at night.

'But he was a gentleman in his own way. Of this, as he stood in my room that morning, there could be no doubt. He spoke a very good English, too, though hesitantly, so that the whole fatuous performance was drawn out painfully, to its fullest possible length. With his hands he indicated to me the size of the china bowl he usually worked with; then he went on to tell me what his usual procedure was. "I fill the china bowl with water in the bathroom," he explained, "and then I bring it into the privacy of my room. And there in my room, I wash the fish."

' "You wash the fish," I repeated. My tone was as grave as his. It had to be. If I had permitted it to be anything else it would have been a yell, a scream, a jabber.

' "Yes, I wash the fish in the privacy of my room. But this time, when I had already bought the fish, I broke my bowl!"

'I looked alarmed at his loss; he stared at me almost as anxiously as he had when I had burst into the common bathroom to find him degutting and washing a pair of mackerel in the hand-basin. That hand-basin which was, as he now pointed out to me, "shared by not less than three other people, a public basin in fact, not a basin in which fish should be regularly washed."

'But what was he to have done, he asked me. The fish were for his dinner. Furthermore, he suspected that they were not as fresh as they should have been, so he did not want to keep them in his room overnight. It was summer, after all, was it not? And did I know what could happen to a fish over a single summer's night?

'For all the meaning his words had for me, the man could have been speaking Norwegian. I stood there politely and attentively, with my head inclined, and a sense inside me that something violent, final, and unpredicted was going to happen to me soon. I wanted to lean towards him and say, "I am a lost man," or "I am not what I was"—quietly and respectfully, without smiling. It would have least have given him something other than his precious fish to think about.

'Eventually he came to his conclusion. He assured me that he had bought a new bowl, and that there would not be a repetition of this deplorable occurrence. I told him that I believed him, that I forgave him. He thanked me; he bowed; he left the room. It seems to me that I must have remained motionless for minutes after he had left—though that can't be so; I felt that I must have dreamed the whole encounter. Or had I dreamed the other: the girl I was going to find, my own calm, the decision I had made?

'No, not that: I was out of the room in a moment, and on my way to the West End. Now, looking back, I feel I would have behaved more honourably, and more sensibly if I had followed the Norwegian into his room and demanded to see his new china bowl, discussed with him the price of it, the price of mackerel—anything, as long as I didn't take that bus.

'And you'd have thought that among all those streets, all those houses, there'd be places where a girl could hide and never be seen. Perhaps there are; but Isabel Last hadn't taken advantage of them. It was as if the bricks parted themselves like water in front of me, to lead me to her. And there was something watery about the light that day: queer, yellowish, it was, and smooth, with neither a sun nor any cloud in the sky, only a haze. The cars and buses seemed to move through the light with no more effort than their own reflections in the shop windows.

'I went to South Africa House. "Yes sir, what can we do for you?" You can find a girl for me, whom I want to see for reasons I don't understand, or understand so well I prefer not to think what they might be. "Yes," the woman said in effect, "we do have just such a girl on our lists." I went to the address the woman gave me. Miss Last no longer lived there, but had left a forwarding address: the Dominions Girls' Club. The Dominion Girls' Club knew all about Miss Last; they gave me another address, the school where she worked. Again I rode through the yellow light. They day looked as though it wouldn't change until nightfall: the sun was hidden, the light was even, there was nothing within it to move or change. I stood outside the school; and walked away; I wouldn't be going in after all.

'I was back in the afternoon; I would be going in after all. I went in. I came out an English teacher. That was nothing. I was an English teacher only because I'd seen her. Seen her eyes, her forehead, her hair. And that grave glance of hers. To look at her you'd think her someone cool, self-absorbed, ungenerous.

'What would you think if you looked at me?'

Kenneth could write no more for the moment. He put down his pen and stared at the last line he had written. It filled him almost with horror to see it; for who was the 'you' he was addressing, if not himself? Yet had he not constructed this audience in order to escape from himself? Sometimes he tried to turn the 'you' into someone he had known: his brother Peter, his father, Miss Bentwisch, Isabel, even Martin Bullivant, in hope that the other would say something surprising, something he had never heard before. But how could the other truly surprise him when he was seeing nobody but himself, hearing only his own voice, writing down the words that came from his own mind? There was no end to the selves that were himself; but there was no freshness in them either: each day they rose up in shabby and shambling multiplicity from the soiled bed in which they had lain; they went back to the same bed at the end of each day. They were clumsy, they jostled one another, they argued, they fell back into their stupid plodding walk within him.

Kenneth went to the window, and looked out. The street was narrow: the tall and hideous red brick houses hemmed it in on both sides. There was nothing to see out there: red brick, black slate, blue tar. He turned, walked back to the table, sat down at it. He stared again at the last sentence he had written. The rhythm of the words ran on in his mind, as if they had been a song. A voice suddenly did sing them: a high, distant, wild voice, whether male or female he could not have said. He sat listening, waiting for the voice to sing again; but all within his mind was dark and silent now. He thought that that was something to be grateful for, breaking into the darkness and silence with the very thought itself, and regretting immediately that he had done so. He picked up his pen and wrote rapidly: 'What they call self-consciousness is in fact a sign of the disintegration of the self.'

It was Kenneth's secret dread that he was going mad. He crossed again to the window, looked out, came back to the desk. He picked up his pen, and wrote, 'I cannot blame anyone but myself for what has happened to me. There must always have been a weakness within me, a will to be abased, a conviction of my own worthlessness, to which I now give the names of loneliness and idleness, as if they were external to me. As if I have not willed my loneliness and idleness! Was I not willing this—this, what I am now—when I refused to tell Isabel Last who I was, when I took the job—asked for the job—that that crazy Randall gave me? And all the weeks thereafter; and the months after that? I had come to Isabel Last because I had to speak to someone who knew who I was, what I had been; someone who knew me in Lyndhurst; who knew Lyndhurst—streets, dust, trees, iron roofs; who knew Miss Bentwisch. I felt frightened only at the thought that she mightn't be living in London, or that even if she were I wouldn't be able to find her.

'I found her, all right—the one to whom I came to restore to me my own sense of identity, to tell me again who I was. It could have been so simple, I could so easily have won from her what I wanted: recognition, affirmation, restoration. And instead . . .

'Instead, I took that job. I held my tongue. I said nothing of who I was. I watched her. Why? Why?

'No, I can't acquit myself. If I had not been filled with self-contempt I would have said to her, "My name is Kenneth Makeer. I come from Lyndhurst. I am one of Miss Bentwisch's protégés: she sent me to London, so that I might learn all I was capable of learning, the better to carry on the struggle of my people in South Africa. It was through you that Miss Bentwisch heard of me; I worked once for your father—I don't know if you remember that at all—so it is through you that I am here. I have come to tell you this; I have come to talk to you about Miss Bentwisch, about myself, about you, about Lyndhurst. You'll understand why I need to do this when I tell you what has happened to me."

'And perhaps it really wouldn't have much mattered what she would have said in reply—if she'd said, "I'm not interested," or "How funny!" or if she'd burst into tears. Instead I gave her no chance. I saw to it that there could be no help of any kind from her. I wanted to be where I am now, because I believed I deserved no better: in this mess, this smell, I wanted this taste in my mouth, nothing else.

'It didn't seem like that at first—of course it didn't. It never does. When I left the school that afternoon I felt better than I had done for weeks. True, I'd been calm all day; but the calm was like a membrane pulled tight over something quite different—a membrane that anything could have pierced. That Norwegian, the gentleman, the philosopher, the fish-merchant, he damn nearly pierced it: if he'd gone on for another five minutes I might indeed have yelled and jabbered at him. But when I left the school the calm I felt was altogether normal. I was in touch again; I thought I'd succeeded in what I'd come for; I was what I had been before: Kenneth Makeer, with a struggle on his hands, a fight, a future. And even the joke or trick I was playing on the girl was in its way a part of the fight. Simply by being what she was, and without even knowing what I was, she had done what I had wanted her to do. Or so I thought. And I was grateful to her; I was even grateful to her for the bitterness I felt towards her.

'And I went to the Society's office for the first time in weeks. The Free Africa Society, it says outside—all very respectable, an engraved plate against a black brick wall in Bloomsbury. And really it's respectable enough inside, too: free-thinking Jews and devout Anglicans in the usual admixture among the whites, and earnest students and untrustworthy politicians in the usual admixture among the blacks. "Hullo, Kenneth, where have you been, we haven't seen you for weeks? Hibernating?" I told them you could call it hibernating. I asked them if there was anything going on. They told me I could address the West Ealing Branch of the Labour Party on South Africa; that I could review a book for the *Free Africa Weekly*; that I could come along and listen to a man from Kenya who'd be speaking at some hall or other. Which did I want? None of them very much; but I was grateful for the offers. Everything was so normal, so much taken for granted, so much like it had been in the first months, the first months of my stay in London. With me writing a letter home every fortnight, and a letter every fortnight to Miss Bentwisch.

'Surely it should have been a warning to us, the way I wrote! I had to tell her everything of what I saw, where I went, the people I met, the things I felt. But if it was a warning, I never took it, and nor did she. "If only you could be here," I wrote to her, more than once, "so that I could show what you have done for me." I wanted her to come to England, I begged her to come, so that I could appear before her in my dark suit, carrying my umbrella and briefcase, standing anywhere in London, and say to her, "Look what you have done for me. Look what you have made me. Look what you have given me."

'What she had given me was everything my eyes fell upon, everything I did from the moment of my waking to the moment I fell asleep, everything I was. "It is all your doing," I wrote to her. "I owe it all to you. I am what you have made me. I thought you had done enough, too much, when you sent me away to school in the Eastern Province: but look, look here, look at me now!" I had dreamed of power, of light, of understanding: and on my first day in London I stood in Trafalgar Square at the foot of Nelson's

Column, and stared down Whitehall, down the tree-lined Mall, the "vistas of empire." I was free to go where I chose! Freedom in Cape Town or Johannesburg would have dizzied me; but freedom here, in London——! That day the sky was all yellow, and very low behind the Houses of Parliament, so that the buildings on both sides of Whitehall were like dark blocks, and the spires of Parliament were like shafts flung upwards that did not fall. Being there, being free, I felt that I had come into power, I had come to understanding, I was in the light at last.

'That was what I felt, that was how I wrote to her, and so often; and neither she nor I was warned. I did not know that I was afraid, and even when I received my father's letter, and sent that cable off, asking if I should come home, I still did not know what it was I feared. And I couldn't have done anything for her, anyway, even if I had gone home. In his very next letter he wrote, "I am afraid the bad news I wrote in my last letter has become worse. I am very sorry to say that Miss Bentwisch has passed away—peacefully, I hear, though suddenly. She was in no pain at the end," he wrote. "RIP." '

Kenneth's reaction to the news of Miss Bentwisch's death was at first one of sheer incredulity. It was impossible, it was a mistake, such things didn't happen. Death came at the end, not in the middle, when there was still so much to be done and said, when he had barely made a start with the life she had given him. His incredulity was so intense that at first he felt no grief: what he did feel was almost a kind of resentment, as if she had in some way affronted him, or betrayed him. How could she have done it!

Later he did feel grief for her: the sense of her absence came most piercingly upon him in his very attempt to reproach her. She could not be reproached—that was it, the very point of grief. And he remembered with guilt and pity how she had been when he had last seen her, in the weeks when she had been working so hard, using all her influence and wealth, to get him a passport: so determined, and beneath the determination so much changed, so much afraid. Had she known what was to happen to her? How much had she known? And how could *he* not have guessed? Why had he not sensed more, done more? Then Kenneth's guilt met his grief, but he remained stiff within himself throughout: even the pity he felt when he thought of her was without release, a harsh stillness which he carried in his breast as he went about his tasks. Because it was his duty he wrote a letter of condolence to Martin

Bullivant; he wrote of what Miss Bentwisch had done for him, and how much he had admired and respected her, for how much he had to be grateful to her. In reply he received a brief, formal acknowledgement, and no more.

Incredulity passed, grief passed, guilt passed. But Kenneth was not set at rest. He thought much of his mother's death, of Miss Bentwisch's death, of the death of those he saw about him in the streets; his dreams were troubled with images of decay and dissolution, sometimes horrifyingly so. But that wonder and dread, too, passed slowly. It passed as his grief had done, leaving behind it still the unease, the fear. About his own immediate future Kenneth was not at all worried: the allowance that Miss Bentwisch had been giving him had been so generous that what he had currently, together with what he had saved, was enough to last him at least for another year or so. Then there would be only one more year, before he would be admitted to the Bar, and Kenneth was confident that he would be able to scrape through that year somehow. No, his unrest was much deeper and more insidious than any money worry.

And as the days went by, Kenneth came to know that his present fear was not of death, but of life. For the fear was accompanied by an excitement that he could not understand, an eagerness he could not recognize. It was as if there was within him something rising, moving, lifting itself towards the light, towards the air—the ever-shifting light, the thickened air of London.

After Miss Bentwisch's death Kenneth again took to walking about the streets as he had done his first few weeks in London. No longer did he go about in a state of dazed and incredulous excitement, drifting and loitering, staring into shop windows and standing outside tube stations to watch the crowds come and go, staring at the buildings marked in the guide-books, at the disfigured statues of people he had never heard of. Now he walked swiftly and as if purposefully, though there was no purpose that he knew of in his activity. Through parks and alongside railway yards, over bridges, down famous streets and streets so little distinctive that they went out of his mind the moment he turned a corner, along roads that glared with lights and squealed with the sounds of traffic, across squares so intensely shadowed and silent that his footsteps clapped like stones flung into a placid water, through alleyways, arcades, courtyards, subways, over railway bridges—Kenneth toiled, night after night, as though this were the work he had come to London to do. Dark-headed, dark-hatted crowds swayed, eddied, ebbed about him; the lights threw a wide yellow radiance against the clouds at evening, and the buildings stood up against them; brick and leaf and mushroom-white stone gleamed above pavements; tiled roofs humped themselves over endless terraces of suburban houses; London receded from Kenneth as he went about it, vast in its details and vast over all, echoing, incomprehensible. London horrified him and frightened him, it was so much beyond anything he could have imagined before seeing it; and there were times when Kenneth felt that seeing London merely made it altogether unreal, altogether unlikely. Who could walk through a corner of its great dreariness and find credible what he saw? Who could believe in the existence of all he knew to lie beyond the fragment he had seen?

Ultimately, what most impressed itself upon Kenneth in the course of these wanderings was the unending persistence and size of the social effort that was demanded of a people, any people, by their history. Kenneth came from a country where 'history' was measured almost in single years; and where the future was valued only for the solutions it might bring to the problems that fatigued the present. Here in London he saw that hundreds of years could pass and still the moral and physical effort towards community had to be made. One could not plead exhaustion; one could not plead the achievements of the past; one could not even point to the graveyards and the bombsites and plead the futility of all effort; still less could one look to the future and look for ease there. The present and the past were intermingled inextricably in London because the present could neither free itself from the past nor rest on it; and what was true of London was true of any place where people lived; what was true of Kenneth's time was true of any possible future.

This was a large reflection; but it did not come as such to Kenneth—it was part of his incredulity, of his surprise, of his fear, of his grief. And it was a part, too, of the exhaustion he came to feel: a personal exhaustion that had much to do with his aching feet, his lack of sleep, the nervousness that sent him into the streets at night; and that yet was above and below these things, which were symptoms merely. He felt drained, powerless, without reserves. He grew more tired still; and when the evening at last came when he went back to his room and stayed there—not reading, not working, doing nothing, simply sitting still, with no compulsion on him to go down the stairs and into the streets—when that evening came, he felt positively grateful for his tiredness. Whatever it was that had agitated him was now as exhausted as the rest of him, he felt; now he could rest. And after rest there would be the real work he had come to London to do, not this phantasmagoria of activity, the energy expended to no purpose, the pilgrimage without faith or devotion. And then there would be his return to South Africa, in the end.

He sat in his arm-chair, smoking; he closed his eyes and dozed; he stirred himself to make a cup of tea, he lit a cigarette and smoked again. In the house there were the usual radio and television noises, but they were all blurred; and it was quiet in the street outside. The thought of the tar, the even-spaced lamp-posts, the dark crammed bulk of the houses on both sides of the street, was no temptation to him. He was safe, alone in his room. He savoured his loneliness and the ease of it; he stared towards the window, where the glass reflected darkly the light within his room, showing nothing beyond it but the few drops of water clinging to the pane, from a shower that had fallen earlier. The silentness of the rain in England always surprised Kenneth: one never knew it was raining until one saw the drops against the windows, saw them sliding down slowly, hanging, splashing minutely. In Lyndhurst the rain always came in storms, and fell with such ferocity that people indoors had to raise their voices to be heard. Kenneth thought vaguely of Lyndhurst; then again of London, as he had been seeing it over the last few weeks. London seemed to Kenneth, sitting exhausted in his room, not a great metropolitan and ordered city; it was not even a group of towns; nevertheless it retained in his mind a kind of abstract unity even with the lowering and smoke-shrouded suburbs that lay around it for so many miles. He could not have said what the unity was: it was like that of an entire country—mountains of brick and asphalt, plains, plateaux, secret valleys, all of brick and asphalt.

The knowledge of what he had been struggling against and struggling towards for these past weeks came slyly and quietly into Kenneth's mind, with no warning. Now it hung there glittering, and he did not move from his chair, as if afraid his movement might shake it off. He was indeed alone in the room, alone in London—now. There was no one in London who knew how he had come to London; there was no one who knew why he had been sent; there was no one who knew what he had undertaken to do. Miss Bentwisch was dead; and Kenneth was answerable to no one. He was free, truly free now, free in London, to live as he pleased.

So simple it was; and so atrocious. It was the simplicity that first engaged Kenneth's attention; he wondered why this knowledge should have been so slow in coming to him, should have had to wait for this present exhaustion and isolation before making its entry. Now it was here—here with him in his room; and it would be with him when he went out again into the streets. He would, after all, be walking in the very streets that his knowledge now offered to him. No wonder he had written as he had to Miss Bentwisch, asserting and reasserting his indebtedness to her, and his intention to repay the debt! It had been in fear, not in gratitude, that he had written to Miss Bentwisch demanding of her that she should remind him who he was and why he had come to London, insisting over and over again that he should be known to her. Even then, while she had been alive, his will had sniffed this freedom in the smoke-smelling air.

Early in the morning Kenneth woke; he had fallen asleep without knowing, in the arm-chair. It was somehow ghastly to waken and find the light burning above him at that hour: it made Kenneth think of sickness, emergencies, departures. At the back of his mind there was a vague impression that some dream had woken him; but he could remember nothing of it. When he went to the window he saw that the sky had grown lighter; the rooftops were cut sharply against it, and quite flat. Later the roofs gained depth, gained colour; but the sky lost by the dawn, for the morning came up smoky, misty, indistinct, with no true surface to it. Kenneth had not moved from the window, though he had grown cold, and there had been nothing outside for him to see: only parked cars gleaming with the moisture on them, or shrouded under tarpaulins; a cat slipping past a low brick fence; the raggedness of rhododendrons and laburnums and hydrangeas being exposed to another day's light, another day's smut. Then at intervals Kenneth caught across the empty street the distinct, sad little sound of alarm-clocks ringing, from this direction and from that. A man came out of one of the houses and started a motor-bike with a sudden guttural roar; and as he rode off on it, the noise joined all the sounds that had been growing erratically in volume, from the Finchley Road to the north. By the time Kenneth turned away to make himself a cup of tea, the noises were continuous and indeterminate, each muffled by the others.

He fell asleep heavily again, and woke towards noon. It seemed days before that he had stood at the window, watching the dawn come to his fragment of the city. And it seemed days before that that he had made for himself, out of loneliness and exhaustion, an image of freedom, of lawlessness, of irresponsibility. But how many years was it since he had dreamed of co-operation and love and redemption! How far was he now from Lyndhurst, from his family, Miss Bentwisch, the self that he had been when they had known him. What had before been hope and promise for him was now something that he had deliberately and harshly to will into remembrance; for promise and hope had shifted, changed their aspect, spoke in another voice. His will could remind him only of pain, humiliation, brutality, of a stupidity more dangerous and baffling than any malice, of impotence, of rage—all to be suffered endlessly by himself. And to what end? To keep faith with Miss Bentwisch? But she was dead, silent, indifferent, she knew nothing of faith or faithlessness. To keep faith with himself? But who was he, if not this man in London, whose faith had silently stolen away from him? To redeem a people, a country? And here the promise had no shame: the promise told him that he had seen for himself, looking deep into London, that there was no redemption for any people in history, only a continuation. This was the subtlest voice of the promise, for it showed him that it did not pretend to a finality and security no human could expect. It offered him a life, no more, no less. He could take part in the continuation—here or elsewhere, as he chose—but if that was the most he could hope for, then why not here, why not here?

Should he then keep faith with his father and brother? But he had broken faith with them years before. What had he been thinking of all this time, imagining himself and them 'together'? It was extraordinary to him that he hadn't before realized what he had done, so many years before, when he had left home. He had managed to delude himself that rhetoric and abstraction could fill his place in the emptied house, could work with his father in his jobs around the town, could go with his father to watch the tennis on Saturday afternoons . . . What nonsense it had been! What cruel nonsense it had become—Kenneth thought, remembering his father's shame at the visit of the police to him, his tears, his terror. So much for his loyalty to his father and brother: so much too, Kenneth felt, for the intelligence and concern on which he had prided himself. Now Kenneth wondered merely how he had managed so successfully to conceal from himself the truth of what the relationship between himself and his father had already become. Apparently one illumination waited upon another; now he was in the light: the simple, broad light of the day that had been given to him.

So the arguments ran; and where they ran they made a desolation. But the desolation was all of the past: the future was another matter altogether. The future was in the smiling faces of girls, the courtesy of bus-conductors, the banter of his fellow-pupils in Chambers, the bow of a commissionaire, the kindliness of Mr Prance; the future was casual, available, filled with hurrying crowds of people going about their business, none of whom would wonder that Kenneth Makeer had joined them. The future was atrocious, foul, abominable; and the more so for its very simplicity, its attractiveness, its ease, its inconsequence.

'I felt that if she could not remind me of what I was,' Kenneth's journal records of his going to Isabel, 'I was a lost man. I came to her as a beggar, a supplicant, hoping she would rouse in me some kind of truth, of honour, of duty. She was the girl whom Miss Bentwisch had thought of as her heir; the girl who was responsible for my having come to London. Then let her be the girl who would send me back to South Africa! And when she roused my desire and spite, I told myself that that would do, just as well. Or even better. I knew myself again, I thought: I was again my true unforgetting Lyndhurst self.

'My true self! I cannot reproach Isabel for what she showed herself to be, in the end. If she felt it to be shameful to have been with me, were not my lies her justification, the evidence of my own shame at what I am? However low her motives were, they were no more vicious and wrong than my own actions had been, my own deceits. She betrayed me; but I had betrayed myself earlier. I gave her every reason, every excuse for believing me to be foul, a man to run away from: had I not tried to run away from myself? So I turn and turn, and there is no blame, no anger, no hatred that does not turn, too, turn upon me. I am a man who kicks and struggles and chokes as he drowns in a swamp; I am the swamp, too, in which he is drowning.

'Isabel, if I'd loved you when we walked out of the school together, what I was doing would have been unforgivable. But I didn't love you then, I loved only the mockery I was making of you, the blindness, the malice, the irresponsibility of what I was doing. It was to save me from irresponsibility and lawlessness that I had come to you; and then, like a madman I plunged further into it, dragging you with me. And you said that first evening, when we walked out of the school, "Where are you taking me?" and I replied, "Somewhere nice, somewhere you've never been before."'

11

'I'VE BEEN EVERYWHERE,' Isabel said.

'Have you?'

'I mean everywhere around here. There's nowhere nice.'

'Oh, you mean cafés and things. Coffee-bars.'

It was late in the afternoon; the crowds in Oxford Street were already beginning to move faster, with that hunted jerkiness of movement which marks the approach of rush-hour.

'Well, let's get out of here, anyway.'

As they walked towards Grosvenor Square, Kenneth asked, 'Why did you stay in the school for me?'

Isabel's reply had a curious and paradoxical air of simplicity, of finality. 'I don't know,' she said.

Then she asked: 'And why did you stay for me?'

'Because I liked you.' Somehow his reply seemed more evasive than hers.

They walked very slowly, almost loitering, a pace or two apart, their hands having fallen to their sides. They passed along one side of the square, its trees and close-cropped grass and red cliff-like buildings stretching away from them. In a street farther down they found a coffee-bar. Several hours passed before they came out of it.

Later Isabel was to try to remember what they had said to one another during those hours. But it was difficult for her to remember, for the time they spent together in that café soon became confused in her mind with all the time they were to spend in other cafés. It was extraordinary how much time they did pass in cafés and coffee-bars and restaurants: to Isabel it sometimes seemed she spent days watching waiters and watresses and cashiers going about their work, or staring through plate-glass at pavements, her talk with Kenneth punctuated by the small crash of money being run into tills and the clatter of teaspoons and teacups.

It was a bad summer: this in itself usually made it necessary for them to arrange their meetings indoors, and kept them indoors once they had met. But there were some afternoons when the sun cleared itself from the clouds, and a light blazed over streets and parks, setting Isabel and Kenneth free to wander where they choose. On such afternoons the rays of the sun seemed to be reflected darkly off the clouds which still massed themselves in the corners of the sky, and nothing that the light fell on was not enriched. Even the grime on the buildings seemed merely to concentrate the darkness that the light already contained; trees in full leaf did not just throw their shadows on the ground but held moving columns and cages of shadow within themselves; the grass, where it lay in the sun, had an underdark to it, almost liquid-like. Hyde Park, Holland Park, Regent's Park, Hampstead Heath: these were the places where Kenneth and Isabel walked, often on weekdays, when there were few people about. Then the rain would come again, and they would be confined to cafés, cinemas; they used to go sightseeing, too, at such times, in the galleries and among the City churches, the museums; Kenneth showed Isabel the Middle and Inner Temples, and Lincoln's Inn and Gray's Inn.

Kenneth's vacation ended. Isabel made no effort to find another job. She was always the first to arrive at their rendezvous in the late afternoons; but she did not resent this at all. In a way she enjoyed waiting for him, especially when they had arranged to meet at some tube station. Standing at the head of the escalators that ferried the crowds upwards from below, Isabel's sense of identity was stunned and disrupted by the numbers of people being drawn in chains towards her; but it quickened immediately into life when she glimpsed Kenneth: frail, harsh-featured, looking out for her with a curious confidence, and an even more curious wariness. Sometimes she lingered for a moment, the better to watch him, letting him stand there, not knowing that he was being watched. Then she would approach. Always, he smiled when he saw her, the smile coming more quickly to his lips than to his eyes.

Often they barely spoke, after they had greeted one another. It surprised Isabel how long they were able to be together without feeling the need to say anything to one another. But then, there was so much in their relationship which surprised Isabel. Even the combination of boredom and excitement which she so often felt when she was waiting for him, or when she was sitting silently with him, was itself a matter for surprise: she had not known that boredom and excitement could be combined into a single state. Yet frequently they were, through afternoons of rain, mornings when Kenneth was at classes or working in the Temple library:

the tedium of these times was as intense as the anticipation with which she looked forward to seeing him, the eagerness with which she watched him, the unhappiness she felt when his eyes softened at seeing her.

Isabel knew that she was falling in love with Kenneth, the stranger, fellow-South African, fellow-sojourner in London, whom she had been for so long watching, and who had come to her when she had needed him. And for her the most surprising thing of all in their relationship was not that she should have been falling in love, but that her love should have been so placid and incurious. Before, she had hungered for the love-relationship with a curiosity that was much stronger than any desire; now that she was about to have it, she was curious no longer. She was expectant, but calm; eager, but patient; alert, but incurious. For the moment it was enough for her that they should be seeing each other so often; to know that Kenneth was as willing to be in her company as she was to be in his. 'Falling in love'—Isabel repeated the phrase to herself; but it seemed ludicrous, irrelevant. She wasn't falling into anything; what she was most aware of was the stillness within her; and her thoughts and ambitions moved delicately, and warily, afraid to disrupt the stillness. How strange it was for her, who before had always been so anxious, who had never acted without looking behind and looking ahead, to be at rest now: how strange and how wonderful.

And the credit, she was sure, was Kenneth's. She loved him, she believed, for the qualities which she had noticed and admired in him, even when she had hardly known him, while they had been at the school. It was his quality of reserve, his independence, even his appearance of being lonely and his ability to bear loneliness without complaint or apparent discomfort, that most attracted Isabel. His quietness of demeanour, the moderation of his voice, the spareness of his smile, the carriage of his shoulders—these seemed to Isabel to be the indications of an indifference in him that was allied, in a way she could not understand but only felt grateful for, with an intense and unfatigued concern about people and a sympathy for them. He was observant, he remembered what he saw and what had been said to him; he was unbegrudging and unashamed of his admiration for things that seemed to him admirable; and he had a capacity for relating one thing to another, which to Isabel seemed in itself a kind of courage. When they went to museums or ancient buildings, he did not see the objects in front of him as things, frozen, dead, in isolation—to him they were as much a part of the living London as the buses or cars or traffic lights. What he saw he seized in a single understanding, which was the reward, Isabel believed, of that same self-reliance which made it unnecessary for him ever to talk at length about himself. And Isabel did not press him to tell her more than he chose to. For the moment it seemed enough to her that they should be seeing each other so often, drawing slowly closer and closer together. Kenneth seemed to know few people in London, and he was not anxious to meet the people she knew: he obviously did not need her friends, and now that she had him, she did not need them either.

The kind of strength Isabel ascribed to Kenneth was one that at this time she particularly envied and admired; that she sought for so eagerly because she believed herself to be without it. The truth was that Isabel had suffered a moral shock which her year in London had done little to alleviate, had even aggravated. After a life in which she had tried as well as she could to do as much good as she could, she felt that the people whom she had most wanted to please had rejected her. It was true that her father had very reluctantly consented to her going to London; but his reluctance had been a sop thrown to the past he and Isabel had shared together; his eagerness was all turned to the future he was going to share with Hettie. Isabel could not blame him for this, but she felt nevertheless that she had been cheated in some way, or deprived; she felt, at the very least, that she had not been adequately rewarded for the work she had done for him. As for Miss Bentwisch, on whom Isabel had relied so much, from whom Isabel believed she had learned her profoundest moral lessons—Miss Bentwisch had in the end simply betrayed these lessons. Isabel was under no illusion as to why Miss Bentwisch had behaved to her so coldly; Isabel knew that it was because she had thwarted a deep dear plan on which the old lady had set her heart. No, not her heart, but her will. Miss Bentwisch had accused Isabel of being self-willed; but Isabel in turn had seen the old lady as someone whose will was implacable precisely because it was denied; because it seemed to seek nothing for itself, but only to give what it could to others. Especially, perhaps in this case, where Miss Bentwisch had wanted to give so much, as much in the world as she possibly could.

Isabel had found herself cut adrift, set loose, thrust out; it would have been easy for her to turn round and blame her father for what had happened, blame Miss Bentwisch for what had happened. But Isabel being the kind of girl she was, she blamed neither Miss Bentwisch nor her father; she blamed herself. She even blamed herself for having seen the lust for which her father was sacrificing her, and for having seen how Miss Bentwisch lived in ignorance of herself; Isabel felt that if she had loved the others enough, she would somehow not have noticed these things, or not have noticed them as demerits. Indeed, if there had been enough love in her, Isabel believed, she would never have permitted the occasion to arise when these demerits would become visible: she would have married Martin; Miss Bentwisch would have been pleased with her; she would have walked voluntarily and cheerfully out of her father's house, and everyone would have been happy. More and more her rejection of Martin began to seem to Isabel to have been arbitrary, unwise, selfish, reasonless. She liked him well enough; she liked him better than any other young man she had ever known; what had got into her to send him away? And poor Martin himself deserved some consideration; he had been so decent about it, so much more decent than she had, really.

That was the one pole around which Isabel's thoughts cohered. The other was one of a confused resentment, selfishness and cynicism, a determination not to be misled by ambitions that were beyond her. She *had* tried to live for others, in the way that had been open to her; and her life in London was the mark of her failure. In any case, it wasn't as though she had been satisfied or fulfilled while she had been trying: had she forgotten the tedium and impotence of her life in Lyndhurst?

So the debate went on. And it wasn't any the less of a debate, or argued less fiercely, for being a false one. Because in her heart of hearts Isabel knew that the very fact that she thought of the one side of the debate as being the side of selfishness, cynicism, and self-will, showed that it could never win. To be truly selfish you had to be unconscious of what you were: you could not be selfish and think of yourself as selfish: Isabel could not, at any rate. And this knowledge wearied her beyond measure, because it meant that she would never know what she really wanted, she would always be trying to do more than she could, she would always be uncomfortable for not doing more, and even more uncomfortable if she did less. She would always be dependent on the people around her, for their approval and disapproval of her actions, dependent on them for their very needs. Marry Martin and be done with it, said one voice. Wait, was there no other way, said another.

Then Miss Bentwisch died; and a few weeks later she met Kenneth. Isabel would have thought that after their frank and tremulous confession of attraction towards one another they would have been quick to embrace, to hold fast to what they had claimed in one another. Isabel would have been ready enough to respond, had Kenneth seized her; but no, he did not, and Isabel respected his slowness; she believed she knew what it was that restrained him. To grasp too eagerly, to hold too tightly, would have betrayed a doubt or insecurity which Kenneth did not feel. Kenneth could afford to wait, until their season had reached its fullness. Then he would gather her, and Isabel watched the hands that would touch her, the arms that would embrace her, the lips that would press against her own. He would be gentle, she thought, and firm; quick and restrained. Sometimes she could not help taking his hand in her own, or coming against him when they said good-bye, and pressing her lips briefly against his; once she said, smiling and yet serious, as she turned away from him, 'You don't have to wait for me.' Their hands were still clasped together, and he pulled her back to him; she freed her hand and touched the back of his neck. 'But I'm not impatient,' she said.

He kissed her again, and then held her off. He was smiling. 'You know nothing about me,' he said, as if warning her.

'I can only learn by knowing you more.'

'You might not like what you learn.'

'I must learn as much as I can.'

'You will learn as much as I tell you,' he said.

She met his gaze with hers, and something about the stare he gave her made her say: 'You won't frighten me.'

'With what I'm going to say?'

'Or with the way you're looking at me.'

His expression did not alter. 'Kenneth Makeer, the mystery man,' she jeered. But she was a little afraid of him, just then.

'That is cheap, isn't it?' Kenneth said, suddenly mild. 'To make a mystery of oneself, deliberately, I mean.'

'Don't you?' she asked directly.

He did not answer her for a moment. 'I can't answer you. I don't know what's deliberate and what isn't in anything I do.'

'Shame!' she mocked him.

Kenneth was not offended. He held her hand more tightly; he said, almost wistfully, 'Ach, if only I could blame you, too, for some of it.'

'Blame me for what? I'm not talking about blame. I'm talking about——' She looked for a word; then she found it. 'Gratitude. I want some gratitude, too, for what we've been doing.'

He said eagerly, 'I am grateful, Isabel, for everything that's been good. I blame only myself, for everything else.'

'What else is there?'

He gestured to the street around them; they were at an entrance to a tube station, but there were few people around, the street was empty, dark, glistening in patches. 'Everything else.' Then, as if remembering, he struck himself softly against the chest. 'No, not there. Here,' he said, and struck himself again. 'It's all here.'

'Kenneth,' she said, 'Kenneth——' uttering the name like a word of reproach. Then she kissed him again, and left him.

Kenneth stared after her, watching her go to the ticket-booth, turn from it, wave to him and then pass through the barrier and step on to the moving stairs. She was carried away from him: but in his imagination Kenneth followed her down, into the concrete tunnels beneath; he stood with her on the platform she reached and heard with her the cavernous and ghostly roar of a train as it passed unseen through another tunnel, and stirred the sluggish metal-scented air; he watched her as the men in raincoats on the platform watched her, covertly, their cheek-bones gleaming in the electric light. Then the air roared again, and her train rushed out of its dark hole, sloped in alongside the platform, came to its halt, sighed as the doors opened, sighed when they closed again. Like an animal bounding, rhythmically, the train went noisily away, and the platform was empty: Kenneth stood unconscious at the head of the moving stairs to which he had run to see her go, too late. Still the stairs heaved, rattled, groaned, opened wide, shrank into one another, slid out of sight; and Kenneth turned into the street, and as he walked he spoke aloud, and gestured with his hands, and then fell silent, hurrying as though he wanted to be where he was going, as though in his room he would be any more at rest than he was here in the darkened and indifferent streets.

For Kenneth all had changed, though he did not even know when the changes had come upon him, or how they had come. Some, the earliest, he could date: he could remember the night some weeks after Miss Bentwisch's death when he had felt himself free, and had been terrified of his freedom; he could remember the afternoon when he had first seen Isabel, and had grabbed blindly and unreflectingly at the opportunity to stay close to her; he could remember the evening when Isabel had cried, first taken his hand in hers.

But thereafter all was a slow irreversible modulation of feeling that he could neither control nor understand nor foresee; so that when he asked himself, 'When did it happen?' or 'How did it happen?' he did not know what he meant by 'it' or even what he meant by 'happen'. Nothing had 'happened': there had been merely all the afternoons and evenings he had spent with Isabel, the first caresses he had exchanged with her, the things he had said to her and she to him, the places where they had met and the sights they had seen together. And could he at any time have found out how much in his feeling for her was resentment of the past, how much was hope for the future? Could he distinguish the desire he now had for her from the shame he had felt when he had been a Coloured builder's boy and had fallen on the ground in front of her? Could he tell his secrecy from his pride, mark off his love from his fear?

Stay with her, be with her, take no risks with her, his heart had called out to him, the first day he had seen her, and the days that followed. And so he had said nothing to her of who he was or where he came from or how he had come to London; he had kept his silence gratefully when he had seen that Isabel had taken it for granted that he was a white man, and had believed him when he told her casually that he came from Cape Town, and had been sent to London by a rich aunt. And when his conscience smote him for the lies he was telling, he was able to silence it at first by the truth that he was acting as much in resentment, in contempt, in scorn, as he was in hope or desire. He would have been a fool not to take advantage of her, with her 'liberalism' and charity, her pity for the underdog and her kindliness and her scruples; her money and her white skin; with that house behind her and those 'problems' of hers that she had told him of—her father, the rich randy old man, her stepmother, her Martin, her Miss Bentwisch. In exacting a vengeance from her he *was* being true to himself, Kenneth could claim, and to the fury and bitterness of an imagined revenge he had been glad to surrender, remembering what it was to have seen his mother die in a tin-roofed, tin-walled shack, and his father bow and scrape in front of every white man; to have been shown into the kitchen of every white home he had entered, and to have heard the note that came into every white voice when he was spoken to; to have been ignored, like a piece of furniture, or to have been noticed like a dog, or like a child; to have been at the mercy of every train conductor, policeman, white woman in the market-place who called out, 'Come here, *bruingoed*, carry this bag'; to have heard the voices saying, 'God, you see that little one, he could pass for a white man,' and heard the laughing casual reply, 'Take down his trousers and you'll see his balls are blue—that's the sign, the infallible sign'; to have seen Lyndhurst not as a town, a city, where people could live, but as a kind of battlefield, a place of exclusions, traps, dangers, forbidden routes, inaccessible places; to have stayed in the house, as he had so often done, out of sheer weariness of spirit, unable to face the humiliations that were built into every building outside, that clothed every human being he passed, were posted up on notice-boards and headlined in every newspaper. Let Isabel Last have burned with these humiliations, ached with impotence; let her spirit have been tortured, mangled, degraded endlessly—and then let her show her scruples, when she at last had one of these torturers, manglers, humiliators at her mercy, as now he had her! White bitch, white slut, white whore, white fool, white female, *witgoed*, he called her: lie down, let me prance over you, with my blue balls and my brown c——, my brown hands and brown blood.

These bouts of anger and hatred horrified and exalted him, left him feeling weak, shattered inwardly; they came again and again, making him caper about his room, or stand with a distorted face in front of the mirror in his wardrobe, mimicking Isabel's face when she lifted it to kiss him or be kissed; they came even when he sat silently, quietly, at his work, or in a bus going to keep an appointment with Isabel. He could be a corner away from her, a flight of steps down from her, and still he would be cursing her, hardly conscious that his lips were moving, his hands twitching in small gesticulations. At such times he felt himself to be demented; and yet when he saw Isabel the dementia would fall away from him: he would speak calmly to her, smile, return the clasp of her hand. And many weeks of rage and hatred passed before Kenneth was able to bring himself fully to admit, in the end, that what he went to Isabel for was just this very reassurance. What Isabel told him—with her smiles, her unabashed friendliness, her eagerness for his company—was that rage and hatred were not all his life. She told him that his dementia was indeed a dementia, and no more; that she was not responsible for what he gibbered in his room, and had nothing to do with it—just as he, when he was with her, had nothing to do with it either. When he was with her, he was free, in London; all of the town was open for him to enter, and then the need to humiliate and abase her would seem no need at all, but an imposition, alien, unwanted.

And as Kenneth grew more and more to know what it was to accept her friendliness with his, to respond to her eagerness with his Kenneth began to feel in despair and a different kind of anger, that this was precisely what he would never really know. Only when he had told her the truth about himself would he be able truly to meet her as she met him, with innocent eyes, with innocent hands when he touched her. Only the truth would set him free to love her as she loved him.

But good God, didn't he love her now? Was it not his love that forbade him now to speak to her: to tell her who he was and how he had come to London, to tell her of the part she had played in his life, and what Miss Bentwisch had done for him, to tell her about the work he had hoped to do in South Africa. If he told her now, after so many weeks, so many lies, after so much had passed between them, surely she would think of him as nothing but a liar and impostor, worthless, unreliable. (And beneath that fear there was another, which made his skin shrink in patches, as if it were exposed, and then glow unbearably: the fear that she would turn away from him in disgust because of what he was.) It was impossible that she would still love him, when she had learned the truth about him: what Isabel loved was someone else, a stranger, a figure he had constructed and held up for her to see, intending one day to cast it aside, in a climax of scorn. But now the figure lived; the figure grasped *him* by the hand, and would not let go. And he did not want it to let go. For as long as he could hide behind it, just so long could he be with Isabel.

It was a trap, he had been trapped. When had the spring been released, when had he been caught, pinioned, held down for division and self-division again? Sometimes he thought it was that first afternoon at the school, when she had lifted her head and he had come forward to her desk; or earlier, much earlier, in the streets of Lyndhurst, and in one sandy lane in particular; more often he believed the trap to have finally been sprung just when he had last seen her, last watched her laugh, look up, frown, felt her touch his sleeve with her finger-tips, heard her voice with its curious colonial smallness and stridency, watched her figure walking away from him or seen her hand waving against the glass window of a bus, as he stood on the pavement looking up to see her go.

'Save me!' he called upon her now, when he was alone. 'Help me! I can bear it no longer!' as if there might be a word she could utter to him, a spell she could make over him, so that he would be able to come to her free, a changed man, the man she thought he was. But there was no word she could utter. And though when he was alone he called upon Isabel to send him away, he went eagerly to his appointments with her, proudly, like a lover. When he was with her the streets of the city did not run endlessly and meaninglessly, one into the other and beyond; but wheeled around a certain centre of life, and the centre sustained them, though they were so massive and immovable and indifferent, and she, Isabel, whom he loved, was so small, so frail, so soft, so quick to move. Time moved in rhythm of days that laboured to bring them together and days that parted them in certainty of their coming together again. The uniqueness and the privacy of the love they were beginning to know, was Kenneth's pride; and so, too, was the commonness of what they were doing, their submission to a fate that was shared by every couple they passed in the street. And all that Kenneth felt was for him enriched by the fact that it was in London that he had come to know what love might be: now the possibility of peace was united with power in the visions he had of the sprawling city, with all its lights and corners, its grime and splendour, the swarms of smoke that hung above its chimneys and the trees that moved in its green parks.

One afternoon Kenneth and Isabel loitered, at a loss and content to be at a loss. They had nowhere to go, nothing to do: they felt themselves to be on holiday; though a whole city of others were at work. London truly seemed a country to the two of them, and they wandered freely down its lanes, crossed its rivers and canals, idled through its villages. They were unknown; there was no danger that they would be seen or recognized; their own foreignness was their seclusion. Every face was the face of a stranger; every street rose up as if from nature before them; every voice was alien and indifferent. A band played on the pavement, and disabled men in blue suits rattled money-boxes in time with the cheerful, desolate music; the shop windows were lurid with goods and neon; the traffic budged, winked, suddenly shook itself free and moved, before halting again. Kenneth and Isabel went in peace, their hands clasped together; when their glances met, delight huddled in their eyes. Where, how did all the others live? Kenneth and Isabel did not know; they knew only that the living of the others seemed for a moment as innocent as their own. Delight ran before them, flashed with the traffic, blared with the music of the one-armed trumpeter.

Later they felt what they did not wish to feel—fatigue, hunger, the brute affliction of sight upon the eye, of sound upon the ear. They had drawn apart. Isabel's feet were sore, Kenneth was empty, irritated, the more so for the content they had lost. Ruefully Isabel smiled, and he smiled too and shrugged, recognizing her weakness and admitting his, in the same movement of his lips and shoulders. Time might seem to pause, or to move only with their own breathing, but mercilessly they, too, were whirled by it from moment to moment, mood to mood, street to street.

Was it wrong, Isabel wondered, for her and Kenneth to try to be happy just within their own happiness? No, not wrong—impossible merely that they would ever succeed, when they were so quick to change, frail in passion, incapable of resting where they most wanted to rest. Isabel remembered how in Lyndhurst she would have answered the question sternly that it *was* wrong to try to be happy with your own happiness. But it had been easy for her to make that answer then, for she hadn't been happy. Now she could not be stern; she was saddened and stirred by the thought of an isolation and permanence that were unattainable.

'Do you feel that it's wrong just to be happy with your own happiness?' she asked Kenneth, while they were having tea in a café they had entered, as much for the rest as for the food.

Kenneth smiled at the question, which had broken a long silence between them. 'Well, if you aren't happy with your own, you won't be happy with anyone else's either.' Then he added: 'Not that I know. I've never been happy.'

'Not even now? You have been, this afternoon.'

'Yes, happier,' Kenneth admitted.

Isabel's expression mocked at his caution. But she went on seriously. 'Before I would have thought that it was wrong even to try to be happy on your own. Now I think: oh, if only we could be!' She dropped her hand on the table, as if in surrender. 'In Lyndhurst I tried to be happy by making others happy, and that didn't work either. I was cheating, I suppose, trying to get something from what I did, instead of just doing it for its own sake. At least I'm not cheating now.'

'Sometimes when you talk of your days in Lyndhurst you seem to make out that back there you were living a life of poverty, chastity, and obedience,' Kenneth said, almost angrily. 'You weren't. You wouldn't, if you went back to Lyndhurst. You'd still have your white skin, a great deal of money, a big house, a car, you'd still be the grand young lady——'

'That's it!' Isabel cried. 'That's just it. That was what was so false about it.'

'You mean it wasn't self-sacrificial enough for you?'

'Yes,' Isabel said defiantly, her colour rising. 'If I had to sacrifice myself, I would want it to be for something really worth while, and I would want it really to hurt me, to kill me even.'

Kenneth looked at her curiously. 'Who knows, you may still have your chance.'

'No, now I don't want that chance. That's how selfish and indifferent I've become. Now I just want to be with you.'

'That's what I mean,' Kenneth said.

Isabel did not understand him, and kept silent. Yet he warned her, 'Remember what I've said.'

They looked at one another, across the checkered table-cloth, in the café in a street whose name they did not know, and Isabel said, 'I will remember.' And she knew she would even remember his hand upon the cloth, and her own above it; she would remember the wondering, half-doubtful expression on his face, that was wholly dear to her just then; she would remember her own calm and her own excitement, and how they seemed to pace in measure within her until they had taken possession of all, of her hands, her eyes, her skin, the depths of her body. 'I love you, Kenneth,' she said. Strangely, it was the first time she had said these words to him, but she did not feel shy or bold: what else was there for her to say? 'I love you.'

He seemed to listen even after she had spoken. But when he replied it was merely to repeat, 'Remember what I've said.'

'I will. And you must remember what I've just said.'

'I shall never forget it,' Kenneth said.

When he spoke again his voice at first was low, calm, in contrast with the violence and unexpectedness of the question he asked her, 'Isabel, have you ever done anything that you were—that you are—really ashamed of?'

'Kenneth——?'

'No, don't look at me like that, listen. I mean really ashamed, a shame that's in you, like a taste in your mouth? Have you ever been so ashamed that sometimes you opened your newspaper—I know this must sound mad—expecting to *read* there what you have done?'

'I've never expected to read anything about myself in a newspaper.'

'It was my ambition once,' Kenneth said bitterly, 'to have my name in all the papers. Perhaps that's why it's my dread now.'

'Now?' She caught at the word, repeated it questioningly; she held his gaze until slowly, as if under the pressure of it, he lowered his head, he nodded.

'Now,' he admitted. 'Not that I've done anything which could get my name in the papers, I said the whole idea was mad. But, Isabel, have you ever done something that you can't bear to think about, something big and foul, and at the same time small, crawling, low—equally foul, Have you? Have you?'

'I don't care what you have done,' she answered.

Kenneth felt weak with love and shame. 'Are you really what you seem to be?' he asked. 'I suppose you are. It's only me, I'm the lost one—lost here with you, where I most want to be. The stupidity——! Tell me, Isabel,' he implored her, and he did not know what he was asking of her except that it was too much to ask—even here, even of her.

Again he felt his own love for her, when incapably, without understanding, knowing only that he needed her help, she did her best to help him. Her voice was small, she spoke hesitantly, abasing herself, hoping that good might come of her abasement. 'When I'm with you,' she said, 'the thing I'm most ashamed of is what happened to me just after I came to London.'

'What happened?'

'I had an affair with a man.'

'So?'

She looked up to see him. 'It was someone I met on the boat.'

'A shipboard romance—eh?'

'And afterwards, too. He was a man from the Colonial service, from Tanganyika. He was coming home on his long leave. That's why I took a little flat when I first came here, I wanted a place he could come to. And that's why I gave it up afterwards, I was too lonely in it.'

'He left you?'

'Yes. He had to.' Isabel lifted her head and spoke more clearly than before, though not with less shame. 'He was married. He was coming ahead, his wife and son were to follow him when he had found somewhere for them to stay. I knew about it, but that was nothing. The worst is that I was glad he was married. I didn't really like him, I was just using him. I was so eaten with a kind of horrid curiosity, it was raving inside me, Kenneth.'

'So you took him.'

'And I learned nothing. How can you learn anything about love when you come to a man like that? We're not to be made use of by each other.' It seemed as great an effort for Isabel to stop as it had been for her to begin. She sat crouching, her head bowed, the nape of her neck exposed. She said, 'Whatever you have done can't be so much worse than what I did. I don't care if you have another girl that you've never told me about. I don't care even if you're married. I don't blame you.'

Kenneth forgot his own shame in the tenderness and pity he felt when he heard her. He reached across the cloth and took her hand in his. 'My poor girl, is that what you've been thinking? It's not true,' he told her. 'That isn't it. Believe me, Isabel, I have nobody in the world, except you. Nobody, nothing, I'm on my own and you're all I have. If I lose you I am lost. That's why I can't let you go.'

Isabel was silent; then she stirred, and asked softly, 'Can I come with you to your room tonight?'

'If you want to.'

'I've wanted it ever since I've been with you.'

Again, they lapsed, as if they passed with time, were carried with it, in a movement that was motionless. Then Isabel signalled to the waitress: while Kenneth smiled painfully and brought out his money, Isabel went to the coat-rack. Her coat was a pale, almost creamy colour, and she buttoned it up to the neck; the blood was high in her cheeks, and she looked severe, almost angry. She stood aside, waiting for Kenneth. When he, too, had put on his coat they moved together to the door of the café.

The evening had come up windy: all the clouds were in motion, and those in the west were swirling about the sun, like smoke around the fire from which it comes. One ray of light did suddenly break through the clouds, and shone from every window, gleamed in long uncertain lines on the tar; but by the time Kenneth and Isabel had turned at the first corner the light had already gone.

Kenneth's lips were hard, even his tongue was hard, seeking her out; he bit at her, so that she cried out, unable to pull her head away lest his teeth should tear the tender flesh of her inner lip. When he released her there were tears in her eyes, but he did not seem to notice them. He took off his coat; slowly she began to unbutton hers, from the neck downwards. She did not look about the room, was aware of it only as the living-place of the man she was with.

Throughout he was hard, as if taking revenge on her. At first she implored him to be gentle, but he would not listen, he shook his head blindly and dragged her to him again. Then she let herself be dragged, though there was no pleasure in it for her. When he had done, he moved brusquely out of her, away from her, and lay at her side. Where he touched her she felt his heat, but everywhere else she was chill, and the division on her skin was too intense for her to bear: she felt she had been disrupted, did not know herself. 'Please cover me,' she asked, turning her head; his ear was against her lips, but she could not kiss him, or show him any sign of affection. Without a word he took one of the blankets from the foot of the bed, and covered her with it. Then he, too, climbed under the blanket. Now he lay a little farther from her; they touched only at the knees, and where his one arm lay across her bosom. Isabel lay on her back, as she had been when he had left her; she hadn't moved. And nor did he, once he was beneath the blanket.

'It didn't have to be like that,' Isabel said at last, clearly.

He did not speak, made no movement. And Isabel, too, was silent. Perhaps she slept, for she was surprised to see how dark the walls of the room had grown; the only light now lay against the ceiling, and even that was hardly a light, merely a paleness. She must have moved, for Kenneth's arm instinctively drew her closer. She did not yield.

'I love you,' he said. It was the first time he had said it to her.

'I no longer believe you,' Isabel replied.

They spoke after long pauses, as if the words were at a distance from themselves, had to be fetched out of the darkness beyond them.

'I love you, Isabel.'

Isabel turned her head. She could not make out his expression; it was too dark, and in any case his face was half-buried in the pillow. She lifted one hand, awkwardly, from her side; her elbow still lay on the bed, and it was as if over her own shoulder that she felt his chin with her fingers. Slowly, lightly, her fingers made their way to his mouth, touched his moustache and withdrew, then came back again, touched his nose, his cheek. Violently he thrust his head deeper into the pillow, but it was too late; she had already felt the moisture under his eyes.

'Kenneth!' This time it was she who fell upon him. She held on to his shoulders, she sought his face with hers. She uttered her words like little appeals, calls, half-unconscious of them; and fell silent only when he turned to her. They kissed lingeringly now, seeking each other and finding each other, hiding only to be found again, at last lying still, sure of what they had found. Then, when the stillness could content them no longer, they moved together, he into her, she to receive him.

Kenneth's endearments afterwards were strange to Isabel's ears: he called her 'child', 'life', 'anxious one'; he told her that he had seen her, that he knew her, that he remembered her; he thanked her for changing everything, bringing him where he was, speaking for him; he told her that he would never leave her, never leave London. He called her 'refugee', 'lost one', 'cheated one', 'innocent one'. 'What else could I do?' he demanded of her. 'Would you do differently if you knew where it would bring you?'

Isabel smiled to hear him; she did not understand what he was talking about, but she had no fear of it; she could hear the love in his voice. She tried to close his mouth with her finger-tips, but he shook himself free to tell her that what he was doing was true—if ever there had been anything in his life which had been true, this was it, he swore.

'I know my love,' Isabel cried, almost in tears, though understanding nothing of his passion. 'I believe you. You are my love.'

'I am. I was. I always have been. I knew you for my own. I knew the girl you were—oh, Isabel, so well. I wanted you, I can't tell you how much. I hungered for you; I had to seize you when I saw you. You sat behind the desk, and it was as if you said to me, "You can be with me now if you want to. You are free to do it." Can you imagine what that was for me? What it is for me? To be with you—you!'

Isabel cried with compassion to hear him; he seemed to speak with such desperation, out of such deprivation. 'Kenneth, my sweet, what were they doing to you? Why did we wait so long before coming here?'

He did not answer. A little later he said, 'When I lay here afterwards—the first time—I thought it was all finished. It was because you couldn't give me the impossible thing that I was so angry, that I hurt you.'

'What impossible thing, my love?'

'Trust.'

'But I do trust you. How can you say that I don't trust you, when we're lying together like this?' Isabel's hand pressed against his ribs, moved up, grasped his neck. 'I can feel the pulse in your neck,' she said. 'And the tendons. I've always wanted to touch them.' He was about to speak, but she silenced him. 'Lie still, just lie with me, Kenneth. Don't worry, my love, there's nothing for you to worry about, while we're like this.'

'We can't always be like this.'

'No, but we are now.'

✣ 12 ✣

Dear Sir (the letter ran), *I trust you will forgive a total stranger writing to you on a personal matter. As you are no doubt aware your daughter has been until recently in my employ, as a secretary; and it is only because I thought so highly of her that I am taking the liberty of addressing you now. In the time that she was working in my office, your daughter impressed me greatly as a girl of great intelligence and upright character; but I fear that being alone in London she is exposed to many dangers, socially and morally. Moved as I am by her plight, I feel it incumbent upon me to inform you of an undesirable association she has formed, trusting that you will believe my motive for doing so is entirely that of concern and anxiety for her welfare. I am referring, sir, to her association with a certain young man Kenneth Makeer. This man was also in my employ until his dishonest and scandalous behaviour forced me to insist on his instant dismissal. He is a South African, and claims to be a member of the Middle Temple: I know certainly that he is of bad reputation and insolent demeanour; and I suspect, furthermore, that he is already married. Were it not for his association with your daughter I would have taken certain legal steps against him; as it is, anxious to avoid unfavourable publicity which may involve your daughter, I have suffered injury in silence. My patience, sir, is not inexhaustible; but my respect and regard for your daughter is. Accordingly, I am writing to you in the hope that you will be able to save your daughter from the consequences of this friendship. I may add, sir, that your daughter spoke of you in terms which aroused my greatest respect; and this has emboldened me to write to you, as one gentleman to another.* The letter was signed, J. Randall BA (Hons) (Oxon).

With a hand that shook a little, Martin gave the letter back to Mr Last. 'The man sounds a bit cracked to me.'

'I'm glad you think so. That was my first reaction, too. It was only afterwards that I began to wonder about it. Quite honestly, if Isabel had just mentioned the name Kenneth Makeer in any of her letters I wouldn't have worried at all; but as she hadn't, I was really very puzzled by the whole thing. And you say she's never mentioned the name to you?'

'No.'

'Perhaps the whole thing is just a fantasy. For all we know this Randall might have been after Isabel, too, and is now just trying to make trouble for her. Except that from the way Isabel wrote about him I would have thought that he's an old man—well, my age, at least.'

'Old enough to be her father,' Martin said slyly.

'Eh? Oh, I see what you mean. That would make it pretty disgusting, wouldn't it?'

'I think Isabel can look after herself.'

'She can, yes, I'm sure she can. Hettie would think it absurd if she knew that I was worried about Isabel,' Mr Last said, and he admitted embarrassedly, 'I haven't showed this letter to her, I haven't dared to. She says that the girl has to grow up; that I always fussed about her too much; that being alone in London is the best possible thing for her. And I'm sure Hettie is right; she knows much more about these things than I do. She sometimes makes me feel that I've lived a very sheltered life, though I would have laughed if anyone had said so to me, before. And she certainly believes that I tried to shelter Isabel too much. But I suppose under the circumstances it was inevitable, really . . .' Mr Last stared at the fire at which the two men were sitting; as an afterthought he added: 'I'd be glad if you wouldn't mention any of this to Hettie, by the way.'

'No of course not, I wouldn't think of it,' Martin replied. He had always found it amusing that Mr Last, who had previously been so independent, so much master of himself, should unmistakably have been afraid of his wife; but Martin kept his amusement out of his voice.

'Perhaps neither you nor Isabel will thank me for having shown you this letter,' Mr Last went on to say, a little more easily. 'But look, Martin, you know well enough that I like you and would have been glad if things had worked out differently between you and Isabel. And I don't think I'm wrong in supposing that you're hoping that that might still happen.'

'No, sir, I am hoping——'

'That's as I thought. And that's why I'm talking to you like this. You were close to Isabel, she must write to you about—about—well . . .'

This further appeal for information was so naked, it angered Martin. How could he know what Mr Last wanted to hear? 'I think Isabel writes to you as much as she wants to,' Martin said rudely, giving nothing away. And having said it, Martin was angered that he should really have had so little from Isabel to give away: her letters to him had all been cautious and non-committal; she had certainly never mentioned this Kenneth Makeer. Then, as if apologizing for his rudeness, Martin added: 'Actually, I may be able to tell you at first-hand about Isabel, fairly soon. I've decided to go back to England.'

'What?'

'Not to stay. At least I don't think so. But things with my aunt's estate have more or less been seen to here; now there's some work to be done about it in England, and I think I should be there. So I've applied for leave, and they've been very decent about it, and have given me a few weeks. I'm flying at the end of the month. And, of course, Isabel is one of the first people I'll be seeing there—probably the first. As a matter of fact, I've already told her to expect me.'

'Oh.' The news made Mr Last feel that Martin had somehow made a fool of him. 'Why didn't you say so before?'

The truthful reply would have been that Martin had wanted to hear what Mr Last had to say before he broke his own news; in any case, Martin didn't find it as disagreeable as Mr Last that the latter had been made a fool of. But Martin couldn't say anything of this, so he said nothing at all.

In the end, Martin found it easier than he had anticipated to persuade the older man to give the letter to him, to do what he thought best about it when he was in London. Mr Last was glad to pass the responsibility on; and then, Martin definitely had a knack for getting his own way in such matters. Martin drove back to his flat feeling that he had done a good evening's work, and determined to do yet another, in connection with the letter he now carried.

On the day after his visit to Mr Last, Martin went back to his aunt's house, which since her death had been shuttered and boarded up. The garden looked as it had always done, there was so little of growth and so much unchanging sand in it; indoors the house was cold and dark, and suffused with a dry and dusty smell. Martin went from room to room, seeing that everything was in order; he moved with a curious stealth, oppressed equally by the silence of the house and the noises that he himself made. In one room a window had been broken, and Martin started back in fear from the cold breeze that came against his face when he opened the door; when he closed the door behind him the air in the passage immediately fell dead still.

Compassion did not come easily to Martin: his 'knack' of understanding others did not depend on it. And he had never been very fond of his aunt; he had rather taken her for granted, even in the respect he had felt for her as someone from whom he stood to gain. Now, alone in the house, he was moved to uneasiness by the thought of her: he was troubled not by her absence, but by what he felt of her presence, in these rooms and corridors; he felt guilty and abashed when he thought of how little he had bestirred himself to learn what she felt, wanted, even what she did with herself, between these walls. He wished that he had learned more from her now for one reason; but there were other reasons, too, more obscure.

Martin had come to the house to find out what he could about Kenneth Makeer: he had remembered, even while he had been speaking to Mr Last, that he *had* seen the name at the foot of a letter of condolence he had received from London. The name was that of one of his aunt's hangers-on, Martin had remembered: but of what kind? And what kind of relationship could there be between Isabel and such a hanger-on? Martin had the key to his aunt's desk in his pocket, and intending finding out as much as he could; but for the moment he lingered, standing outside his aunt's bedroom, but not going in; he stood at the head of the stairs, looking down; he stood in the front hall, as if he were waiting for someone to come through the front door; he stood with his hands in his pockets in front of a great, glassed-in bookcase, staring idly at the titles on the spines of the books. A kind of disappointment stirred within him that he could not simply ask his aunt what he wanted to know; he felt a vague disappointment with himself. He had missed something in the house, he felt; there had been an opportunity here that he had declined; he had accepted too easily his easy, dull role of nephew and heir, had never tried to get beyond it. What a queer old bird his aunt had been, Martin thought; it was his favourite phrase about her, but it failed for once to bring him the comfort it usually did. She might have been a queer old bird, but her blood flowed in his veins: perhaps he would end up a queer old bird, too.

No, Martin knew he would not; and in the empty shadowed house the realization came to him with a queer and unexpected sense of loss. He would always be what he was, and the prospect seemed to Martin at that moment a lonely and meaningless one;

he felt himself detached, rootless, lonely. What was it that his aunt had had, that her presence should haunt the house, should make him reluctant to thrust his fingers among her papers, as if afraid of what he should find there? Martin drifted away from the bookcase, went back into the hall again; it was with an effort of will that he at last grasped the handle of the door to his aunt's study, and thrust it open.

By the time he had finished with his aunt's papers, Martin knew better what it was that his aunt had had. He could sneer at her, he could see easily enough the lusts for power which she had managed to hide from herself and from others until the last year or two of her life; he could feel that she was lucky to have died when she had, when every day was revealing, even to herself, more and more of the bone of her desires. But when all the judgements were made, all the sneers had been uttered, there remained something that a man was poor without; there remained the passion of self-regard which Martin envied his aunt, as he sat at her desk, his fingers playing with the pins she had thrust through old accounts, the ribbons she had tied through old letters; as his eyes fell on the words that her living eyes had read.

Martin read all Kenneth's letters to Miss Bentwisch; he read the letters that Isabel had written when she had been a schoolgirl, away from Lyndhurst on holiday; he read some letters from others among his aunt's clients. And what was true of his aunt was certainly true of Isabel and Kenneth Makeer. They cared about themselves and what happened to them, whether it was wise or foolish for them to care; and Martin was filled with an envy of their lack of shame, their ability to care. Reading their letters, he had been made to feel that he was the ghost at the desk, not his aunt; and when he thought that Kenneth and Isabel were now, in London, sharing with one another their common concern, exposing to each other their seriousness and awareness, mingling their passion, Martin's envy became a sharp and degrading jealousy, the sharper and more difficult to resist because it was a jealousy of a Cape Coloured pauper and a colonial girl who had grown up in a town like Lyndhurst.

It took Martin a long time to burn the letters he carried across the room and threw into the grate, but the job absorbed him; and by the time it was done he felt calmer, easier. He went back to the big desk and closed up all the drawers; the rest of the letters still there could be burned at another time, by another hand. Kenneth's letters he had kept aside; he had them in his hand when he left the house, slamming the great front door behind him.

Jealousy became wonder when Martin stood with Isabel in the Visitors' Room of the club in London; and the wonder was not so much at what Isabel had done or at what Kenneth had done, but at the power Martin now felt he had, at the opportunity for conquest that lay before him. But he had to move cautiously; he had to make sure of his ground before treading on it.

'And this fellow doesn't know that I'm here?' he asked.

Isabel shook her head.

'Why haven't you told him? Didn't you think I was worth mentioning at all?'

'Martin——'

'Probably I am not worth mentioning. But it seems strange to me that you shouldn't have mentioned *him* at all in your letters home. I mean—you know nothing about him that should make you afraid of mentioning him.'

'Afraid? Why do you use that word ?'

'Well, I'd say your secretiveness forces me to use it.'

'Martin, I haven't really known him for so long. I didn't want to write when everything between us was so unsettled.'

'From what you've just told me I would have thought that it was pretty settled. You say you love him.'

'Yes, I do.'

'And you say that he loves you?'

'Yes, he does.'

'Then what remains to be settled? Honestly, Isabel, I know you'll think I'm being interfering, but you must try to understand how I feel, too. And how your father will feel when he hears about it. What are we to think, except that there's something about him that you're ashamed of?'

Isabel shook her head dumbly, her lips pressed together in a flat and pale line. She sat in an arm-chair, Martin stood over her; and they talked in low voices, because there was another couple in the far corner of the room, near the window. 'Yet everything you tell me about him is respectable and decent enough,' Martin went on, insistently. 'You say that he comes from Cape Town?'

'Yes.'

'And that his aunt sent him to London?'

'Yes.'

'And what else do you know about his family?'

'His father is a builder, or something.'

'And what else?'

'His mother is dead. He has a brother at home.'

Exultingly, Martin knew that he had to strike now, if he was to strike at all. He had to show Isabel who this Kenneth Makeer was; and in that one stroke show her, too, who he, Martin, was; he had to win her respect, her gratitude, her love.

It is hard to believe that that is what Martin thought he would succeed in doing; but it is the truth. Perhaps there moved in the back of his mind the vague and vulgar idea of 'catching her on the rebound'; perhaps it was simply that he felt that Isabel, on learning how she had been wronged, would fly into the arms of the person who had shown her what had been done to her; perhaps he was so puffed up with his knowledge as against her pitiful ignorance, that he felt himself to be irresistible in his wisdom. What is certain is that at that stage in his conversation with Isabel, Martin sat down in an arm-chair, put his attaché-case on his lap, and produced what he referred to in his own mind as 'the documents'.

By the time he had done, Isabel had risen, she stood bent, sideways to him, one shoulder thrust forward, one arm crooked behind her, like something fractured, her face as old and as heavy as her father's. She bent still lower, until it looked grotesquely as if she were bowing to him, bowing more deeply still; noises came from her throat: low, incoherent sounds of whimpering, muttering. Then suddenly she was silent, and white: only her eyes were dark, staring forward. Instinctively Martin moved closer to her, to grasp her.

She fell against him with a force that thrust him back. But he clung to her, and filled with the wonder of his own strength, began to kiss her hair, her neck, her hands, kissed the tears on her face, in a passion that the moment could not abate. 'My sweetheart, Isabel,' he said, 'stay with me, don't leave me, I need you, too.'

Very soon afterwards Isabel said good-bye to Martin, assuring him that she would see him the next day, the day after. Then she walked about the squares of Bayswater, she came back to her room in the club, she crept into her bed. Again and again she went incoherently over all she had seen and known of Kenneth, from the day he had come into her office at the school to the sick, dream-like moment when she had first seen in Martin's hand a letter, a whole bundle of letters, in Kenneth's handwriting. Now when she closed her eyes it was still the letters she saw, and in her mind there ran repeatedly the phrases, promises, oaths she had read in them, in Martin's presence and later—fluttering through the pages, clutching them, throwing them aside, recognizing in what she read characteristic turns of phrase, even hearing Kenneth's voice, as though the letters had been addressed to her and not to Miss Bentwisch. And the fact that Kenneth should have come from the Coloured Camp in Lyndhurst; that he should have known Miss Bentwisch, and been a protégé of hers; that he should have known who she, Isabel, was; that he should persistently and deliberately have lied to her—all this was so monstrous, so surprising, that Isabel was hardly able to feel anger with him: her astonishment swallowed anger, swallowed reproach, swallowed all but grief, and the nagging insatiable question *Why? Why?* Once or twice, lying in her bed, Isabel started up from her pillow, like a dreamer, thinking that what she suffered now was a fantasy; and then in a misery which ebbed away from her, out of her, and yet did not grow any the less within her, she would remember again that it was this suffering which was the only truth.

What had the other been, then: the hours she and Kenneth had spent together, the love they had exchanged, the animal warmth they had given, each of them to the other? Had that all been a lie? She could not believe it, would not believe it. He loved her, she knew, he must have loved her, he could not have deceived her eyes and hands and breast as he had deceived her mind. But how could he have lied to her, then, with his tongue—the tongue which had filled her mouth so many times, touched at her breast? Why had he lied to her? Why? Why? She asked her question aloud into the darkened room, and frantically turned her pillow over, seeking the cooler side, and making hot that side, too, so that again she rose, flailed at the bedclothes. Why? Why? And at first when she asked the question it seemed to her to have no meaning, no relationship to Kenneth, her lover, whom she knew so well, so deeply, to whom she had so often spoken about Lyndhurst and Miss Bentwisch, telling him of streets and people he had never seen. Yet, more and more, as the night passed, and still she asked the question and failed to find an answer to it, Kenneth became unreal and shadowy to her, almost as if she herself had made up his image, and there was nowhere outside herself where she could go to see him. Then another figure became more real and full to her than that of the Kenneth she had known in London: it was the figure of a Coloured youth, who, growing up in deprivation and squalor in the Coloured Camp, Lyndhurst, had been given an opportunity to fight for a change in the lives of his people. Eagerly the boy had seized at it—how eagerly, with what devotion of purpose, she had read in his letters, in his own words; and Isabel remembering again the lanes and alleyways of the Camp, remembering the harsh sunlight and the hideous shadows, the loud embittered lives among the shacks of tin and sacking, could not wonder at his eagerness, could only sympathize passionately with it. For him, for the boy who had written those letters, the work of redemption and release had not been a duty, an obligation imposed publicly from outside, or even by any single thing within himself: it had been his life. How could that direct and unambiguous person have become the other she had tried to grapple with during the night: the shadowy, equivocating one, who loved her and lied to her, who pretended to be what he was not and never spoke to her of what he was, who asked her questions to which he knew the answers, and answered her questions with what he knew to be untruths? Of the two men, one stood in the light, the other edged into darkness: one spoke of his motives and acted on them, the other's actions were without reason, like a madman's. One figure she could recognize, though she had never seen him; the other she had embraced, and yet he now seemed altogether strange to her, monstrously surprising, a new creature, even to the features of his face, which she could not summon up before her when she tried. One she had to admire with all within herself that most respected; the other could make no claim upon her but the claim of a past which his own actions had made unreal, even shameful. Why had the one figure become the other? Why? Why? Once only did it occur to Isabel that the man had lied out of shame and fear, thinking that she might find him repugnant if she knew he was Coloured; and no sooner did the thought come than it was thrust aside as unworthy of him, unworthy of her.

Isabel thrashed in her bed, seeking for an answer to her question; but when the answer came she lay quite still, feeling only her own heart beating. She was the answer! She was to blame! For her the man had changed himself, denied himself, corrupted himself! He loved her, and loving her, could not become what he had most wanted to become; had been forced to become something different, something that he perhaps writhed against even now, though he loved her, because he loved her. The man had dreamed of a life of action and self-sacrifice, he had given himself to it, and then he had come to her, embraced her, and lost himself and his own purposes. She was white, soft, wealthy; he could not have her and be what he wanted to be; he could not be what he wanted to be and yet have her. The law alone in South Africa prevented that: made it impossible for them ever to meet in that country, ever to kiss, embrace, lie in love. So he had surrendered himself, tried to cast himself behind, in order to be with her. Never, even in her grief, even in her astonishment, had Isabel doubted that Kenneth had in his way truly loved her: but now the knowledge of that love was for her confirmed and confirmed again. He had been weak, rash, dishonest; but she, *she* was the guilty one. Guilty again, guilty to him as she had always been to his people, in her very skin, just in being what she was. She had forced him into this corruption and debasement; she could not permit him to remain in it.

Across a waste of shadows and institutional furniture in the Visitors' Room of the club Kenneth and Isabel spoke again to one another. Outside, beyond the tall windows, a haze made murky the far side of the square, and muffled every sound; the branches of trees leaned away from one another, their leaves grey with the fine rain that all day had seemed to rise in the air, rather than fall. Kenneth stood beneath the windows, Isabel near the door.

'You know——!' Kenneth stared at her, unable to speak, aware only of the shame that seemed to burn on the skin of his hands, his neck, his shoulders. He could not move, and the flame went over him, then sank, guttered, left him charred, sick that he should have still been alive. 'How do you know? How long have you known?' He shook suddenly, in a spasm he could not control. 'What do you know?' he shouted. 'Who told you?'

'Martin Bullivant told me. He was here yesterday.'

'Martin Bullivant? Martin . . .' It seemed grotesque to Kenneth. 'I have never seen him. He knows nothing about me.'

'He knows everything about you.'

Isabel was pale, but composed. She paused, before she went on.

'I know what you were before you met me,' she said. 'And I know what you must be again.'

'What I was before I met you,' Kenneth repeated, dazed, 'What I must be again.' His shame burned, less fiercely, because he was so much less than he had been. He could not defend himself, he could not attack; yet a cry broke from his throat: 'You too——! You too——!'

When he saw Isabel move towards the door he called her —'Isabel!' But what could he offer her, or ask of her now? 'Go!' he shouted suddenly. 'Let it be the end! For God's sake, for my sake, go!'

Isabel turned, she walked out of the room. As she made her way up the stairs she heard him calling her back, but she did not halt. At the landing she hesitated, before walking down the passage towards her room. 'Isabel!' came the cry again, from the hall. Then Isabel heard the sounds of an altercation, the voices of English menials raised in self-righteous remonstrance: 'No, sir, you cannot go upstairs, gentlemen are not permitted, it's against the rules.' There came a yell, then, that was incredible to hear, it was so shameless, so filled with despair. It rang down the corridors into the little rooms where the girls lived; Isabel heard it in her room; she lay on the floor; 'Kenneth, Kenneth,' she answered, and the despair in her voice was as great as the despair in his, though the sound of her voice went no farther than the floorboards, and her own fists, crushed against her mouth.

In the days that followed Martin was helpful, considerate, understanding. Martin had no more immediate ambition than to get Isabel to return to Lyndhurst: he was sure that if he could get her there, he would finally conquer her. And Martin wanted to conquer her more than he had ever wanted anything else in the world, and her subduedness, her dazed and chastened acquiescence in the arrangements he made for her, merely inflamed him the more. She was life to him, she was passion, she was the world he had to grapple with—and look, he could say to himself when he saw her, look what I have done to it already! He instructed her where they should meet and what they should do; he spent money freely, with the comment that there was plenty more where that came from; once or twice he surprised her again by kissing her fiercely and publicly. And though Isabel disengaged herself from his embraces, she did it sufficiently slowly for Martin to grasp at her and to tell her without fear or self-consciousness, 'Ah, I love you. I need you Isabel.'

Isabel heard his declaration with attentiveness: she listened as if he were saying something obscure to her, and yet of absorbing and unexpected interest. Then she asked, 'Do you? Do you really?'

How he loved her voice when she spoke, with its flat little South African vowels. 'I do. I want you, Isabel. I won't let you suffer again.' She came to him, when he grasped her; and Martin's compassion was all the more sincere for the knowledge that he was the one who had inflicted the hurt on her. He had punished her, but she came to him: this was power, a grown man's power, and Martin exulted in it. 'Darling,' he whispered to her. 'Sweetheart, Isabel, this time I'm not going to let you go. Never.'

Because the limpness and bewilderment which Isabel showed so much suited Martin, he did not ask himself what she must be suffering; he did not really ask himself what she was feeling, or if she felt more than she showed. Martin was full of himself, full of pride at what he had succeeded in doing; and the very day before he and Isabel left London, Martin fulfilled an ambition that he had secretly permitted himself to nourish ever since Isabel had finally surrendered to him, and said yes, she would return with him to Lyndhurst.

Martin had not told Isabel of his intention; nor had he written to Kenneth that he would be calling. He simply went to the address that had been given to him at the Temple; he rang at the bell which bore Makeer's name, and waited, rang again and waited. When he heard behind him footsteps coming up the short path that led from the pavement to the door, Martin turned; he saw approaching a man with a stocky figure, a lined face, and a strong youthful head of blond hair. Was this Makeer? This man was white, a European, an older man than Martin had expected.

'Can I help you?' the man asked.

The faint foreignness of his accent increased Martin's apprehension. 'Mr Makeer?'

'No,' the man said. 'He lives in the room next door to mine.'

Martin was relieved to hear this. The stranger had a key in one hand, and with it he opened the door. 'Will you go in?'

'Well, if Mr Makeer isn't here . . .'

'Come in anyway.' The man hesitated, then suggested, 'Perhaps you would like to wait in my room.'

'That's very kind of you. But won't I be putting you to trouble?'

'No, no trouble. I cannot slam the door in your face?'

'No, but I don't have to wait here on the doorstep.'

'You are welcome to wait in my room.'

Martin followed the man up the stairs. As they went up, the stranger told Martin that Mr Makeer was a good friend of his, that they had had some interesting conversations on various topics, that South Africa was an unhappy country, no?

'Yes.'

'Norway is not such an unhappy country as South Africa. I am from Norway.'

'Oh, I see.'

They entered the room. As if the sight of his room had reminded him of his longing, the Norwegian said, 'I would like to live in Australia.'

'Why Australia?'

'Ah,' the man said wistfully, 'it is so far away. That is the best thing about Australia.'

'It is the best thing about South Africa, too.' Martin said, amused, struck by the thought.

Martin was to remember the Norwegian with a certain fondness; the man not only helped him to pass the time while he waited for Makeer, but turned the visit into something of a social occasion. When they heard Makeer's footsteps on the stair the Norwegian did not simply usher Martin out of the room, to confront Makeer stone-cold on the landing. Like a host he thrust his head through the door and called out, 'Mr Makeer, I have a friend of yours waiting for you in my room. We have been having an interesting conversation about South Africa and other lands.'

So that when Makeer stepped into the room, he was on someone else's territory—which Martin was grateful for. 'Here is your friend,' the Norwegian said. Martin had stood aside deliberately: both the others in the room had to look for him for a moment. And during that moment Martin had had his chance to look at Kenneth. Of course Martin had been warned, he knew that Makeer was Coloured; but how, he wondered, could Isabel ever have taken him for a white man? There was something characteristically degraded, it seemed to Martin, even in Makeer's attitude; only a Coloured could have looked at once so hangdog and yet so wary.

'I am afraid,' the Norwegian said to Martin, 'I do not know your name.' Then he laughed loudly. 'But of course I do not have to introduce you to each other. You are friends.'

'No,' Kenneth said, 'we are not.'

'My name is Martin Bullivant.'

Kenneth looked at the other. 'And you know mine.'

Of the three of them it was only the Norwegian who seemed embarrassed. 'Ah, but I thought you knew each other. Forgive me, I have made a gaffe.'

Kenneth did not take his eyes off Martin. 'I forgive you.'

Martin said, 'Mr Makeer and I know of each other, but we have not met before.'

'You have acquaintances in common,' the Norwegian said, anxious to please.

'Indeed yes,' Martin said. 'We do have acquaintances in common. Close acquaintances. Dear acquaintances.' Then Martin said, 'Thank you very much for letting me wait in your room, you have been most kind, I really do appreciate it.'

The Norwegian was distressed to hear this. 'But you are going? So soon? I was hoping that we could continue our interesting conversation. There is so much we can learn from one another, when we come from such distant parts of the world. From the north and from the south, as you might truly say. And it is only by meeting and mingling that we can understand one another's problems, yes?'

'Yes,' Martin said, walking to the door, nevertheless.

And Kenneth wasted no time, once they were in his room. 'Why have you come?'

'I wanted to see you.'

'What about?'

Martin hesitated. 'On a personal matter.'

For the first time Kenneth smiled. 'I didn't think you'd come on business.'

'Well, I have, too—in a way.'

'What do you want? To buy me off?'

'I don't need to,' Martin said pointedly.

For a moment Kenneth was silent. Then he asked, 'You're seeing Isabel?'

'Yes, every day. I'm leaving with her for Lyndhurst tomorrow.'

The texture of Kenneth's skin seemed to change, to grow coarser, as if the pores were showing themselves up. Then they contracted again, shrank. His whole face seemed to shrink. He said again, 'Why have you come? What do you want of me?'

Martin hesitated. 'I want to help you.'

'What?'

'Yes, it's true.'

'It's unexpected. Why should you help me?'

'I feel it's my duty.'

Kenneth did not comment on this. 'And what makes you think I'd let you help me?'

'You let my aunt help you.'

'Your aunt? Yes, I let her help me—God help me. But you——?'

'I'm her heir.'

Kenneth was silent. Then he shook his head. 'I know. And don't think that that didn't show up your aunt to me. Why did she want to leave her money to you, when you meant so little to her? So that the world would know she wasn't a bastard!' The outburst sounded curiously as though it had been rehearsed, prepared for.

And so it had been, in all his soliloquies, self-examinations, silent arguments. 'Where was her independence, then? She was white enough and rich enough and lonely enough to have told the world to go to hell. But she did not. None of us can, none of us ever does.'

'Then why are you so bitter?'

'Wouldn't you be bitter, if the world had made you what it has made me?' Kenneth turned away, unable to face the man.

'And you thought you could make yourself over,' Martin said quietly.

'Yes, here in England I did. And in South Africa I thought I could make the world over. The stupidity of it, both ways, both times! What help do you think you can give me? To help me become the great revolutionary? I don't want it, I can't become one. To help me become the young English barrister? I don't want that, I can't become that either.'

'So what future do you see for yourself?'

'None,' Kenneth replied bluntly, without shame or pride. Then he faced Martin again. 'And now have you finished? While your aunt was alive you took no interest in what she was doing, but now you come and tell me that you want to help me! I know all about you; I've heard what Isabel had to say about you, and what your aunt had to say about you, too. You go here, you go there, you do what you like—you know you're safe, you're rich, you're white. But if you ask me what future I see for you, I can tell you in one word.'

'What word is that?'

'None.' Kenneth was jeering, his mouth wide open under his black moustache. 'That is what you came to hear, isn't it? You wanted my advice, didn't you? You wanted me to prophesy for you? You wanted something you could take away with you.'

'Yes,' Martin admitted in a low voice.

'Well, I've made my prophecy. And I know it's true precisely because you had to come to me, you couldn't keep away. Well, I've given you what I can, I've told you what to expect.'

Martin waited, bowed forward, listening for more; he had been touched where he had most deeply wanted to be touched; and even the pain and anger he felt was a profound relief, darkening his mind, relieving him of responsibility. At last he said, 'I'll marry Isabel, all the same.'

'She's another!' Kenneth shouted suddenly, his face working, his hands clasping and unclasping. 'She's another failure, we all are. And you know why we fail? It's because there's nothing we believe in. Nothing. Not in ourselves, not in the world outside. So we go from the one to the other, from disbelief to disbelief and back to disbelief again. And to every one of our disbeliefs we give a name; we call one an ideal; we call another a duty; we call a third love; but they're all names for the same disbelief. If we felt just one of them, truly, deeply, do you think we'd be where we are now? Do you think I'd be talking to you, and you'd be listening to me? And yet we both claim to love Isabel; and Isabel claimed to love me.' Kenneth stared fiercely forward. 'But where does it end? How do you come to an end of disbelief?'

'There's no end,' Martin said.

Still Kenneth stared forward; something about his posture made Martin think he might reel away, fall. 'Ah, you know,' Kenneth said, almost whispering. 'You would know. And you've said it.'

Both men were suddenly weary, anxious to be done. And yet there remained something to be said; they waited, before Martin spoke. 'I won't tell Isabel that I've been to see you.'

'For whose sake? Yours or mine?'

But Kenneth was grateful, and Martin replied without anger. 'For both our sakes.' Martin added: 'I will give you money if you need it. I meant what I said.'

Kenneth shook his head, and a few minutes later Martin left. The last he saw of Kenneth was that he was standing in the middle of the room, staring down at the carpet, like a man unconscious that a visitor had just left, or indeed that a visitor had been with him at all.

13

WHEN THINGS GO really badly with us, they go badly altogether, all round; and even our virtues become sources of infection, lending their strength to make more insidious our weakness. Having done wrong, we suffer; and we suffer the more because we believe we deserve to suffer. But suffering has a life and will of its own, and in itself becomes the signal to us of our own demerit: conscious of that demerit, we punish ourselves further, refusing to believe any good of ourselves. And so we tread the mill of punishment after self-condemnation, and condemnation after self-punishment. Thus it was in Kenneth's case, and all aggravated unendurably by the sense of sheer waste and humiliation he felt when he thought of Isabel.

He could not recall her by any act of will as an image in his mind; and when she did come to his imagination unbidden and unexpected, it was never with any completeness, but in fragments only. He would feel on him the touch of her hand; he would remember the grey of her eyes, the frown of her brows, or the way she had bent her head one afternoon in a park; he heard her voice uttering words, never sentences; he remembered the line of her neck, her bosom in a blue jersey and her arms folded protectingly and tenderly over it. He saw, and felt these things with an hallucinatory vividness, but they fled from him the moment he tried to grasp them, to bring them together; fled into the grey and brown and formless wastes of the room he lived in, the streets he walked in.

So the days, the weeks, passed. To Kenneth it was incredible that an existence as miserable and as futile and as full of self-hate as he felt his own to be, could go on for so long. He told himself that time would cure his state; but time itself seemed to be his disease. Time had no end, it went on and on, accumulating upon itself, coiling down more and more heavily upon him, crushing him. He sought distractions, of course; he went to his classes, until he could no longer bring himself to do so; he went to meetings of African societies of one description or another, until the faces and voices sickened him; once he picked up a girl in a tube train, once in a public library, but let them go. He went to the cinema, sitting through the same programme more than once in an afternoon; he worked at his lawbooks in fierce spells, and afterwards could remember nothing of what he had so painfully and doggedly committed to his memory; he wrote in his journal. (*'If she felt it to be shameful to have been with me, were not my lies her justification, the evidence of my own shame at what I am? However low her motives were, they were no more vicious and wrong than my own actions had been, my own deceits. She betrayed me; but I had betrayed myself earlier. I gave her every reason, every excuse for believing me to be foul, a man to run away from: had I not tried to run away from myself? So I turn and turn, and there is no blame, no anger, no hatred that does not turn, too, upon me. I am a man who kicks and struggles and chokes as he drowns in a swamp; I am the swamp, too, in which he is drowning.'*) Kenneth slept, woke, tasted in his mouth his own bile, bitterness, evil. More and more his thoughts turned to the darkness and silence of extinction, where there would be an end to the time that was crushing him with such persistence, with such implacability.

. . . . .

Then the evening came when Isabel returned to his room. He cried out to her to get away, that he was better off without her; but when she pulled him to her and kissed him on the lips, he could not resist, and when Isabel made her way to his bed and lay down on it, he lay with her, too weak to move or speak or embrace her. He seemed to his own sense to faint, to pass away, to lapse into a darkness that had on it only the greyest, most distant horizon of light, and no more. This was the end, and it had no end; the darkness was globed, encircling him utterly, containing him. And Isabel lay quite still, too, her eyes closed, as his were.

Light returned slowly, before he opened his eyes; the horizon expanded until the globe was irradiated with silver from below and above, and his eyelids fluttered and opened to the light of the room. But there was no shrinking of the horizon when he saw the walls around him, for the room contained Isabel. For a long time he stared at her, while she lay unconscious of his scrutiny: he looked at her mouth, her chin, her brow, at the tender oval swellings of her closed eyelids. It was unbelievable to him that she should have been there for him to see, her hands and face and shoulders not now glimpses, hideously disconnected and impalpable, but part of a breathing and natural body. It was the simplicity and completeness of her physical presence that most moved him: in awe he wondered that she should have been wearing the shoes that she had put on that morning, and the stockings, and the navy-blue skirt and the pink jersey that her open jacket revealed. She lay with her hands to her side, and he, half-risen, did not stir, because he wanted her to lie as she was, hands lying where they had fallen, her head thrown back and her neck exposed. Hearing her breathe, and smelling in his nostrils the precise and indefinably commingled smell of her, which he had not known he knew, until he smelt it again—then Kenneth felt that there was nothing worse than parting. Severance was destruction: he was not strong enough to survive it; no one was; we lived together or died alone.

'Isabel,' he said at last. With one movement her arms came up and enfolded him; her hands were around his neck, her face was against his own. And the particular warmth and dryness of her hands, the particular smoothness of her cheek against his own—these he would have known from any other in the world. The sweetness of her presence was too much for him; and he lapsed, though not so deeply as before. Not so deeply that he couldn't feel within him the welling-up of happiness, which came unasked for and unexpected. How easy it was to be happy, how little trouble it was; how simple and quiet was the joy he began to feel. 'God, God,' he said. 'God. God.'

Isabel drew him closer. She still had not spoken, had barely moved but to put her arms around him; and now, too, he neither spoke nor moved, but lay quietly with her. There would be time for movement later; there was time now for stillness, which was rarer.

So easy it had seemed, those many weeks before, for Isabel to leave London with Martin. The taxi ticked in the street, the Club porter carried her luggage, Martin opened the door of the cab. For the last time Isabel had looked back at the tall-windowed house she had lived in, looked around at the green-leaved square, as the taxi turned and began making its way towards the Bayswater Road. And that was all. In a dream Isabel saw Hyde Park, wide and empty on this weekday morning, and the congested flashing of the traffic at Marble Arch; she saw Hyde Park Corner, where the traffic swirled between one park and another, and hideous lumps of statuary stood on islands in the roads, the mouth of a pallid piece of concrete artillery gaping upwards. A clutter of dirty streets and dingy brown buildings passed to the right, and at last the taxi sidled alongside the slab-like terminal building. There was more opening of doors, passing out of luggage, exchanging of money, issuing of instructions. Docilely, still in a dream, Isabel went with Martin to show their tickets at the counter; she went with him to the counter where their baggage was weighed.

Then they sat down to wait. And there was no awakening for Isabel, not even when she turned to Martin and said to him, 'I can't go through with this.' His pale face was close to hers; his mouth opened wide, but she could not hear what he said; there was a noise of loudspeakers in her ears. She was caught, as if in some sluggish and unreal passage of time; she could not even run, for the passage would stretch itself out as fast as she ran. So it was in sheer weariness that she said again to Martin, 'I can't go through with this.'

He did not move, did not let go of her wrist; and hours later, when they were vibrating, helpless in their padded seats in the plane, Martin said reassuringly to her, 'It's all right, you know, I won't tell your father or Hettie anything about that fellow. I mean—I won't tell them what he is, you know. You needn't worry about that.'

After a long silence, while she looked closely at Martin, and he smiled at her encouragingly and sympathetically, Isabel replied, 'I will tell them then.' Had he imagined that *that* was why she had shown fear, had tried to draw back?

The smile went from Martin's face. 'I advise you not to.' He added, 'You've forgotten what it's like in South Africa.'

Indeed, she had forgotten what it was like in South Africa. The feel of the night air, the shallow sunburned faces of the officials at the Johannesburg Airport, the straggling yet sudden blaze of the suburban towns they passed through on their way to the city; the city itself, residential streets open and yet empty, the towers of the town-centre and the pavements beneath them empty, too, deserted, depopulated—they were all strange to her. Of course, no one loitered in Johannesburg at night; the city was fear-bound; and this, too, Isabel had forgotten, after her year in London.

The train journey from Johannesburg to Lyndhurst was one that Isabel had often done before, and it was with a recollective melancholy that later that same night she watched the southern suburbs of Johannesburg passing alongside in rows of street-lamps and an occasional bus; saw the deep pall of smoke that hung over Newclare location; followed with her eyes the railway lines that diverged and ducked beneath half-lit subways or strode above them. Then the streets and the lamps were left behind, and the train began to trundle through the veld, carrying with it flat windows of light that rode over the rocks and grass, and stood momentarily upright against the walls of narrow culverts. There were halts at little unroofed platforms, where bluegum trees stood unstirring; and within the sudden silence of each halt, Isabel heard the slapping sound of the drinking-water inside its tank at the end of the coach-corridor, the clear voices and footsteps of lantern-carrying railwaymen outside.

Her meeting with her father in the morning moved Isabel more than she had expected it to do: seeing him, she felt a grief that was strangely impersonal, a pity for her father and herself and everyone else who was caught up in the passage of time. On that bright winter morning in Lyndhurst there seemed to Isabel nothing safe, nothing secure, nothing lasting in the world: already time had turned her childhood into the mere pang of memory; and what she felt now as she clung to him would become that, too, in time. And yet part of the sadness was that nothing had changed: her father seemed no older, nor did Hettie; the house, the garden, streets and roofs, sand and sky were the same. And she was, too: she who had been so far away, and to whom so much had seemed to be happening.

Of London, of Kenneth, of her own future, she did not think. The swift and violent journey she had just made seemed to stretch itself in length, in days, in effort, and when she did look back it was the journey itself that she remembered: London was no more than the place she had left; Lyndhurst was merely the place she had come to. Surely no new effort would be demanded of her now; she felt she had done enough, in moving. And so she let the days pass over her, and was grateful that her father and Hettie did not worry her, but left her to herself; and that Martin, too, did not intrude upon her. 'There'll be time,' her father had said, 'there will be time for us to talk—all the time in the world.' He was happy to have Isabel at home again; he felt somehow set at rest, even justified, by the fact that she had been away and had come back. Hettie was friendly and ironical, and kept her distance. It was easy for Isabel to let the days pass. They talked of going down to the Cape together, later in the year. In the meantime, Isabel hardly went out of the house. She slept, she read, she sewed. Occasionally, she was troubled to wonder for how long she could go on in this idleness or suspension of spirit; but then she would think that she had not really been home for long; she had hardly been home at all —though the days still passed, one after the other, each like the last.

Until one evening—when Isabel was sitting silently on the front *stoep* with Hettie, while the older woman was having a sundowner, waiting for Mr Last to return from his office—the servant came through to say that there was a man at the back who wanted to see the missus.

'What kind of a man?' Hettie asked, getting to her feet.

'A Coloured,' the servant replied. Then he said, 'He wants to speak to the young missus.'

'Oh,' Hettie paused, looked inquiringly at Isabel. 'Do you want me to go?'

'No, I'll go,' Isabel said, putting aside the magazine she had been glancing at. She felt puzzled for a moment, before she felt fear, though she met Hettie's gaze calmly, and then slowly followed the servant through the house.

On the back *stoep* there was standing a tall, well-built, and neatly-dressed Coloured. He was looking aside; Isabel could not see his face fully; but she was sure she had never seen him before. 'Good evening,' she said.

He turned to face her. 'Good evening,' His voice was low and pleasant, and he spoke without embarrassment. 'I think you should close the door, madam,' he said.

Isabel was afraid, but not of physical violence; so she closed the door, shutting out the servant who had been standing just behind her. 'Yes?' Isabel said. The light was harsh, and yet without strength, for the *stoep* was open, but for the roof above them; there were no walls to reflect or contain the light, which soon lost itself in the dimness of the evening. And the Coloured stood near the steps, at the edge of the light, his forehead shining, his nose and mouth in shadow, his shoulders without definition. 'What do you want?' Isabel asked.

'I want to speak to you, madam.'

'Who are you?'

'My name is Peter Makeer.'

'Oh——' Isabel breathed.

'I am Kenneth's brother.'

Hesitantly, Isabel came forward a step. 'Are you really?' she asked.

The man smiled at the note in her voice, at the question itself. 'Yes.'

Isabel did not draw closer to him. 'How do you do?' she said.

'Thank you, madam,' he replied.

Isabel did not know what to say. 'Won't you come in?' she asked.

'Where?' he asked. 'Into the kitchen?'

Isabel knew immediately what he meant by the question. 'I'm not frightened,' she said.

'I am,' he replied.

'There's no one, there's only my stepmother.'

He stood where he was. 'Thank you. But we are more private here, anyway.'

'How is Kenneth?' Isabel asked suddenly.

'I don't know. That's what I came to ask you.'

They were both silent then. Isabel moved irresolutely, but her voice was sharp when she spoke again. 'Did Kenneth send you? Is that why you've come?'

'No, Kenneth didn't send me. Kenneth doesn't know I would think of coming to you.'

'Then how do you come here? How do you know I have anything to do with Kenneth?'

'Kenneth mentioned you in one of his letters, a long time ago.' Now Isabel heard the strain, the fear, in his smooth, pleasant voice: he was afraid even to mention to the white girl in Lyndhurst that she had kept company with his brother, a Coloured. But he went on nevertheless, 'And then weeks ago my father saw in the Social and Personal of the paper that you had come home'. He paused, and added, 'My father always reads the Social and Personal in the paper.' Isabel did not respond to his brief smile; she stood, waiting. 'We haven't heard from Kenneth for so long,' he said. 'My father is very worried about him. He used to be so good about writing; we were getting a letter from him every two weeks, before. Now there's nothing. So my father worries. And I worry, too. And I thought that you *had* seen Kenneth, and would know . . . a little. And I thought also that if you had been friendly with Kenneth you wouldn't mind if I came.'

'Because I'd also be friendly to you?' Isabel asked sharply.

'No.' He shook his head. He put his hand against his chest in a gesture that was curiously slow and weary. 'To us,' he said. 'To me, too,' he admitted then. 'To anyone—' he looked back and pointed, stretching his arm out—'who comes in through the back gate. My father would say that I am being cheeky coming here to you like this, but I thought that you would feel differently. So I came.'

'Of course,' Isabel said.

He seemed to relax slightly. 'So I am here.'

'I can tell you very little,' Isabel said.

'You can tell me how he was when you saw him last time.'

'He was well,' Isabel said.

'You don't write to him?'

Isabel shook his head. 'No.'

'Why doesn't he write?' the man asked quietly, as if to himself. 'Is he in trouble? Has he done wrong?'

Isabel trembled; she spoke before she knew what she was going to say. 'No he hasn't done wrong. Almost, he did, but he will save himself.'

Immediately he was on his guard: upright, wary, searching her out with his eyes. 'What do you mean? Save himself from what?'

'From me.'

'From you? I don't understand.'

'Don't you?'

They stared at one another in silence: then the man shook his head. 'No.'

When Isabel spoke the note in her voice was one of supplication; unconsciously she clasped her hands together, stretched them out to him; the tears smarted, stung in her eyes. 'You know why Kenneth was sent to London. He went there to learn so that he could come back stronger than ever, to fight for himself and for you. He wasn't sent there to stay. But he would have had to stay there, if I had stayed there. He loved me. Yes, he did, he loved me, and I loved him; but when I learned who he was and why he had been sent to London, I left him. I couldn't stand in his way. I left him, so that he could come here again, do you understand? You must understand, you must tell me that I have done right. Because it was for you that I left him, only for you, and for all the others ——' Isabel came forward, her hands still stretched towards Kenneth's brother, the tears running down her cheeks. 'I had to give Kenneth back to you,' she said. 'I am so glad you have come, so that I can tell you.'

Suddenly, his hands shaking in front of his chest, as if he wanted to strike her, the man shouted: 'F—— you! Who the hell do you think you are? And what do you think Kenneth is?' He shook his fist at Isabel; his voice rose still higher as if he spoke from a distance, and the words were carried to Isabel in the gusts of his rage. 'What do you think *I* am? Yes, me? You think I've got no life, except what Kenneth gives me? Who needs his saving? F—— him! F—— the pair of you!'

Isabel was pushed away from behind as the kitchen-door opened; Hettie shrieked; Mr Last blundered forward, lunged clumsily at Peter, grasped him by the collar, shook him, let go, almost fell himself as Peter staggered down the steps, into the darkness. Mr Last clung panting to the pillar that held up the roof, and Hettie screamed in Afrikaans, '*Weg! Weg, jou Hotnot!* We'll call the police!'

'There you are,' Peter cried to Isabel from the darkness. 'You hear her? Is this how a man must live? But we still live, do you hear me?' Then Mr Last lunged down the steps, and again Hettie screamed as the servant rushed past her and the three men grappled. For a moment they seemed to have Peter down, but with a wild thrust of his body he managed to throw them both off. He appeared in the light, struggling for breath, his face scratched and bleeding, his tie torn; Isabel saw Hettie looking at him with horror and fear. And Isabel cried out and ran down the steps and grasped at Peter: in the darkness she smelt his smell, felt the cloth of his jacket in her fingers, and then blindly she embraced him, crying out for him to help her, not to leave her. When her father and the servant came forward again she screamed at them, 'Go away! I need him! Oh God,' she cried, sobbing, holding on tighter to the man, beating her head against his breast, being dragged with him farther into the darkness, 'Stay with me, don't leave me——' She did not hear her father call her name; she did not stop her entreaties until she felt that Peter was holding her—tensely, with strain, with his fingers only; but holding her. Then she fell silent at once; when she looked back she saw the faces of her father and Hettie: clear, white in the light. And Peter was whispering to her, fiercely and compassionately, 'If you really love him, go back to him. I love him, do you hear, he's my brother; but as true as God if he comes back here because he thinks I need him, I'll never forgive him. I live my own life, let him do the same. Do you hear me? You hear what I say?'

Again there came the shout of Isabel's name from the *stoep* above them. And Hettie added her voice, hysterically, 'Come back you mad girl! Don't touch him! Do you know what he is? Do you know what you're doing?'

'Do you?' asked the voice closest to her, softly. For a moment longer the fingers held on to her; then she was released. Isabel looked up and saw her father and step-mother staring at her, as if she were a stranger to them; and the servant nonplussed behind them.

'Brother,' Isabel said, 'Peter.'

He touched her hand with his, and then he was gone.

As Isabel began climbing up the steps, wearily, draggingly, her father and stepmother moved away from her. At the door to the kitchen they paused; they looked at her, and then without a word turned their backs on her and went into the house. Again Mr Last looked back; but his wife grasped his wrist and pulled him on. Isabel waited until they had gone through before she followed them; then she went straight to her room.

For days, weeks, thereafter she suffered in silence their abuse, pleas and threats; finally, Mr Last came and told her that as she would not apologize, nor promise never to see her Coloured friends again, she must leave. Hettie had said that if Isabel did not leave, she would; she was not prepared, Hettie had said, to live in the same house as a woman who slept with Hottentots.

'I want to go,' Isabel said. 'I want my fare and then I will go.'

Her father wrote out the cheque for her. 'Don't tell Hettie I've done this,' he said. And he added, 'I'll send you more, you needn't worry. But don't mention it when you write to me. If you write to me.'

'I will write to you. And I won't mention it, Daddy.'

Like conspirators, they embraced, holding each other, speaking in whispers. And then Isabel left her father's house. Martin had not been to the house since Hettie had told him that Isabel wanted to go back to her Hottentot boy-friend. 'So there's your payment for keeping a secret from us,' Hettie had shrieked. 'But a girl like that—you're better off without her!'

'No I'm not,' Martin replied; and for his pains was never invited again to the Lasts' house.

All through the night of her return, Kenneth and Isabel were awake and asleep; they made love, and drew apart, and talked and dozed, and came to each other again, and cried out with the pang of their passion, and lay awake in silence.

Once Kenneth said, 'I know what I am, now I love you again.'

'We know ourselves through each other.'

'But only when we are true to ourselves, apart.'

'What a mystery it is, my love.'

'A sweet mystery.' Kenneth held Isabel's arm at the elbow; then he kissed her there. 'Your sweet arm, where it bends,' he said; there were no other words he had for the wonder of her presence.

At last they fell deeply asleep. They woke to the warmth of the bed, the warmth of each other. Waking, they looked into one another's eyes, and seeing anguish, but no reproach, they knew that they had triumphed. Kenneth's limbs were full, heavy, languid; and Isabel nestled against him.

'We will find our way,' Kenneth assured her.

14

TWO YEARS LATER, Mr and Mrs Kenneth Makeer arrived in Cape Town on the *Kimberley Castle.* For fourteen days the horizon had swung up and down, up and down, beyond the great creaking windows of the public rooms; for fourteen days a white wake had unravelled itself behind the stern of the boat, and all sides around it the sea had plucked itself into shifting, restless, driven heaps. Now the boat was still; and still, too, was the view of the great bulk of Table Mountain, dwarfing the city beneath. On board, the passengers were subdued, quiet; the only voices raised were those of the Cape Coloured porters, humping the bags from each cabin, loading them into great nets which were gathered together and swung overboard by cranes.

The cabin-class lounge was almost deserted, when Kenneth and Isabel went to present their passports and immigration forms to the officials there: most of the passengers had already been in, and the officials were working with an air of lassitude, their task for the morning almost done. Kenneth and Isabel were soon beckoned forward, and they moved together, Kenneth putting down the papers in a single little heap. 'Welcome home,' a uniformed official said indifferently, seeing that they had South African passports. Neither Kenneth nor Isabel answered him. The silence of the lounge, the rigid stillness of the windows, was oppressive to them after the journey; but it was not this which had dried their lips, made their faces pale, forbade them from responding to the words of the immigration official and the glance he gave them before he busied himself with their papers. By his side there sat another official, in civilian clothes, with a list of names in front of him.

The uniformed official treated Isabel's papers first; he glanced through her passport, then at the immigration form; he stamped the passport and passed both documents to his colleague, who checked her name against his list. 'Mrs Makeer,' the latter said, stamping the immigration form, putting it together with a pile of others on the table in front of him, and holding the passport out to Isabel, 'thank you.'

Isabel took it without a word, and stepped back a pace, waiting for Kenneth. In the meantime the uniformed official had gone through Kenneth's passport; cursorily, he ran his finger down the immigration form, and was about to slip it into the passport and pass on both to his colleague, when suddenly he paused, and looked again at the form.

Kenneth had stepped back to join Isabel; the official glanced quickly at them, then showed the form to his colleague, pointing with his finger at a particular entry on it. 'Here, you see?'

'What's this?'

'No, look man. Here, look.' He jabbed with his forefinger again. 'There.'

The other looked; then both raised their heads and stared in surprise at Kenneth.

'It says here that you're Coloured,' the uniformed man said; he smiled momentarily, almost apologetically, for uttering the word.

'Yes,' Kenneth said. 'I am.'

'What?' It was an exclamation from them both.

'Yes.'

'But——'

'Let me look,' the uniformed man said, and again stared at the form.

'And this lady——?'

'Is my wife.'

The face of the official began to redden under his peaked cap. And the other shoved himself away from the table. 'What the hell——?'

'The hell!' his companion exclaimed, picking up the word, his face still darkening. 'You know what you're saying to me?' His eyes went from Kenneth to Isabel. 'You know what you're doing?'

'We're South African-born,' Kenneth said. His voice was high, but steady. 'You can't bar our entry.'

'Don't you tell me my job! Jesus Christ!'

The official in plain clothes got to his feet. 'Will you come with me?'

'Why?'

'Because I say so!' the man roared suddenly. 'You think you can come here and tell me what to do!' He stooped and whispered something in his colleague's ear. The two men conferred for a moment. 'All right,' the man said, straightening himself. 'You stay here.' With long strides, his shoes squeaking angrily on the rubber tiles, he walked out of the lounge.

While he was away, two more passengers came in to be processed. 'I'm afraid you will have to wait until the return of my colleague,' the uniformed official told them, breathing heavily. He was embarrassed, now that there were others in the room, and did not look at Kenneth and Isabel. When one of the passengers protested at the delay the official replied solemnly, 'I am sorry, but something of great difficulty has come up—we will try to be as quick as possible.' Still he did not look at Kenneth and Isabel; he busied himself among his papers.

His colleague returned with an older, thinner man in uniform, and Isabel and Kenneth were led away by the three officials into the ship's library; the passengers remaining behind stared at them curiously and resentfully as they went off, blaming them for the delay. In the library Kenneth and Isabel had to produce their birth-certificates, and their marriage-certificate, as well as their passports and immigration forms, and every one of the documents was examined anew, in turn, by each of the officials, who transcribed details from them on to other forms, consulted each other, wrote again. None of the officials now spoke to Kenneth or Isabel, or even looked at them, except to demand the papers from them. Then the senior man asked them about their next-of-kin, the length of their absence in England, their professions, their intended place of residence in South Africa, their income, their reasons for returning. To the last question Kenneth replied steadily: 'We came back because we are South Africans.'

Only then, and only for a moment, did the official lose control of himself. 'You'll be sorry,' he cried shaking a finger at them. 'You'll regret this day.' But his voice was calm, clipped, and almost ironical when he later went on to tell Kenneth and Isabel that as they were South Africans he could not bar their entry into the country, and was therefore allowing them to proceed. However, he continued, they were perfectly aware that if they cohabited here—and he paused, he dwelt on the word for long enough to make insulting his glance at Isabel, while the others gaped at her openly, vacuously, obscenely—if they cohabited here they would be committing a criminal offence under the terms of the Immorality Act. And if they didn't know what that meant, they would soon find out. Then, with a last whispered word to his aide, he signified that Kenneth and Isabel could go.

The official threat was acted upon that night. At two in the morning there was a bang at the door of the hotel room which Kenneth and Isabel had taken, and when Kenneth opened the door it was to admit a uniformed policeman, a plain-clothes policeman, a Cape Coloured policeman, and the manager of the hotel, in his pyjamas and dressing-gown, who whispered fiercely to the policemen to be quiet, not to bring disgrace on his hotel, and who then himself, in a grotesquely loud and hoarse whisper began raving at Kenneth. 'Filth! Bastard! Hottentot! Coming into my hotel, pretending to be a white man, and bringing your whore with you! Scum! Shit!' The man clawed at his dressing-gown, he choked, he cleared his throat and spat in Kenneth's face; he almost collapsed, tottering to the bed on one side when the uniformed policeman pushed him aside.

Kenneth and Isabel were both dressed, for they had been expecting this visit. Neither of them had said a word since they had been interrupted: all their words had been said earlier, when they had lain shivering together on the bed, fully clothed, waiting for what was now upon them, hardly able to help each other, except by clinging to one another and muttering brokenly of 'love,' of 'afterwards', of 'England'. Now they stood apart, dazed, in a room half-lit and full of men. When Kenneth wiped away the hotel manager's spittle his hand was trembling so much that it rattled against his cheek; when the policeman stepped forward Kenneth flinched, ducked, crouched away from the blow he was expecting.

But no blow came. 'Let's go,' the policeman said, with a small nod, almost like a greeting, as if he recognized them both.

'Down the fire-escape!' the manager gabbled. 'This is a respectable hotel, you hear. Bastard! Whore! A respectable——'

'All *right*, man, take it easy,' the uniformed policeman said in an aggrieved tone. His grasp closed on Kenneth's wrist; he jerked Kenneth towards the door; the plain-clothes man took Isabel and pushed her in front of him. Isabel cried out once, and they were out in the dim corridor, the manager running ahead.

His robe floated behind his pyjama'd legs, the cords of his gown dangled; he whispered, gesticulated, he beckoned them on. When they reached the door to the fire-escape the manager halted, and stood aside; as they went by he spat again at Kenneth; like a demented creature he jabbered and pulled a face at Isabel. The lamplight gleamed on the iron of the fire-escape, and their footsteps rang loudly on it, as they all tumbled downwards; they reached the pavement in a heap, and first Kenneth, and then

Isabel, was pushed into a saloon car that was waiting at the kerb. The policeman followed them into it, and the driver of the car accelerated before the door had been closed.

At a near-by police station Kenneth and Isabel were formally charged with contravening the terms of the Immorality Act, were warned that anything they said could be used in evidence against them, and were told that they could get in touch with their lawyers in the morning. Then they were parted. Isabel was taken away first, to the cell for white women. No sooner had she gone than one of the policemen in the charge office smashed as powerfully as he could at Kenneth's face—wordlessly, though the breath was driven out of the man's own body with a grunt, a deep groan. He struck with an open hand, and at the moment of impact his five spreadeagled fingers covered Kenneth's face; then Kenneth had fallen and the policeman was panting over him. When they dragged Kenneth to his feet he was bleeding at the nose, and already his lips were beginning to swell; a light shone in the slit of his eye, but he was barely conscious.

He was pushed into the cell for Coloured men. One light burned weakly behind an iron guard; there was neither bench nor blanket, and a single open bucket stank in the corner; the walls were of crude concrete blocks, and the prisoners leaned against them, sitting on the floor, or lay full-length; some walked up and down, some wept, sang, spat, talked in low voices, quarrelled fiercely; and all fell silent each time the iron door was opened and a uniformed arm thrust in yet another ragged fluttering figure, that flew in like paper, and fell into flesh and blood on the floor. And so the night passed for Kenneth, in a daze, in a dream, where his own fear and horror so numbed him that he barely felt fear and horror, felt only the mask of pain on his face, and his own strangeness from himself, like a sick man or a mad one.

Isabel in her cell was calmer, sustained by resources that Kenneth was without: her white skin, her wealth, her disbelief that what was happening to her was really being done by forces that were stronger than herself. And though her cell was smaller, there were bunks in it, and she shared it with only two other women, both of whom slept until the morning, as she did too, eventually. When she woke, she knew immediately where she was; yet she thought of Kenneth and worried about him, pitying him as though she were free.

. . . . .

In the short speech he made from the dock before sentence was passed, Kenneth spoke both for himself and Isabel, clearly and without hesitation. 'By arresting us and bringing us into this court,' he said. 'the State has made my love for my wife, and her love for me, a public and political act. For this reason we cannot be punished by the court, but only released by it—released from the public and political hatreds, the public and political guilts, which make ugly the most private and secret lives of everyone who lives in this country. We hope that our families will forgive us for having come back; I know they will forgive us for leaving this country for England, when we have served whatever sentence this court imposes upon us.'

Justice —— was on the Bench; he listened impassively to Kenneth's statement, and when Kenneth had done he proceeded impassively to pass sentence. Kenneth was sentenced to six months' imprisonment, with hard labour, and twelve strokes of the cane; Isabel to six months' imprisonment, with hard labour. A sigh went up in the courtroom; but still impassively, Justice —— announced that the twelve strokes of the cane imposed on the prisoner Makeer were suspended, on condition that the prisoner did not again commit the offence while he was within the jurisdiction of the court. A sigh went up again; but whether of relief or disappointment it was impossible to say.

One of the defence counsel turned to his colleague in the case. 'That'll be four months, if they behave themselves,' he said, and the other replied, 'It could have been worse, could have been worse. —— is a good stick at heart. And thank goodness he took no notice of Makeer's speech.'

'Everyone else will.'

'I hope so. I hope so.' But he said it *sotto voce*.

Almost everybody in the court was on his feet by now. Kenneth and Isabel were separated by a barrier; a policeman held Kenneth's arm, a policewoman Isabel's. They did not smile at one another, did not speak, did not even open their lips: they simply looked their full, looked their last. Their expressions were grave, reflective, and peaceful.

Then they were led away. As Kenneth went past he leaned towards the senior counsel. 'Thank you,' he said, touching the man's shoulder with his hand. A moment later he had disappeared, a door swinging behind him. Another door swung open and closed and Isabel, too, had left the courtroom.

And so it had come to its end; those who remained standing in the courtroom looked vaguely disappointed: they seemed to have anticipated a more dramatic conclusion to a case which had become so celebrated, and which had been so sensationally reported in the press, both locally and overseas. When the two lawyers who had been defending Kenneth and Isabel walked out of the courtroom they found a more than usually large group was hanging around in the corridor outside, at a loss: there was nothing to say, nothing to do, now that the case was over, yet none of them could leave. One a bench sat Kenneth's father, and over him stood Peter Makeer and the girl that Peter was going to marry: a bright attractive girl with a loud voice and a dark skin. The lawyers stopped to say a word to them.

Cornelius did not get up, but he did manage to say, 'You did your best, sah.'

'We tried to.'

'Kenneth did well,' Peter said. 'His wife, too. They were very brave, right to the end.'

'Very brave.'

'One day perhaps they'll be able to live here, like me and Betty.' Peter had his arm around the girl, and she smiled at him.

'I hope so.'

'For sure,' he said, but without much hope or insistence in his voice. They were all exhausted; and in the minds of each of them was the thought of Kenneth and Isabel being carried in vans to their respective prisons, to be stripped, shaved, shouted at, bathed in lysol.

'Be comforted, sah,' Cornelius Makeer cried out.

One of the lawyers looked up, surprised; but it was not to him that Cornelius had spoken; it was to Mr Last who was limping by on his own. He stopped at the word, and stared, recognizing only the counsel, who had been briefed at his instructions. Then he recognized Cornelius and took a pace forward, as if he were about to go on without a word.

'Be comforted,' Cornelius repeated.

Mr Last's face was twisted, ugly with anguish. 'Why?' he asked. 'What comfort is there?'

'The comfort we can give to each other, sah.'

'From you?' Last struggled with his pride, his face still distorted, his weight still on one foot. He shook his head. 'No, there is no comfort.' He took a step, but halted again.

'Think of the children,' Cornelius cried.

'I think of nothing else.'

'They will comfort each other.'

Isabel's father had been prepared to spend almost any sum of money on the defence of them both; he had even managed to silence his wife's opposition to the aid he had given them. And he could not move away now.

'You are luckier than I am,' Cornelius said. 'You will be able to visit them in England, afterwards, when they come out. Not me.'

Then Mr Last said, 'You'll visit them, too. I'll see to it.' He limped away, to his wife, to the cottage at the Cape he had taken for his retirement: he could no longer live in Lyndhurst, where people whispered and looked after him in the streets.

'You see there is comfort,' Cornelius called after him; but when Mr Last had gone he broke down and wept. And the only consolation they could offer to him was the cause of his grief.